JESUS AND FAT TUESDAY

and other

short stories

by

Colleen J. McElroy

CREATIVE ARTS BOOK COMPANY, BERKELEY
1987

ACKNOWLEDGMENTS

These stories appeared in somewhat different forms in the following publications: "A Brief Spell by the River" in CONFRONTATION and SHORT STORY INTERNATIONAL; "The Limitations of Jason Packard" in BACKBONE 2: NEW FICTION BY NORTHWEST WOMEN; "Sun, Wind and Water" in CALLALOO; "Farm Day" in BELLINGHAM REVIEW; "Imogene" in SEATTLE REVIEW; "Exercises" in CHOICE: THE TWENTIETH CENTURY ANNIVERSARY ISSUE; and "Under the Equinox" in IRON COUNTRY: CONTEMPORARY WRITING IN WASHINGTON STATE.

The story, "Sun, Wind and Water," was awarded first place in fiction in the CALLALOO Creative Writing Awards for 1981.

A special thanks for permission to reprint lines from—
      "Combing" in TO FRIGHTEN A STORM by Gladys Cardiff (Copper Canyon Press, Port Townsend Washington)

For information contact:
      Creative Arts Book Company
      833 Bancroft Way
      Berkeley, California 94710

Typography: QuadraType, San Francisco
Cover Art: Charles Furman Design

ISBN 0-88739-023-4
Library of Congress No. 87-70508

To the late John Gardner, for his encouragement in helping me hear the language of poetry in fiction, and to Al Young and especially Peter Beagle for endless support.

TABLE OF CONTENTS

JESUS AND FAT TUESDAY

and other

short stories

A Brief Spell by the River

ARLY THAT MORNING BEFORE THE SUN COULD clear the line of scrub maple just east of the crab apple orchard, Cressy Pruitt had stepped into the shadowy area behind the hen house where the old biddy hen, Eelly, liked to nest. Cressy had shooed Eelly away from her cache of eggs, collected all but two of them and placed them in her apron pocket. Eelly cackled and defiantly settled back onto the two eggs. As Cressy walked through the barnyard, she'd selected a fat, lazy brown chicken, swooped it up with one hand and held it at arm's length. Mama Lou had already decided on a stew pot for supper and Cressy knew that taking one hen meant the others would get jumpy. The birds skittered in all directions. Before their harsh, frightened clucking could reach its full pitch, before Titbeak, the rooster, could squawk a second warning cackle, she'd snapped the hen's neck.

Later, as she walked along the edge of the railroad tracks, she noticed the red taint of blood staining the grit beneath her fingernails. Cressy frowned, then spit on her wide, blunt fingers and rubbed them through the woolly mass of hair behind her left ear where one of her thick braids had pulled loose. She'd have to redo her hair before she returned from Miz Greenlove's with the goose grease and witch hazel Mama Lou had sent her to fetch. But she was only half a mile from Big Creek River and she could wash her hands real good once she got there.

In the fringe of trees bordering the railroad tracks, she heard the cry of a redstart or a warbler. Cressy paused for a moment. The bird repeated its call. She heard a cow mooing in the pasture beyond the thicket of trees. Insects buzzed a shaded pool of stagnant water just beyond the gravelled edge of the railroad hump. There

1

were other sounds, barely audible and indistinct. The bird trilled again and she heard a rustle of leaves as it left the tree area. She decided it must have been a redstart when she saw it flit into the next patch of elms, its flight as skitterish as a butterfly's.

She swung the croker sack of potatoes and onions onto her other shoulder. "Don't drag that sack through the mud," Mama Lou had warned. "Miz Greenlove won't take no chewed up roots in trade and your papa needs that medicine. He got the croup real bad."

Miz Greenlove's house was west of Pap Thacher's place. Miz Greenlove and Pap Thacher were the oldest folks in the valley. Some said Miz Greenlove was nearly ninety, but no one knew exactly how old Pap Thacher was. He'd always looked as grizzly and rusty black as he did now. Mama Lou said folks talked about Pap Thacher clear down in South Carolina. Pap Thacher had been one of the first black freemen in the valley. Twice he'd been run out of the valley by Quantrill's raiders; early in the Civil War, he'd helped slaves cross the valley on their way north to Canada, and when Cressy's family had moved into the valley from Alabama, the year Cressy was born and two years after the Civil War, Pap Thacher had helped them settle onto the craggy ten acres they now farmed. He was a wily old man and didn't really believe any presidential papers could keep one lone black man safe from the rebel raiders who'd crossed the Missouri border all too often. So he'd carefully culled a thin string of families from the many black people fleeing north or heading west across the Plains states. Six other families now farmed land around Pap Thacher's place and black folks dotted the shores of Big Creek River from Granville to Deepwater.

Pap Thacher knew everyone and everyone knew Miz Greenlove because at one time or another, everyone, including Pap Thacher, had been sick enough to visit Miz Greenlove for medicine. Sometimes Mama Lou just sent Cressy to Miz Greenlove's with food, but sometimes Cressy had to go fetch medicine like everyone else. At any rate, Cressy went to Miz Greenlove's every week and every week Mama Lou warned her to be careful.

For Cressy, the trip to Miz Greenlove's was a time for her to forget all the chores she had at home. She stepped onto the iron rail and for the next quarter of a mile walked the hot ribbon of tracks, balancing her pace against the bouncing weight of the croker sack and the burning strip of metal that connected all the towns behind her to Sedalia to the east and St. Joseph to the north. Then she felt the rumble of the afternoon train vibrate against her bare feet. Cressy walked the rails for a few more yards before she hopped clear of the cross-ties and gravel bed. She could hear the echo of the great lumbering thing as it entered the tunnel near Pap Thacher's farm. Cressy walked over to a fallen tree, sat down and waited. She swung the croker sack onto the ground in front of her feet and picked a few of the bright buttercups growing in a clump just behind the tree trunk. By the time she'd gathered five or six of the flowers, measuring each stem to make sure they were all the same length, the train was out of the tunnel and heading up the gorge toward the hill where she sat. She cocked her head, waiting for the whistle that signalled the train's journey across Big Creek River. The pulsing throb of the driving wheels let her know that the train had gathered speed. She could even see the billows of smoke as the engine plowed toward the uphill grade, but the whistle was silent.

Then she heard the gunshots.

They were muffled at first, but as the train drew nearer, she heard seven or eight shots in rapid succession. Cressy stood up. All of the sounds around her seemed to be sucked in to the space between the train tracks. She saw the engine slice through the shadows that marked the thicket of trees where she'd heard the redstart, then it barrelled past her, its funnel belching puffs of black smoke as it headed up the line toward Sedalia or St. Joseph. But there was no face in the cab window and no one pulled the whistle as the train sped by. She heard another gunshot, the sound so close she jumped, clutching the flowers until one or two of the stems broke. Then she saw him. A tall white man crawling the rim of the boxcar halfway down the length of the train. When he stood up, she could see the shotgun in his hand, long and evil as a snake.

The backwash of wind from the train lifted the edge of her cotton skirt. This movement must have drawn his attention, because at that moment he stood straight and stared at her. Cressy did not move. The whoosh of wind lifted her skirts again, this time pulling the hem from her dusty ankles and bare toes almost to the tops of her knees. The black-clad figure lifted his hat, nodded his head, then turned, dropped to his knees and swung into the car through a door on the other side of the train. But for that second, Cressy was sure his eyes had stared clear into her soul. Almost as soon as he'd disappeared, she heard more gunshots. Another figure loomed up over the edge of the first three passenger cars. Cressy heard someone shout, then a scream and more gunshots. She grabbed the croker sack and ran. She didn't stop running until she'd reached the footbridge at Big Creek River.

She didn't think her knees would stop trembling, but her chest was pumping air so hard, she had to stop. She fell to the ground at the edge of the creek and leaned forward to scoop water into her hands. That's when she realized she was still clutching the flowers. The reflection of her sweaty black face and that scraggly bunch of flowers trembling in her clenched fist caused her to laugh. She laughed so hard, she rocked back on her heels and toppled over. Then she released the flowers, righted herself into a kneeling position and looked into the water again. She was still laughing softly, but this time the face was familiar.

"Look at those little round cheeks," Mama Lou would say. "And that mouth. Lips stuck out like a poke-mouthed trout sucking scat flies," she'd laugh.

Cressy crossed her eyes, wrinkled her broad black nose and blew up her cheeks until they were round as fat purple plums. She grinned at the dusky image unfolding on the water's surface, then tried the face again. When she'd eased the tight knot in her stomach, she leaned forward and rippled the water to clear the scum. She was about to scoop a handful of the clear water when she saw the long thin line worming its way downstream. It was as bright red as a ribbon and Cressy remembered how she'd seen blood seep from the deer Papa had shot last winter. He'd caught it off guard sipping water from Indian Pond and when it fell, it had landed in the marshy shallows of the pond. Cressy remembered how the current had pulled the blood away from the body and how it had trailed into the deep part of the water like a finger of bright red vine.

She looked upstream. At the base of the railroad trestle, there was a clump of couch grass, its spiky blades mildewing at the edge of the wash. There, the line of blood muddied the water into a deeper shade of red. She squinted. The grass was dark and solid, waving slightly under the force of the river's current. Then she heard the horses.

Cressy was already into the trees on the other side of the footbridge when the men rounded the corner. She could see them clearly, but unless they moved to the middle of the footbridge, she was well hidden.

"Down here," one of the men called. The others followed him, one of them leading a riderless horse.

"I don't see him, Bradshaw," another yelled. Then Cressy recognized the man who'd stared at her from the top of the train.

The horses stopped and the men leaned forward. Cressy couldn't be sure how many there were. She hadn't learned to do her figures too well and she really had trouble anytime someone rushed her. But she recognized the man from the train and she knew where those men had come from.

Pap Thacher had worked on the railroad when it was being built. He'd told her how the train had to slow down when it reached the spur about two miles down the line. "That's when they got to make their move," he'd said. "East to Sedalia so they can dump the cattle heading for Kansas City, or north to St. Joseph. Up there in St. Joseph, they got a big de-pot. But they got to figure out which way they gonna go when they reach that spur down yonder by Big Creek."

Pap Thacher had told Cressy that the train slowed down enough when it reached the spur to allow a man to hop on or off. Cressy was sure the men had jumped the train down by the spur, and now they'd doubled back looking for whoever made that bloody line slide down the middle of the river.

"Bradshaw, you move on down there a piece," the man with the shotgun yelled. "Me and Clint gonna check further up."

Before they could swing their horses around, another man, the one leading the riderless horse, waved a purple scarf and yelled to them. He was standing at the base of the railroad trestle and Cressy knew he'd found what they were looking for. The others moved toward the trestle, but the man Cressy recognized swung off his horse and kneeled by the spot where she'd been only a few minutes before. The man's horse blocked her view, but when he stood up, she could see his head—that black wide-brimmed hat, the mustache, long and sleek, hanging to the edge of his chin, and those eyes narrowed to a slit. He was looking across the river, peering at the trail that led away from the footbridge.

The other men called to him again. Cressy could see them lift the

limp figure of a man from the grassy bog. They propped him onto
the horse and called to the man standing by the river bank. He
waved to them but did not turn his head away from the trees where
Cressy was hiding. She held her breath. Then she saw him swing
back onto his horse. And she saw the tattered bunch of buttercups
in his hand. He lifted his hat in her direction, smiled, replaced the
hat and moved toward the marshy spot at the base of the trestle.
Cressy snatched up the croker sack and ran. This time, she did not
stop until she'd reached the porch of Miz Greenlove's house.

The whole valley was buzzing with the news of the train robbery.
Some said the men had killed everyone on the train, while others
said all of the robbers had been killed. A few even talked about how
the train had been blown up before it left the tunnel at North
Forks. Cressy didn't say a word. She knew better than to interrupt
her papa when he was talking. Even though she was fifteen and
"pret-near a woman," as Mama Lou was always saying, she knew
her papa would swat her backsides before he'd let her sass him. But
Cressy had seen the men and she closed her ears when she heard
folks saying how many of them had been killed.

Pap Thacher took the buckboard over to Pittsville and talked to
some of his railroad friends. He came back two days later and let
everyone know that only one person had been killed on the train.
"A young buck from Texas," Pap Thacher told them. "I hear tell
he'd been causing trouble anyways. One of them fool Rebels still
bragging about Sherman and how he's gonna make his darkies
work twice as hard as his papa did."

All the old folks said um-hum and Lord-Lord and Thank-you-
Jesus, so Cressy knew they didn't hardly mind hearing that man
was dead. Pap Thacher's story shut up those who wanted to say everybody on the train had been killed and nobody paid any attention to that business about the train being blown up anyway, but
Cressy was the only one who knew what happened to the robbers.

"They wanted in six states," Pap Thacher said. "Tell me they
been robbing trains since they was nigh on to twelve years old."

"Tell me them James boys come back," Miz Ada's boy said.
"Brung some of Isom Dart's boys with them."

Pap Thacher glowered at him. Everyone knew how Pap
Thacher felt about Isom Dart. Pap Thacher lived by himself now.
His wife had been dead for five years. His oldest son had been

killed in a brush war up in the Dakota mining territory, and his only other son had run off to join the black outlaw, Isom Dart.

"Naw," Pap Thacher spat. "Weren't none of them more than ten or twelve years old. White bucks. Half growed, I hear."

Cressy smiled and counted buttercups.

But for the next few weeks, Mama Lou crossed her thick black arms over her chest and wouldn't let her go to Miz Greenlove's. Mama Lou was Cressy's grandmother. Cressy's mother had died the year she was born, when it was too cold to even find firewood, and Mama Lou would let Cressy do most anything she wanted to do. Cressy's papa yelled a lot and sometimes took a willow switch to her, but Mama Lou told her she looked too much like her mother for her papa to really get mad at her. Still, they both kept her away from Miz Greenlove's after the Wichita-Sedalia/St. Joseph train was robbed.

"Hear they still hanging round down by the spur," Mama Lou said, but after a new moon had passed, Cressy made the trip the way she always did and Mama Lou warned her to keep the croker sack out of the mud the way she always did.

Cressy thought she'd nearly forgotten the man with the shotgun until Mama Lou and Papa took her to Granville. They didn't go to Granville very often, so just the thought of going into a store or walking down the street where the houses were lined up against the road like buckboards when the travelling preacher set up his tent at North Forks, made her so excited Mama Lou threatened to leave her at home. Cressy tried to keep herself calm all morning, but by the time Papa had the horse harnessed to the wagon, she'd had to cross one foot over the other and knot her dress up in her hands so she wouldn't leap up on the seat before Mama Lou got comfortable.

They'd been in town nearly all day when Papa took her to Applegate's Feed and Grain store. Papa was buying a new curb bit for the hinny mule when she wandered down the street. If Papa had been paying attention, he would have told her to go back and sit in the wagon with Mama Lou. "Don't be forgetting who you are," Papa always told her whenever they went to town. "Folks don't think no more about stringing you up like a chicken than they do about getting up every morning. They still remember how it is to put a branding iron on black skin."

But Papa was busy looking at a box full of saddle rings, so she'd wandered down the street. She was staring at some pictures on the wall outside of the saloon when she saw his face. A white woman came to the door and fanned herself. When she saw Cressy looking at the pictures, she said, "Don't you be talking to none of those men, gal. They don't know good from bad. I reckon they shoot little darkies like you for practice," the woman laughed.

Cressy stared at the man's face. His picture was set dead center of a group of pictures, but none of the other men had a mustache as long as his and none of them had eyes that cut straight through her. She knew it was him even without the wide hat and shotgun. The woman began to tell her what all of the men had done.

"That one robbed a bank. And that one killed forty men over in Abilene. That one rode clear from Texas to Wyoming just to shoot a lawman. Think they'd have enough marshals in Texas. And that one, the one with the buck teeth, he done run clear out of new trouble. Now he's trying to make money on other folks' trouble." The woman held her stomach and fanned even faster, laughing at Cressy's wide-eyed stare.

Just then, Papa called her back to the feed store, his arms folded across his chest and his stocky black figure planted in the middle of the walkway like those tree stumps he was always pulling out of the fields.

"I got to go," Cressy told the woman.

"Don't you want to hear about them others?" the woman asked. Her finger was inching closer to the picture of the man Cressy had seen holding buttercups down by Big Creek River.

Cressy shook her head. "My papa be real mad if I don't come directly," she said. She took one last look at the picture, then walked away.

Papa yelled at her all the way home, and the next week Mama Lou said Papa didn't even want her to go to Miz Greenlove's cause she was so hardheaded, but after Mama Lou made her promise to be careful, she sent her to Miz Greenlove's anyway.

Cressy knew Mama Lou was watching her, so she hoisted the croker sack onto her shoulder and held the end of it with both hands. As soon as she'd rounded the bend in the road, she relaxed. She had just reached the clearing near Big Creek River when she remembered Mama Lou's warning. But it was a quiet day. She'd passed the edge of the fields, walked the length of railroad tracks and turned into the woods without causing even a flutter in the movements of the small animals and birds that made their home in the valley. Since the robbery, she'd learned to cross the river quickly and no matter how thirsty she became, she never stopped for a drink. When Cressy reached the other end of the footbridge, she turned and looked at the opposite shore.

She didn't hear him. He was just there, the air filled with the pungent odor of sweat, horseflesh and tobacco.

She knew who it was before she turned around. He had one hand on the horse's bridle and the other, extended toward her, was clutching a cluster of yellow flowers. The man was smiling. Cressy shifted her feet in the loose dirt of the path. She stared past him into the trees, the bushes beside the path and the dense woods beyond them.

"Ain't nobody," the man said. "Just me."

Cressy's head jerked as she tried to shy away from the sound of his voice, but his eyes held her still. He stabbed the air with the flowers, thrusting them to her as if she hadn't seen them. Cressy shook her head. The man sighed and dropped the horse's reins. He moved forward. Cressy moved back a step. It was as if her movement had startled him as much as his voice had startled her. They were both still for a moment, then the man threw back his head and laughed.

Cressy stared at him. She hadn't heard so much noise since the last time Mama Lou had taken her to the revival meeting at the travelling preacher's tent. A host of wood sparrows swirled away from the trees and squirrels chattered in the uppermost branches as the sound of his laughter billowed into the air like wash on a clothesline. When the man laughed, his mustache moved away from his lips in half circles like two thin black slivers of a dark moon. As abruptly as he had started, he stopped, swallowing the sound in large gulps as if he'd needed to swallow a hunk of dry corn bread. Then he looked at the flowers in his hand, grinned and tossed them in the bushes beside the path.

As he lifted his hat and wiped the sweat from his forehead where the band had bleached a ridge into his skin, Cressy turned to run. Before she'd managed three steps, he grabbed her around the waist and pulled her against him. She swung the croker sack over her head and heard it thunk as it slammed into his back. The man did not flinch. Instead he grinned. Cressy hit him again, swinging the sack over her shoulder and letting it take a full arc towards the small of his back. When she raised it the third time, he said, "Stop it," his voice as deep and strong as her papa's when he worked the horses around the tree stumps. Cressy let her arm go limp.

The man pulled the croker sack from her hand, then lifted her off the ground. He carried her easily, one hand around her waist, the other under her knees. Cressy felt her stomach churning up into her throat. The man smiled, his eyes never leaving her face. When they reached the bushes, he slowly eased her to the ground. Cressy wanted to move, to run, but she couldn't remember how. The man took off his hat and vest. Then he pulled the end of his shirt from his pants.

Cressy heard a small sound, like an animal mewing. The man put his hand over her mouth. "Hush," he said. Then he began to unbutton her blouse.

Cressy wanted to hide. No matter how many ways she moved her hands, they would not cover her body. The man moaned and drew her skirt up over her waist. She thought he would kill her. She wanted to die, to close her eyes and wake up on another morning in her own pallet in the corner of Mama Lou's room. But nothing was that easy. For that time, while the man pressed her against the prickly underbrush, she knew no other sound except that of his breathing. He smelled of tobacco and liniment, the dusty smell of horses who have run too long under the oil of saddle leather. He smelled of strong swamp smells like the trails possums leave when you surprise them at night. Cressy's stomach filled her throat and her mouth burned with the taste of bile as she heaved into the tangle of weeds beside her head. The man groaned and lay still. When he felt Cressy begin to heave again, he kneeled beside her and wiped the sour fluid from her lips with the tail of his shirt. Then he moved away. Cressy kept her eyes closed. She could hear him pulling and tugging at the rough material he wore, then she felt a damp coolness fall onto her bare chest and heard him move away.

Long after he'd gone, she opened her eyes. The buttercups lay against her bare black skin like the light gray moths she sometimes found in the morning lying on the dark wood of the kitchen table. Cressy turned away from the ugly pool of vomit next to her head and cried softly. Finally, she limped to the river and washed herself. She pulled the stickers from the thick braids of her kinky hair and dried her face with the hem of her skirt. When she saw that her skirt was stained with blood, she waded into the water until she was waist deep. After she located the croker sack, she hoisted it onto her shoulders and walked to Miz Greenlove's.

The man met Cressy in the woods on and off all summer. Each time he just appeared. Each time he brought a small bunch of flowers. At first she cried, but she did not run. Soon she no longer cried. He'd hold her hand and lead her back to the path. Once he explained why there had been blood the first time. Once he lifted her onto his horse and she'd ridden behind him almost to Miz Greenlove's door. After a while, Cressy learned to give Mama Lou new reasons as to why it took her so long to return from Miz Greenlove's.

All summer, news of train robberies reached the valley. Cressy said nothing. By mid-summer, Pap Thacher made another visit to Pittsville. He came back with the news of a bank robbery in Holden, a train robbery near Odessa and another one near Liberty. Cressy listened when the man told her about the hot dry fields near Odessa. She said nothing about Liberty and Holden, but when she didn't see him for several weeks and when she heard there'd been a series of hold-ups near Atchinson, she knew he was moving north.

Sometimes on her route to Miz Greenlove's, the afternoon train passed her as she made her way to the footbridge. She'd stop and watch it slide by, smiling at the gloved hand that waved to her from the cab. By mid-October, she grew listless and even the sound of the train's whistle couldn't cheer her up. Mama Lou sent her to Miz Greenlove's and although Cressy took the medicine Mama Lou had sent her to fetch, she didn't feel any better. One morning, Mama Lou saw Cressy heaving her breakfast into the trough behind the outhouse. Mama Lou began to watch the girl as if she expected her to grow larger by the minute. But it was November before Papa noticed any change.

"Musta been one of Miz Ada's boys," he yelled. "You gonna tell me which one?"

Cressy said nothing.

The next week, Papa sent for Pap Thacher. Early one morning,

Cressy saw the old man's buckboard round the bend of the road at the end of the yard. She walked to the front porch. Mama Lou was already standing in the yard and Papa was in the doorway behind her. By the time Pap Thacher had climbed down from the buckboard, Cressy had reached the barn. She fed the milk cow and cleaned its stall. When she heard Pap Thacher coming to the door, she was heading toward the shaded area behind the hen house where the old biddy, Eelly, liked to nest.

"Can't rightly say as I know what to tell you, chile," Pap Thacher muttered. He stroked the stubbly grey whiskers on his chin, cocked his head and looked at her so that his milky grey eye, the one that had been blinded by one of Quantrill's raiders, was in the shadows. "I spect you ought to stay clear of folks till the circuit preacher comes around next spring."

Cressy nodded.

"You the only child your Papa's got," he added. "Surely would hep him to know who you been seeing."

Cressy stared at him. After a while, he limped back to the buckboard and she saw him shake his head. Her papa looked across the yard at her, then Pap Thacher patted him on the back, climbed into the buckboard and rode out of the yard.

After that, her papa seemed to grow tired of asking her the same questions. By spring, Cressy was so heavy with child, she used all of her energy moving from her bed, the one Papa built once he found out what was wrong with her, to the kitchen where she sat most of the day sewing scraps of cotton onto a new bed quilt or into clean even squares for the baby. Mama Lou had collected material from all of the women who had it to spare, and Mama Lou sat in the opposite corner, sighing and singing gospels.

Miz Ada came to the house several times, even brought one or two of her boys with her. The boys looked at Cressy with new eyes, but Cressy said nothing. By spring, Miz Ada was visiting so often, it was as if she herself felt guilty about Cressy's condition.

Cressy got up every morning, dragged herself from her bed to the kitchen and, once the days turned warm, onto the front porch. One morning in late April when the sun was particularly bright, Cressy took up her post on the porch. The sun was still cold, but if she placed her chair directly in its path, she could stay on the porch for hours. She didn't want to go into the house anyway. Miz Ada had come over with some chicken stock and one of Miz Ada's boys was sitting in the wagon waiting for her to finish her visit. Cressy had not spoken to the boy although she knew he'd been staring at her.

She was sitting on the porch, her head turned away from the boy, when she heard them ride into the yard. The boy stood up in the wagon and yelled, "Yahoo," and Miz Ada ran to the door, Mama Lou close at her heels. Cressy could hear the sound of Papa's hinny mule round the bend on the path below the house. She knew he must have seen them when they passed the road bordering the field.

There were four of them, but the yard seemed to be filled with men. Mama Lou brushed past Miz Ada and whispered, "Lord have mercy. What those white men want?" Cressy pulled herself from the chair. When she moved, the horses pawed the ground and whinnied, but the men reined them in and patted their necks until they'd calmed. Cressy remembered the one with the purple scarf, but she didn't recognize the other three. Then she saw another figure ride up the path.

The black hat was pulled down low over his eyes; his mustache drooped to the edge of his chin and he cradled the shotgun in the crook of his arm. She was already moving toward the stairs when she heard her papa call to her to stop. Mama Lou just kept saying, "Lord have mercy. Lord have mercy," and Miz Ada motioned her boy to get down off the wagon.

The man swung off his horse and handed the gun to one of the other men. Cressy leaned against the supporting pole when she saw he was limping, but he smiled and walked toward her. When he reached the porch, he tipped his hat to Mama Lou, saying, "Ma'am" as if they'd met many times before. Cressy could see her papa over by the barn, and when the man saw she was looking in that direction, he smiled even wider.

"Bradshaw," he said, "y'all get down offa them horses. They needs a rest. Just sit a spell. We be going directly." Then the man looked at Cressy again and raised his hand to help her down the stairs.

Cressy had just managed to get to the foot of the stairs by the time Bradshaw and the other men pulled their horses over to the elm tree in the corner of the yard. Cressy took the man's hand and led him around the back of the house to a bench near the well.

At first, he just looked at her and shook his head. Then he asked her if she was doing alright, when the baby would come and if she needed anything. Cressy answered yes, soon and no, but for the first time in months, she smiled. He gave her a brooch, an egg-shaped flat black stone with a flower carved in the center of it. "I'd be pleased if you'd call the baby Sam," he said.

He told her how he'd been shot, the miles of country he'd seen, the harsh winters in the Dakotas and the miles of trail they'd cut coming home across the plains. Cressy let him hold her hand and listened to the sound of Titbeak clucking the hens away from the horses' hoofs.

Then she saw her papa standing at the corner of the house staring at them. The man stood up. "I'm Sam," he said. "Sam Packer." Her papa nodded.

"I come to see. . . ." the man paused.

Cressy saw him frown, look at her, then back to her papa. "Cressy," she whispered. The man shook his head and frowned again. "I be Cressy," she told him.

Before he could say anything else, her papa said, "I spect them others want to go."

Cressy followed him to the front yard. She smiled when he pressed the small purse in her hands and watched him swing onto his horse, grimacing as the pain in his leg caused him to ease into the saddle. Then they were gone. Cressy moved back to the porch, the pin and leather pouch tucked into her skirt pocket. She heard Mama Lou and Papa questioning her, but she did not move. After a while, Miz Ada and her son got into their buckboard and rode off. They stared at her over their shoulders as they left the yard.

Before she went to bed, Cressy gave the money to Mama Lou. She pinned the brooch inside her blouse, and that night she slept soundly.

Some say that over the years, Sam Packer made regular visits to Cressy Pruitt's house. Some say that Cressy and Sam had a score of children, that Sam took some of them off to Oklahoma and Cressy never saw them again. Folks that live near Pap Thacher's, those who still talk to Miz Ada and don't believe one of her boys had anything to do with Cressy's baby, tell strangers they've seen a photograph of Cressy and Sam Packer. According to them, those two are standing on Mama Lou's porch with three, four, can't tell how many members of Sam's gang around them. Talk is those men are as ragged as teeth on a saw blade, lounging against the porch rail or sprawled in Mama Lou's chair like they own the house. Their guns are in plain sight and they're so relaxed, they're not wearing shirts, just long johns, dingy white and cut on each shoulder by broad suspenders. And Cressy is leaning against Sam Packer.

The way those folks tell it, Cressy is expecting another baby, or maybe it's because she's got that first baby straddling her waist as if he's riding a horse. They all agree that Cressy's round as a pumpkin and next to Sam Packer's lanky redbone figure, her walnut face is even darker.

Pap Thacher says he heard Sam Packer caught a marshal's bullet over in Bloomfield, Nebraska, the same week Cressy's child was born, but even though folks in the valley are inclined to believe Pap Thacher, they still wonder if Cressy Pruitt knows where Sam Packer is.

Anyone with patience could have asked Cressy herself.

Cressy's son was four years old the last time she saw Sam Packer. By that time, Jesse James had been dead for three years; Cole Younger and his boys had crossed the Kansas border; the railroad had hired Pinkerton men to guard their trains, and the Wichita-Sedalia/St. Joseph run had not been robbed all summer. Cressy had borrowed Pap Thacher's buckboard and she was riding into Granville to run some errands for Mama Lou. As she drew near the spur north of Big Creek River, she could hear the train chugging toward her in the distance. Pap Thacher's horses tended to be skittery and with the child beside her, she decided not to take any chances on the mare.

The train slowed as it reached the spur and when the engine moved past, pausing for a moment as if the train hadn't decided which fork to take, her son giggled and waved. The screeching whistle made the horse jump, but she reined it in and clucked until it was calm. When she looked up again, the last of the boxcars was sliding past, and the train was moving so slowly, no faster than a horse's gait, that she had a clear view of the passengers' faces in the windows.

He was sitting in the last passenger car, the wide-brimmed hat tipped back from his head as if he'd just shoved it away from his eyes. His mustache framed his mouth in flat, shiny arcs, but he was not smiling. He must have seen her before she saw him. Almost as soon as she spotted him, he raised one hand, then the other. The hand next to the window was as strong as she remembered, but the other was bound to the wrist of another man, the ugly glint of manacles flickering in the light. Then he was gone.

As soon as the train had passed, Cressy whipped the horse across the tracks. The wagon jerked, its wheels grinding against the soft dirt that bordered the railroad hump. The sudden movement caused her son to rock in the seat, but he caught himself and clutched her skirt before he toppled backwards. Cressy heard him giggle again, and in the scraggly tangle of trees on the other side of the road, she heard the angry chatter of startled birds. They flew from the thicket, scattering in all directions, but Cressy did not bother to see if she could recognize them.

The Limitations of Jason Packard

IN 1928, EAST ST. LOUIS WAS LIKE A NICK IN AN OLD rubber band along the highway that stretched between Chicago and St. Louis. In those days, the town resembled a little chewed up piece of something, half one-horse Western and half big city honkey-tonk, that left a crimp in the buggy rut of a roadway serving gangsters on both sides of the Mississippi who needed to move their goods across the state line. It was a town where black gangsters rubbed against white gangsters and they both could make a little bit of money off the good folks who wanted a taste of what made the '20s roar. East St. Louis fit Jason Packard like a glove.

Through most of 1927 and into 1928, Jason Packard had survived by thinking of himself as a shadowy black extension of the ragtime piano in Miz Bea Weeks' back parlor. Before those years, Jason was somewhere between seeing himself as a fancy man, a black man who knew how to hold his own with mobsters, and a drifter, a little no-account something his daddy had left behind the night the old man died in a hobo camp near Macon, Georgia. "A ditch nigger," Jason's father would snarl. "Folks don't think you nothing but a ditch nigger. Born in the dirt and gone die that way." When Jason had discovered his father lying in the wet grass beside the railroad tracks, he had tried to find some traces of himself in the face of the dead man. All he saw was an old man, like all the other bums he'd seen shambling down the back alleys and skid roads. "But the face can't tell it all," as his father would have said.

Jason's father had been the last slave child born on Sudacres Plantation. In 1862, Jason's grandmother had given birth to his father, had clamped her teeth on the rawhide strap shared by all the slave women on Sudacres, and in one final grunt, pushed the baby from her oily wet womb straight onto the dirt floor of that cabin. And in late September, two years before Sherman marched on Atlanta, Jason's grandmother had gathered her bundle of clothing, strapped the baby to her hip, and freed by Presidential Proclamation, walked forty miles of dirt road into the next county before the soft yellow moon could reach its zenith. For the next six years, she'd kept moving, always heading north and east, always moving away from Sudacres. And every time she'd had to stop, she'd gotten tougher. More than once, Jason's father had buckled under her back hand slap, and more than once, whenever Jason dared to defy him, the raw bone strength of Jason's grandmother had filled his father's six foot frame like a mirror image.

"I done busted heads from here to Memphis," he'd say to Jason. "And boy, I'ma learn you well to know where your place is, even if'n I gots to whup your hide and cry all the way to your grave."

Jason thought he'd found his place until he met Regina Blackwell, and while he saw the look in her eyes, curling like a ribbon, like a thin veil or a desert born dust cloud blown across the Sahara, he still didn't see that Regina Blackwell had no intention of settling for East St. Louis.

East St. Louis was a five minute hop over the Eads Bridge to the Missouri side or a quick trip up the highway to Springfield, Bloomington, Kankakee, and on to Chicago. Its prairie-flat streets were equally divided into ramshackle, country town squalor and penny ante low life. Regina Blackwell didn't fit either side. Regina Blackwell had been born on a dirt farm near Cahokia, a town so small, it didn't appear on any but the most historical maps. Jason had been in East St. Louis for seven months when he saw Regina Blackwell. And as soon as he saw her, he went courting.

Until then, Jason's contacts with women had been quick couplings in vacant lots, behind back fences, or in kitchens that served back parlors full of mulatto and black women who earned their keep doing what they allowed Jason to do for free. Jason had a way with those women, not a handsome, smooth talker's way, but a piano player's way, a certain movement he'd make with his head while his fingers slid over the keys and a devilish grin spread across his face. None of that really made him handsome, but it was his cocky, little boy manner that attracted the women. Jason wasn't much to look at, but he could make a woman laugh.

Physically, he bore little resemblance to his father, whose bulk could flood a room with patterns of wooly light, or his paternal grandmother, whose long limbed beauty had not left its mark on Jason. Jason was sand-dabbled and skitterish as a bone-brittle desert rat, a high yellow mosquito of a man. But when he lost himself in ragtime rhythm and his onion-slick head snuffled and bobbed above the keyboard in off-time syncopation, the women sidled up, ready to lean against him or pour him a shot from their favorite bottle.

"I got everything from cake walk to breakdown right here at my fingertips," Jason would brag. "You just bring you sloe-eyed silk to my piano and I'll make her toddle all night long."

But more than anyone else, Jason Packard recognized the weaknesses in his appearance and intuitively, he tried to correct those faults by surrounding himself with a lush landscape of beautiful women. Regina Blackwell was meant to be the centerpiece of that landscape, and for a time, Jason firmly believed he'd captured her, that he had in his possession the link between what he was and what he longed to be. In his world, all women were roughly translated into good and bad, with no in-betweens. Jason had not known his own mother, an Indian girl, probably Cherokee or Choctaw, who had died in childbirth, and he barely remembered his grandmother's face, the image dulled by too many railroad camps after he'd started travelling with his father at the age of eight. By the time he met Regina Blackwell, he'd worked in cathouses and speakeasies from Florida to New York, from New York to Chicago, and from the Texas border to the midwest. He'd worked in places called cribs, dens, boxes, joints and dives, and when his luck had run out and he couldn't get hired as a piano player, he'd do short time as a card dealer, or a runner, though his heart was never in it. But in all that time, he'd never come close to the likes of Regina Blackwell, so it was only natural that he saw her as fitting his mold for good, meaning she had to want what he wanted. It never occured to him that Regina might not be what he assumed her to be until he had nowhere else to turn. The kind of woman Jason wanted was a vague memory, a sudden sound of laughter, a sudden flash of soft skin or the fleshy symmetry of hips and thighs that brought his grandmother's husky, sing-song melodies back to him. Regina Blackwell had been singing the first time he saw her at the Rock of Ages Sanctified Church.

Jason was not a churchgoing man, but one of the girls at Miz Bea Weeks' house had been consumed by the urge to visit the Lord. "A bright fire," she called it. "A light calling my name," she'd said as she pulled a young white customer into her room. Jason had been sure the feeling would pass, but for the next several nights, when she wasn't spread eagle on her dingy bed, the girl had sat beside the piano and begged him, her eyes large as moons and her mouth filled with tiny mewing sounds.

"Ah can't hardly face the darkness no more," she'd said. "Ah can hear His voice. Lilbeth . . . Lilbeth, ya'll com'on, you hyeah?" Then she'd pulled her chemise tight around her waist and shivered. "Won't be no trouble to you, Jason. Ah promise." Her eyes had turned liquid and Jason had seen that faint, willowy thing that danced inside them.

It was to please Lilbeth, he'd told himself at first. Six Sundays in a row he'd gone to the Rock of Ages Church and for six Sundays, he'd never moved his eyes away from the choir's lead singer, a bright copper penny angel of a girl whose voice was so clear, she even commanded the attention of the Sunday school children. When Regina sang, the Auxiliary ladies would puff up like pigeons and not bother to wipe the tears from their oyster-soft cheeks. On Sundays, everyone seemed to forget that Regina walked around in prune-faced silence all week long. On Sundays, Regina's sisters forgot that under the primly starched folds of her blue choir robe, she was probably wearing some favorite item she'd borrowed from one of them and would never return. And Jason sat there through all those Sundays and let the spiralling notes of Regina's fine soprano voice tie him to a life that ended his days as a ragtime travelling man.

Jason Packard and Regina Blackwell were married on August 4, 1928, and although no one in Regina's family accepted Jason, they could hardly ignore him. He was slick to the bone—his suits always crisp, his shirts always stiff and his socks, whenever he hiked up his pants and shuffled his feet to show off a new dance step, were white as cream. But his skin was as withered as an overripe pear from all his years of sleeping days and working nights in smoke-filled rooms where he drank bad gin out of tea cups.

"Hear tell you plays the pianer," Regina's father had muttered when he was introduced to Jason.

Jason had nodded and leaned back, letting his arms span the length of the davenport. He needed a relaxed pose around church-goers, especially those, like Regina's father, who had been bred to hard work and had the muscles to prove it. Jason was reminded of his own father and the men who worked with him in railroad camps and loading docks, men who were so muscular, their skin had rippled like blue-black swamp water when they lifted an axe to split a log or toss crates onto flat bed trucks. When Regina's father leaned forward, Jason shattered the movement by crossing his legs and hooking his hands in his vest pockets. As he shifted his position, the flash of gold from the watch chain he'd bought from one of Lilbeth's customers, released a shower of giggles from Regina's younger sister.

Jason smirked. "Been an ivory tickler since I trucked away from my pappy," he told them. "Boston and eighty-eight. That's my style. Been at it a spell too. Make enough boodle to keep me in bread and butter and then some." He'd smiled as Regina's parents inspected him.

"We believe in Temperance," Regina's mother had said. "The church don't allow no drinking and gambling." The rest of the family had nodded and stared at Jason. They had not believed Regina was serious until they attended the wedding. Once Regina's father had whispered, "Keep her well in hand, boy, and don't take your eyes off the Lord," and twice, Regina's mother had muttered something about postponing the wedding until spring. Regina had nodded patiently.

It was a simple ceremony. Regina and Jason could have been a couple from one of James Van der Zee's Harlem wedding photos come to life: Jason in his best piano man outfit, and Regina under a crowning pouf of French knotted hair that made Jason appear even shorter than he was. On one side of the church, Regina had lined up her family as if they were going to a funeral instead of a wedding. The next of kin were seated on the first row, followed by uncles and aunts, nephews and nieces, first cousins and shirt-tail relatives all the way down the line to Raybird Blackwell, the family's lost lamb, a third cousin once removed who was known to drink and gamble without feeling the least bit of sin. But all of them, from Regina's parents to Raybird Blackwell, studiously avoiding looking at Jason's side of the church where his stingy line of followers were represented by Miz Bea Weeks, Lilbeth, and Buford LaDonk, his close piano playing buddy and the only man who nickel-and-dimed the rum runners more than Jason.

Against the flickering silence on one side of the room and the mercury-quick stirrings from the adjacent pews, Regina answered, "I do," as if the two words were an aria, and soon after, she and Jason were whisked away from the church in Miz Bea Weeks' Lincoln Roadster. Regina's oldest sister never again saw the brocade coat Regina had pilfered from her closet that morning.

The morning that Regina Blackwell became Regina Packard, she never again thought about the farm near Cahokia or the choir at the Rock of Ages Church. That morning, she decided she had outgrown whatever it was the proper Blackwells stood for. "He is the shepherd and we are His flock," the preacher would shout, while Regina's family sniffed down anyone who didn't say "Amen" and "Yes Lord." But Regina had seen that same preacher snatch the choicest pieces of chicken her mother had set aside for his Sunday evening visit. And she'd seen her father wring his hands until they were ashy black, and still not get enough out of a few acres of land to feed his family. She had seen her mother sing the praises of the Lord, beat her children, and chop neck bones and onions as if one chore were no different from the other. Regina had waited until the time was ripe to leave her mother's house, and now that Jason had come along, she wasn't about to turn back.

That first year, they moved into a rooming house about half a mile from Miz Bea Weeks' and although Regina never missed a choir practice or church service, Jason, more often than not, would drag himself from the lamp-black space of sleep to find her staring across the mudflats towards the Eads Bridge and St. Louis on the other side of the river.

"You can't hardly see nothing from here," Jason would tell her. "Com'on, bring yourself to bed and snuggle."

Sometimes she'd let the curtains drop and crawl in beside him without a word. Sometimes she'd stand there, etched in the lacey grey light of a cloudy Missouri sky as if she'd been cut out of thick black paper. Jason was reminded of the silhouette portrait he'd bought from a carnival hawker at the fairgounds that summer. He'd watched the man's fingers quickly bend and twist the paper through the clicking blades of his scissors until, as if by magic, Regina's profile had appeared out of the pattern of snips and curves. Sometimes Jason felt that if he didn't force Regina away from the window, she'd remain frozen against the glass forever, her eyes turned away from him, toward the bridge and the city beyond.

On those days when she seemed destined not to turn back to him, it took him several minutes to break the spell of those castle-grey buildings on the other side of the river. And even then, she teetered on the edge of that hypnotic skyline, reluctant to turn away, to come back to the Illinois side and Jason. Always she gave the city one last caressing gaze.

"My Uncle Cohee works over yonder on Market Street," she'd murmur, and Jason would see her tilt toward that other world. "They got a whole mess of brownstones going up over near Chouteau," she'd tell him. "Say they gonna have trolley cars and everything."

The next month, Jason began working longer hours at Miz Bea Weeks' and sometimes, on sunny afternoons, he'd saved up enough money to take Lilbeth and Regina across the river to shop in the stores along Market Street. Lilbeth always stepped lightly, her head always uncovered to let the sun warm the quarrelling tangle of kinky hair that shadowed her dark face. But Regina, wearing a soft cloche hat, walked some distance away, and although she eagerly spent the money Jason gave her, she rarely spoke to Lilbeth once they'd crossed the river.

"Never know how many of those men we see been in that woman's bed," she sniffed when Jason chided her. Then she gestured toward the benches where several old men dozed in the sun near the Wedding of the Rivers Fountain outside of Union Station. "Maybe she done slept with some of them," Regina whispered.

Still, Jason saw Lilbeth and Regina reach for the same hat or length of creamy ecru lace. Regina no longer dressed like a Cahokia farm woman in shades of brown and beige woven from sensible cotton and wool. Now, like Lilbeth, she favored rayon and crepe de chine in colors that left her dresses moving in a rhythm of their own, and left Jason dazzled by the flicker of bugle beads, seed pearls, or little ropes of black crystals. Once, when a vendor made them buy an apple Regina had picked up and then decided she didn't want, Jason had seen in her face the same kind of stubbornness he saw in eyes of the girls at Miz Bea Weeks'. Regina had held her ground, turning her back on the man, whose English was soaked in sounds from northern Italy as he screamed insults about having his fruit touched by her black hands. But Jason had paid, tossing the nickel onto the lip of the cart while the Italian spit on the ground to ward off any black magic Regina might have cast on his produce.

Still, nothing seemed to cool her fever for St. Louis. Not even the day Buford absentmindedly had taken the car back to East St. Louis and left them stranded on the Missouri side, too far from the colored section of town to find a room, and too deep in the white section to find a taxi. Jason had taught Regina how to sleep in the rain, newspapers folded under her head and the overhang of the loading dock for shelter. Regina had been quiet but he knew she'd never slept. Even in the dark, he could feel her eyes were open, watching him, although she never spoke to him that night, or any other time, about what had happened.

"Miz Mildred's girl's working way out on Lindell Road," she told him. "Say she got a room in back of the house and she can go to town twice a month. Ain't nothing but three childrun to look after. That peckerwood's always taking his wife off somewheres, so Miz Mildred's girl don't have to cook for nobody cept that old man and them childrun. Say there ain't much to do no way. Other folks be cleaning. Say there's another family looking for a couple—man and wife. I told her we was married, Jason. Jason . . . you hyeah me?"

Jason hunkered in the middle of the bed and pulled the blanket under his chin. "Ain't gonna mooch for no white folks," he muttered. "I'll play five fingers on the eighty-eights until hell freezes over fore I do that kind of work."

Jason kept his promise until Buford LaDonk started working across the river as a skin man in one of the speakeasies along Lafayette.

"You got a good woman there," Buford told him one afternoon. "But you look like LICKETY-SPLUP. The more you put down, the LESS you pick up. Better take your box uptown and let Little Eva put some bucks down. You can rake in more coins playing for uptown white chicks than you can beating in Bea Weeks' place. Put some honky-tonk in those keys, Blood. How long you gone stay in Weeks' jook joint? Let her find some other boy."

"Now just hush up, Buford. Jason don't need no honky tonk," Regina interrupted. "We got plans that don't include no honky tonk. Don't we, Jason?"

Jason looked at his hands and tried to imagine his fingers moving without music.

"Can't book no change in the Black Bottom," Buford continued. "East St. Louis ain't nothing but a stopping-off place. Them rum runners just need a spot to buy some poontang fore they head on to Chicago. But man, Pro-HI-bition, it ain't gone be forever. Mark my words."

"I don't know nothing but ragtime," Jason told him. "Uptown, they wants razzmatazz. I just know how to keep them keys moving."

Buford laughed. "You'll learn slick as NO time. And you could do a little dealing. You always good with the cards."

Through the swirl of blue-grey smoke from Buford's cigar, Jason could see Regina squirming in her chair. Buford's shiny black, bald head gleamed like a billiard ball in the light, and the coat of his grey pin-striped was peppered with ashes and splotches of bad gin. In the diffuse light from the window, Regina seemed to flow into the soft collar of her dark red dress. Although she'd left a short flip of curls hanging over her ears when she'd pulled back her hair, she had a thin-faced look that set him on edge.

"My Uncle Cohee's got a son by his second wife name of Raybird Blackwell," Regina began. "Raybird say he can find a house for us, Jason. And I seen a nice horsehair sofa down on Market Street last week."

Before Jason could answer, Buford started to laugh. "I guess I best be making tracks," he chuckled. "Folks start to trotting out their kin on the married side, and I KNOW it's time for an old piano man to be stepping."

Jason rolled his cigarette between thumb and forefinger, and although his narrow head pecked the air in agreement, he made no move to show Buford to the door. Fragments of plans brushed against his skin like a dry itch, like the crackle of phlegm deep in his throat, but whatever Jason thought he was hung by the thin strings of an upright piano.

"Reckon I could still do my time at Bea Weeks' most Friday and Saturday nights," he mumbled.

Buford made a noise, a guttural sound that was almost a word. Jason remembered his father laughing louder than any of the others when he saw his son struggling with the packing crates on the loading docks. "Runt," his father would spit, a hoarse explosion of sound, like the clatter piano keys made when a fight broke out in the back parlor and someone was hurled against the keyboard.

Regina led Buford to the door. "You can visit any time you want, Buford. I spect it won't be long fore I'll fix up one of those big dinners and invite everybody. I already got my eye on a nice big old table. Seats eight. Me and Jason gonna make these rooms like home."

Buford turned to say goodbye to Jason, but stopped mid-sentence when he saw Jason rise from his chair. "Gonna walk Buford cross town," Jason muttered. "Be back directly."

When he brushed past Regina, she said, "Don't stay too long, Jason," and smiled sweetly.

Jason was half-way down the hall before Buford caught up with him. Behind them, they could hear Regina singing as she gathered up the cups and glasses they had used. The louder she sang, the faster Jason walked. They were three blocks away before Jason slowed down enough for Buford to catch up with him. Jason heard Buford talking to him, but he rarely answered and when he did, it was a half-uttered mumble that Buford could not clearly understand. When they reached Bond Street, they took a jitney and headed for Seventh Street and the Eads Bridge. Buford talked and Jason looked out of the window, trying to remember how it felt to know it was time to move on, to leave a town because his time had run out. By the time they'd reached the Missouri side, even the jitney driver had noticed Jason's silence, and he watched him in his rear view mirror, checking him as if to say he'd picked up too many customers headed for the city without money. The man looked obviously relieved when Buford paid him, counting off the fare from an impressive roll of bills.

Buford said, "Ain't gone be long fore you looking for some paying work. Bea Weeks ain't drawing no trade to mention, anyway. Got my eyes set on a hotel job. Do a little pianer on the weekends, but won't be tied to no keys. Be free-wheeling."

Jason raised his head as if he'd heard someone call his name, but Buford did not see the gesture. "Ain't nothing to it," Buford continued. "Just mooch a few coins. Tell me some boys got a running poker game down there on Chouteau." This time, Buford caught Jason's stare, and hitched up his pants until they were pulled tight in the crotch and he could see the full length of his spats, a trademark he'd decided to adopt after he'd heard big time Harlem hoodlums wore them. Then he laughed and did a little two-step shuffle. "Um-hum. It brings in the coins. When you gone cut yourself in for a little, Jason? Maybe you too busy being family?"

Buford ended his two-step in a half spin, and behind him, Jason could see several barges hurrying toward the docks at the foot of Jefferson Street. Behind that, he saw the faint glimmer of lights from the Illinois side of the river. The wind whipped the river into a muddy froth. Jason turned up his collar against the chilly draft. "Regina's a fine woman," he told Buford.

"Ain't never said she weren't," Buford said. "Seen many a FINE woman in my day. Mostly at night," Buford laughed. "You coming down on Chouteau with me?" he asked. "There's a rent party, wide open if you interested."

Jason shrugged. It was not the idea of bathtub gin and cards that made him hesitate. The city was filled with speakeasies and Jason knew bootleggers needed a good ragman to mellow the bitter hootch they sold. But there was Regina. When Jason held her in his arms, she unravelled in the muted darkness, and Jason heard the child in her voice. When she sang for him, his skin prickled against every note, but he could not keep away from her. Those nights he worked at Bea Weeks', Regina's singing seemed to suffocate him. And now, standing on a rainy the corner at the edge of the colored section of St. Louis, Regina's voice was the loudest sound in his head. He shook himself away from the sound, but when he opened his mouth to speak, the wind suddenly blew dirt into the air and he found himself almost choking on the grit that lodged itself in his mouth.

"Easy, Blood," Buford said as he beat Jason across the back. "We got plenty of time. This six and one rent hustle gone last till morning. Gonna pick up some change. There's plenty of room for you, Blood."

He followed Buford to a backroom joint sandwiched in a block full of brownstones. The rent party was in full progress when they arrived. It was a good house, enough people to raise the rent for several flats with money left over to sport food for the next party. In one corner, an upright piano was almost hidden under piles of suit-coats, stacks of used glasses and shallow plates filled with crusted bits of food and ashes. For a moment, Jason was ready to leave, then Buford pointed out Raybird Blackwell. Raybird was pouring drinks into china teacups, each splash of thin gin matched by the clink of coins into the Mason jar placed at the end of the table.

"Well shut my mouth," Buford said. "Seems like some of the Christians done joined over to the other side. Ain't that one of your wife's kin folk I'm looking at?"

Before Jason could answer him, Raybird spotted the two of them. "Hey there," he called to Jason. "I told Regina you gone be coming round here pretty soon. You ready to start working for me? Make it a family business."

"I figure Regina is all the Blackwells I got to put up with," Jason said. Buford laughed out loud, and Raybird snickered. Jason stared at Raybird for a moment, then eased his temper by looking around the room again. When Raybird saw Jason eyeing the pi-ano, he snorted, "We don't make no music here, boy. This here's a MONEY house."

This time, Jason turned his back on Raybird and took careful stock of the rest of the room. Two of the six tables were already banked with poker players, and in the corner, three men waited in the chairs lining the walls for another table to open. A big-boned brown-skinned woman with light gray eyes—devil eyes, as Miz Bea Weeks would say—moved between the tables with a tray of drinks. Her movements were jerky, not the fluid cat movements of the women at Bea Weeks', and when she grinned at Jason, her face did not hold that liquidy smile Jason saw in Lilbeth. This woman's grin was as thin and sharp as a razor's.

"That's Dru," Raybird told him. "She cleans up around here."

"Yeah," Buford laughed, "if you got the stomach for it, she'll clean you up too."

Raybird narrowed his eyes. "You ought to know, Buford. But we ain't here to count Dru's toke. You boys watching, playing, or doing?"

"We doing," Buford announced.

Jason watched Raybird's face change from tight caution to an open smile. It was the same movement he'd seen Regina perform whenever he allowed her to change his mind. Despite Raybird's bloated cheeks and red-rimmed eyes, he was, unmistakably, a Blackwell, and when he smiled, that finely honed Blackwell profile was clearly visible.

"Ain't this out of your league, Raybird?" Jason asked. "I thought your folks was temperance."

"What you see ain't all there is," Raybird said. "I don't have to be drinking to be selling." Jason grunted. "Ain't you learned nothing from watching them white boys on the East side? They don't dip in the till in their own house. You don't get rich drinking your own swill. This here's my house." Raybird paused, and Jason looked at him and shrugged. "You don't think Anheuser and Griesedich got rich drinking their own hootch, do you?" Raybird added. Jason said, "Un-hun," and shook his head. "Well now that you remember how to say Yes and No, you gone look or you gone deal?"

"I'm in," Jason sighed, and watched Buford finally relax.

"Well, why didn't you say so from the git-go," Raybird laughed. "Dru! Hey woman. Open us up another table. Can't be a full house every night," he added as Dru slowly began to set up a third table, "but there's change to be made most nights long as folks got to have a way to raise the rent. Ain't but one thing to remember, the house takes the seventh winner—six to one."

Jason nodded Yes, and that night, and for a month of nights, he tried to let the swish and flutter of cards fill his head with the music he so wanted to play. He tried to think of himself as having moved a step above Miz Bea Weeks, into a money house as Raybid had said. But Raybird's running poker game was cut-throat and coarse. The coins were greasy with sweat and the bills so smudged, Jason miscounted a bet at least once a night. There were no slick women serving Raybird Blackwell's games. No women whose thin voices tickled the back of his neck when they whispered "Hello." There was Dru, her breath always a bit rancid from her daily meal of onions and collard greens, and her lips always a little chalky from the cornstarch she ate as she worked the tables in Raybird's backroom. Dru was a country woman, her skin pebbly brown like old dirt, and her voice thickened by drinking. Jason missed Miz Bea's girls. And here, the piano stood in a decaying heap just out of reach in the far corner.

By the beginning of 1929, Jason worked Raybird's joint at night and ran numbers during the day. Regina still stood by the window, but now, Jason talked about when they'd be able to afford to rent a flat over on the Missouri side. He would talk and Regina would count money, lock it in the cash box in the bureau drawer, then stand by the window, dreaming. Jason had only one dream, and in it, he was always playing a ragtime piano.

Sometimes when Regina turned from the window, she'd find Jason frowning at her. Once, when she asked him about it, he'd said, "You remind me a bit of my grandmother. That woman would get one thing on her mind and run it into the ground. She was mean too. Fulani woman. Believed in roots and spells. Always trying to find some new piece of gold for her ears or her arms. Waited for the moon to tell her when to add a little bit of glitter. Had three or four earrings. Said the number of earrings could tell a slaver how many times you'd escaped. But the bracelets, they were her pride and joy. Arm bands, she called them. Had an arm full, and when she walked, they'd keep a little tune, a little jingle like she was holding old man death out the way."

Regina interrupted. "That's country talk, Jason. Why you want to bring up that country stuff?"

"I was just thinking bout a tune," Jason said. "Little bit like a piano the way them bracelets would jingle. Ping, ping-ping . . ."

"We ain't never gonna get nowhere if all you can talk is stories." She shivered and turned back to the window, pulling the curtains apart so she'd get a last glimpse of the sky before the light faded. "I ain't waiting for the moon to tell me nothing," she said, and shivered again. But when Jason walked to the window and put his arms around her, she held him close, soothed by the warmth of his body and forgetting, for the moment, what she dreamed was waiting for her on the other side of the river.

By the end of 1929, Jason began to see a pattern to his life, one that would have, no doubt, continued if rum running had kept Bea Weeks' business in money. But times got hard, and more than one man was out of a job by the end of that year. And in that year, Buford LaDonk started visiting Regina on those days Jason ran numbers for Raybird Blackwell. Then Buford helped Regina find the flat she wanted, a place, as Regina told him firmly, where the rooms were too small for a piano.

"And I found me a job too, Jason," she said the day she took Jason to see the new flat. Buford and Raybird went along with them.

"It's in a hotel," Raybird added, and Buford said, "You know they hiring more colored folks to do the cleaning now. Say the paddys charge too much money."

"I checked it out myself," Raybird told him while Buford winked and said, "Tell me they need a night man over there, too."

Jason glared at both of them, but Buford lounged in the doorway as if he had not seen the look, his legs crossed at the ankles and his spats dusted grey from city dirt. Raybird just turned away from him and stared out the window at cars heading toward Market Street and the river.

"Ain't much of a job, but we could use it to save some money for furniture," Regina said.

Jason remembered seeing the dung-brown face of the man who swept the portico of the sailor's hotel near the levee. Whenever the man caught Jason's eye, he would flash a snaggle-toothed smile and call out, "Hey, Brother."

"I can save money working the jobs I got. Add some music to Raybird's gaming tables, and he could be raking in the money. There's already a piano he ain't even using," Jason told Regina.

She moved closer to him. "This could be your last night at Raybird's, Jason honey. I already told him. Ain't that right, Raybird?"

"Sho did," he said.

"And I figured we could save us some money if Raybird was to move in with us. He can have the extra room. For a while at least," she added hastily.

Buford nearly purred. "It's all family, Jason. Just a little bit of family business, like Raybird is always saying."

"Miz Bea Weeks never did find another piano man," Jason interrupted. "I could go back there after tonight. Me and Buford, we could trade off."

Buford held up his hand to stop Jason before he could say anything else. "Blood, I'm out of here. Gone head over to Kansas City. Hear tell Moten and his boys playing downbeat. Moving away from ragtime."

"I ain't moving to Kansas City," Regina said firmly.

"You spect me to stay here and work the business with Raybird forever?" Jason asked.

"Got my eye on a new line of work. Gonna hit up to Chi-town. Gone keep my rusty dusty on track," Raybird chuckled.

"You hear that, Jason?" Regina cooed. "Raybird's got plans."

Jason said nothing.

Regina's mouth tightened. "Jason, you ain't never gonna make no money in Bea Weeks' cat house. That woman don't care about you. I'm the only one who cares about you. You don't need to be playing no piano. You best listen to me, Jason Packard."

"Yeah," Buford echoed. "Woman's got a point."

"How much money is left?" Jason asked. "IF we gone stay here, I can find me an old honky tonk cheap. Something somebody wants to sell in a hurry. I'll fit it in whatever extra space we got," he said, and looked pointedly at Raybird.

"I spect it don't do no harm in asking round, Cuz," Raybird told Regina. "Give it some time."

"We'll see," Regina muttered, and as she turned away, the string of black crystal beads arund her neck seemed to gather all the light bleeding through the milky leaded glass of the front door panel. At that moment, Jason remembered it had been some time since he'd heard Regina singing.

A week later, Raybird Blackwell closed his game room and started working the hotel. "All I got to do is clean out the lobby and make sure the ice box is full," Raybird told him. "I still got my morning run on the numbers, but now I got one foot clean with the law."

"Blood, there some cats give anything to be in your place," Buford told Jason. "Regina's the prettiest thing I seen around in a long time. But your woman's got her mind set on HOME. You need to be thinking upon how that grabs you."

Buford offered him a spot with Moten's group in Kansas City, but Jason couldn't face leaving Regina any more than he could face taking Raybird's hotel job. He was trapped, caught between where he was and someplace off in the distance. On those days when he was near the waterfront, he could see Eads Bridge rising out of the wharf and swelling to a hump over the river before it plunged into the mudflats of East St. Louis. He learned to read the shadows of the bridge, how the light changed the colors of the steel rim and how the span seemed to swell into the sky itself if the cloud cover were just the right shade of grey. Regina never looked toward the bridge anymore, and Jason couldn't even draw her attention to it.

More and more, he left the house at dusk and returned in the early dawn. More and more, he came home to an empty house, and puzzled, sat on the horsehair sofa watching the dim lights of cars heading down the avenue toward the bridge or across town toward Union Station. Sometimes he thought about Buford La-Donk, thought about how he could join Buford in Kansas City, but more often than not, Jason sat in silence, his thoughts not directed to any particular place.

One morning, after a night of trailing backroom poker games, Jason came home to find the house filled with more stillness than usual. At first, he was aware of a lull, as if no one had been in the rooms for months. Then he noticed the open bureau drawers and closets, hat boxes tilted at crazy angles above rows of wire hangers, and in the kitchen, a single glass, placed off center of the sink so that water trickled against its rim. When Jason saw Raybird's empty room, he knew Raybird had moved north taking Regina with him.

Regina had left only the large pieces of furniture, whatever could not be quickly moved. And she'd left Jason's clothes, neatly folded and arranged as if that alone represented her last wifely act. For a while, Jason sat on the edge of the wine-red vanity stool and quietly cried, then he left the flat. He was several blocks away before he thought of returning for his clothes, but the wind had begun to unroll toward the river, and Jason followed it.

At first, he told himself that he only needed time to think, that after a while, he'd go back across the river and visit Miz Bea Weeks, but each night, he'd wander through the downtown area and before the moon had turned translucent with grey light, he'd walk down to the levee, to the loading docks and warehouses, and there, under an overhang, he'd find a place to sleep. For a while, he managed to snag odd jobs in some of the joints he and Buford had worked, but always, the piano betrayed him and he'd end the night picking away at notes that had no melody except madness. On those nights, Jason dreamed of Regina, imagined he smelled her scent still buried in the crevices of his own body. And in a time when half the country was beginning to dream of bread lines, Jason had no trouble losing himself in his meager dreams.

Somewhere in the quagmire of Market Street stores, fresh air fruit stands, loading docks, and bars, Jason Packard grew old. Some days when the sun was crested over the waterfront, when it seemed actually to give life to the statues in front of Union Station, frozen mid-dance in the Wedding of the Rivers, when it reflected the glint of gold off some woman's earrings, Jason would sit on the park bench and let his fingers trail the air in half remembered ragtime patterns. Children passing by gave him wide berth, and church ladies on their Sunday strolls, shook their heads and wondered why some upstanding black woman could not have set him on the right path. But the other old men, those who had known bathtub gin, rent parties, and how easy travelling was before times got hard, nodded their heads and sometimes, if they'd had just enough to eat or were fresh from a shared bottle, they'd hike up their pants, crotch tight, and dance a ragtime step to Jason's tunes.

Jeremy Franklin Simmons

JEREMY FRANKLIN SIMMONS IS A FOOL AND EV-
erybody on the block knows it. Fern has told me again and
again to stay away from Jeremy.

"That Simmons boy is just plain no good," she says.

"Acts too grown," Uncle Dell adds.

And Margay is sure to say something like, "Ain't no fool like a
fool's fool."

Margay is my mother, but I never call her Mother or Mommy,
and everybody, even cousins, calls my grandmother Mama, just as
they call my grandfather Papa. I had even been named after my
grandmother, but Papa, who had picked out the other part of my
name, calls me Jo-Jo, and so does everybody else, unless I'm in
trouble, and then I'm called Josephine Ethel Barron. Margay and
I live in three rooms on the top floor of Fern's walk-up. My Aunt
Fern rents rooms on the second floor where my Aunt Maddie used
to stay before she got married and moved to Texas. And my Aunt
Fern and Uncle Dell live on the first floor. I spend a lot of time on
the first floor helping Fern cook or carry things up and down the
stairs when she has to clean the rooms on the second floor. Uncle
Dell is quiet when he's there, although most of the time he's off being a pullman car porter on the railroad, but when he's there he
gives me a nickel so I can go to old man Farrow's store for candy.
Margay doesn't mind that I'm down there so much, but she always
tells me not to make a nuisance of myself.

"If you buzz around in everybody's face like a fly, you get
swatted."

They all think Jeremy is a big old fly that needs swatting, but
Jeremy Franklin Simmons is the biggest kid on the block, a fat,

slick-headed kid who's never invited anywhere but manages to show up everywhere, and everybody is afraid of him except Bumpsy Pritchard and, maybe, Monica Frasier. When Jeremy gets into trouble, everybody else is in trouble too. He's always louder than anyone else, always demands attention, always carries things too far, and always seems to be around when someone gets hurt. Jeremy Franklin Simmons can make the dullest games exciting, but no matter what he does, things seem to go wrong.

So I spend endless hours listening to Fern and Margay tell me how dumb it is to hang around a big fool like Jeremy, how I should know better than to let anyone tell me what to do when that someone doesn't even know right from wrong himself.

"He's too dumb to find his butt in the dark with a flashlight and a map," they say, and I can't tell them how Jeremy's pigeon-toed foolishness can teach me more about right and wrong than any preacher, how just watching Jeremy get into trouble will keep me on the safe side. I can't say anything, and they go right on accusing me of trying to cover up for Jeremy.

"Birds of a feather flock together," Margay says.

Even Uncle Dell had something to say one time when he saw Jeremy clowning around down near Hodiman tracks. Uncle Dell was taking me downtown on the trolley. Woodrow Payne's papa has a brand new 1949 DeSoto, but I'd rather go uptown with Uncle Dell on the trolley than ride with fat Woodrow any day of the week.

"Saw that boy, Jeremy, running down the middle of the street like a chicken with his head cut off," Uncle Dell told me. "Ran right in front of the trolley, ran smack dab down the middle of the street with a big old mangy-looking dog in his arms. Don't you go fooling around on Hodiman, Jo-Jo. These folks get to drinking around here and you don't know what will happen," he said, waving his hands toward the taverns banking both sides of the tracks.

"Them boys always down here, Uncle Dell," I told him.

"You let them be where they want to be."

"Yes, Uncle Dell," I answered, because I knew whatever I said about Hodiman tracks would get me into trouble. You can see some of everything down on Hodiman, even some things you don't want to see. Mama calls the folks who hang around there "low life."

Mama never talks to anybody from Hodiman tracks except Mr. B-B, because Mama says Mr. B-B didn't always live near the tracks. Mama says Mr. B-B wasn't always a rag picker. She says he just fell into hard times, and whenever she sees him, she shakes her head and says, "That poor man sure has had his trials and tribulations." In the winter she always finds a few rags and bottles to give him so his cart won't look so bare, but even so, she won't talk to Mr. B-B when he's walking down Hodiman. She says once folks get in the gutter they do strange things, and you have to stay clear of them.

One time I went walking near Hodiman with Monica Frasier and Rosalind Washington, but we didn't get very far. We'd just turned the corner when some old man leaned out of a doorway, breathing whiskey and years of dirt. "Where you going, you pretty little things?" he said. I remembered what Mama told me, and I got so scared I turned right around and headed for home. Monica said I was chicken, but she and Rosalind were walking faster than I was. Another time, Jeremy and Bumpsy Pritchard got chased all the way home by some old man from Hodiman, and Mama said, "It's sure a good thing that old man didn't catch them."

I guess the worst thing that could happen is to end your life on the tracks, so Uncle Dell really didn't need to warn me, and I surely didn't want to talk about Jeremy or Bumpsy or any of the other boys and what they did out there. They're always finding soda pop bottles and stuff, and the rest of us help sell them. All those pennies buy a lot of comics and Kool-aid at old man Farrow's. I guess if it wasn't for old man Farrow's store, we wouldn't think about Hodiman tracks one way or the other, but I didn't want to say that to Uncle Dell. Besides, Uncle Dell takes me downtown whenever he has more than three or four days off from his railroad job, and I don't want to upset that in any way.

I like Uncle Dell almost as much as I like Papa, but Uncle Dell is so quiet most of the time, I can't tell if he really likes me or not. The only thing he says to me most of the time is, "Hey, Jo-Jo," or "You want a nickel, Jo-Jo?" or "Let's go downtown, Jo-Jo." We ride the trolley all the way to town and back without saying a word, and if we get off he'll buy me something. "You want that, Jo-Jo?" he'll say, but he never really talks to me like Papa does. Papa talks most of the time, showing me all kinds of things and telling me how they work or what they're for. Whenever we go for a walk or down-town on the trolley, everybody thinks Papa is my father, cause we look so much alike, and Papa never says one way or the other. "This is my little girl Jo-Jo, alright." Then he takes my hand inside his big fist and says, "Come on, Jo-Jo, we got people to see." I have to skip to keep up with him. I just know Papa could walk clear across the country without getting tired.

Sometimes Uncle Dell tells me to be careful around boys, as if he has to say that when Papa isn't around, or because I don't have a father of my own to tell me those things, but I think he says it most of the time because Fern tells him to. To make matters worse, Fern half believes the rumor started by Mildred Harris that I like Jeremy Franklin Simmons, and no matter what that old liar Mildred says, I wouldn't have Jeremy Franklin Simmons on a Christmas tree, although I've tried to imagine him grown up by about six years with more hair on his bullet-shaped head. But all that was before Jeremy Franklin Simmons ate that mouse.

It started in August when we'd played the regular summer games so many times that nothing seemed to please us. Rosalind had gone on the train to Chicago, and she was full of "In Chicago they do this or that," "In Chicago you can go this place or that place," "You see this in Chicago, but you never see that," until I swear I thought Chicago was going to become her middle name.

The more she told us about Chicago, the more we tried to see beyond the postage-stamp all-white cemetery, the cinders of Ash Hill, the row of clip joint taverns and the steel rail fence of the state highway. But none of her stories made our eyes get as big as the one about the circus and its tattooed people, its fat-thin-tall people, snake people, fire-eating people, and most of them, Rosalind said, were black.

Sereatha Higgins had been to the circus before, but none of us had ever seen a black man eating fire. We wondered how it could be done, how much practice you needed, and how mighty fine it must be to have the crowds cheer and clap as the flames disappeared down your throat.

"I could eat some fire," Jeremy boasted.

"We could all eat some fire," Mildred added.

But Bumpsy said, "They don't eat fire, girl. That's just make believe."

"Then what is it, Mr. Big Stuff?" I asked.

"It's something they put together to make out like it was fire. Just some food or something."

"Naw. In Chicago they eat fire," Rosalind said. "They wouldn't stand there eating food. Besides, food don't burn and this stuff was burning, flames and all."

We were quiet, trying to imagine the smoke curling around some man's lips and flames licking his cheeks.

"Aw, come on, Rosalind," somebody said, "tell us what they really eat."

We talked and talked until finally Woodrow Payne ate a whole sheet of newspaper, just to prove it could be done, but Woodrow Payne would eat anything, so that didn't really count. Then Monica decided to eat dirt—not just any old dirt, mind you, but special dirt that Monica spent the better part of a perfectly good day looking for. Jeremy said dirt was dirt, and passed off the whole thing as unimportant, but we could see that he was as impressed as all the rest of us. We wouldn't admit it, but we couldn't tell one kind of dirt from the other, although we helped Monica until she found what she wanted in Miz Lucy's garden. Monica said it had a certain smell to it, like clean newspaper, and since everyone had watched Woodrow Payne chew newspaper like Wrigley's or Juicy Fruit, Monica probably knew what she was talking about.

Some of us wanted to quit after Monica ate part of Miz Lucy's garden, and getting ready for the first day of school slowed us down a bit.

"You kids been acting awful strange," Fern told me after she had to drag me away from the neighborhood so I could go downtown to get my school shoes. "I can't understand why you want to stay home when you know we're gonna get some things for school. And here you already got your money for junk pencils and stuff from Uncle Dell, too. He just spoils you rotten."

I leaned against the window of the trolley and didn't answer.

"Miss Frasier told me Monica's been sickly here late. I don't suppose you know nothing about that?"

I watched the streets change from dirty to clean as we got closer to the downtown stores.

"Sereatha's mother found her chewing up rulers. Said she told her all you kids promised to do that. What you want to chew rulers for? Don't be so stupid. Sometimes I don't know what I'm gonna do with you. Margay needs to take better care of you, but she's got to work. You on your own too much. With everybody working all day and sometimes all night, you got too much time for trouble."

Fern went on and on until we got downtown, but all I could think about was how I was gonna talk her into buying penny loafers instead of saddle shoes.

"Maybe school will knock some sense into you," she added, but that didn't seem likely since we thought of crazier things to do in the winter than we ever had in the summer. We had a game we played when the cold wind whipped across the river and the schoolyard was dotted with frozen bunches of kids who were gonna have fun during recess, no matter what the weather. One of us, whoever was brave or foolish enough to be "It," stood against the building and chanted, "Everybody, everybody, pile on me," again and again until they got so cold or scared they finally broke the chant. Then that unlucky fool, back against the brick wall, nose frozen wet, was rushed by a screaming, smelly mass of ten or more kids who ran forward like those mobs of howling heathens the preacher carried on so about every Sunday. The trick was to break the chant and scuttle away just after the mob had picked up too much speed to change its direction.

We played that game each winter, and it was as dumb as trying to learn to eat fire, so nobody was surprised when Jimmy Dufree began to eat erasers the first week of school, smacking on big gummy brown ones like he was eating ginger snaps. Our teacher, Miss Samples, put an end to it right away, but we were off on our circus trip again, and by October, I decided to try hedge leaves.

I really like the smell of damp basement walls better, even licked one once, but it made me spit and spit until my mouth was dry, so I settled on hedge leaves. You have to eat hedge leaves in one move, snitch the fat waxy heartshaped little ones from the rows of freshly cut hedges lining the sidewalks, then open your mouth wide and pop them in like jelly beans, swallowing before you get a chance to bite. In four or five trips, I could pluck at least eight different clumps of hedges before I'd get caught.

That's the trouble. Folks on our block take special care of their hedges, so when I wander down the street, eating my way past Mr. So and So's and Mrs. So and So's, I hear screams of "Get away from there!" and "What you think you're doing?" trail me until I reach Monica's or Sereatha's house, full up to my eyeballs in hedge leaves. It's lucky for me that most people can't really tell one kid from another, but I found out in a hurry that it's better to snitch leaves in early evening, a time when the light is so dim folks can't even begin to know whose mother needs to be told, a time when the leaves get crisp and tingly because the air has just the right tinge of cold in it, like a faucet when the hot and cold water doesn't quite mix but sort of run sideways and inside each other.

Sometimes those old hedges talk at night, and just before I pluck a leaf, I hear what sounds like a whisper. It isn't clear at first, but it gets a little louder as my hand moves nearer. It always sounds like those hedges are saying, "Don't touch me. Can't you see I'm perfect?" That scares me a little, and for a second my hand stops mid-air—then I dry-snap a leaf, pop it in my mouth and wait to see if those old hedges have anything else to say. The talking ones always seem a little bit sweeter.

But Bumpsy Pritchard outdid us all by eating a worm. It was just a little worm, not nearly as much to chew as Jimmy Dufree's erasers, but Bumpsy was the first one to eat something that was still alive, and I thought he was so brave I dreamed about Bumpsy and his dimpled smile every night for a week.

Bumpsy waited until Monday, right after school when everyone was still standing around on the playground. He had carried the worm around in a little cigar box all day, but he didn't let us know what he was going to do until after school. He even waited until Sereatha helped Mildred find her spelling book before he told us what he was going to do. When Bumpsy opened the box, Monica squealed like a stuck pig and Michael Davis started hopping up and down on one leg like he had to go to the bathroom. He had on a little red cap and his mouth was open in an "O" and he looked like that billboard picture of the guy saying, "Call for Philip Morris!" Jeremy hit Michael so he'd keep still, then turned to Bumpsy and double-dog-dared him to eat the worm.

Bumpsy waited for a minute, letting everyone watch that thing wiggle around inside the cigar box. He held the box under my nose, but I didn't jump and squeak like Monica. Then he gave me a big dimpled grin and winked. I almost missed seeing the worm go into his mouth, because Monica saw him wink too. She giggled and nudged me until I dropped my head and stepped back a little so it wouldn't look like I was standing too close to Bumpsy. But I looked up in time to see him pick up the worm and stick out his tongue, licking air, while that slick grey thing hung from his fingers like a fat piece of spaghetti. Then he dropped it in his mouth and smiled.

For a full minute we didn't say a word. Then Monica started screaming and making burping sounds, Sereatha held her throat and ran out of the playground, and Michael said he really did have to go to the bathroom now.

A week later, Jeremy Franklin Simmons decided to eat a mouse. Everyone on the block knew about my hedge leaf snitching, just as we knew about Woodrow Payne's newspaper, Jimmy Dufree's erasers, Monica's cup of dirt and Mildred's dirty old grass right out of vacant lots, but Jeremy Franklin Simmons didn't have any real competition until Bumpsy Pritchard ate that ugly grey worm, and Jeremy, who wasn't about to let anyone else be king of the District, got so mad he ate a mouse and threw up all over the lunch room.

The rest of us were still talking about what Bumpsy had done, but Jeremy had been quiet all week. On the day it happened, Bumpsy was telling us one more time how the worm had tasted, when Jeremy slipped into the seat beside him and opened his lunch pail. You couldn't miss that nasty, squeaky thing, sitting there all slick and pink, like a fat piece of leftover something that nobody wanted. When Monica saw it trembling between his sandwich and half an orange, she screamed as usual. We all knew that mouse came from the fifth grade science room, and that was bad enough, but before we could move away from the table, call a teacher or anything, Jeremy picked it up by the tail, took a deep breath and the mouse was gone.

We couldn't believe it. Bumpsy let out a long awful croaking noise and toppled backwards off his seat. I didn't see him get up because kids were screaming, turning over lunch trays and almost trampling each other trying to get away from the table. Jeremy kept looking bug-eyed and sicker by the minute, then he fell across the table, choking on that awful thing caught in his throat. I'd never heard so much noise, and when Mrs. Wilson, who serves up the soup, threw her spoon clear across the room, pulled her apron up over her head and screamed like a fire truck on the way to a four-alarm, I decided to get out of there without waiting to see how long Jeremy would keep that mouse inside him. I didn't see Jeremy finally get sick, but when we were called into the principal's office I certainly heard about it.

Actually, it was hard to hear anything at first because everybody was talking all at once. Miss Samples kept crying and saying, "I don't know what got into them. I just don't know what got into them," and I had to squeeze my lips tight to keep from telling her, "What got into Jeremy was a mouse." And Mrs. Crutcher, the vice-principal, kept wringing her hands and dabbing her head with a little white handkerchief that smelled exactly like Mr. B-B's breath after he'd been away for a few days. She was careful to keep from wetting her purple-blue dyed hair, but each dab left a little wet spot on her skin. "Oh my good Lord, they're going to cut that child open," she cried.

"You can count on that," Sara Blount said. But she was the nurse and she liked to stick you with needles or pour iodine on a raw spot.

"In the fourth grade," Mr. Martin said, "the fourth grade and you act like you're still in kindergarten." He kept pacing the floor and banging his hand on the desk every now and then like he was trying to remind us how he was the principal, in charge of everybody in the room. "I won't have it!" he shouted. "I won't have it. Shape up or you're out. You know what I mean? You all know what that means, don't you?"

He said it so loud, even the teachers shut up. I tried to imagine what that would mean in the worst possible way, but all I could really come up with was being sent away with Jeremy Franklin Simmons for the rest of my life. Sent away with him sitting on one side and Sara Blount on the other. I looked at Mildred, Monica and Bumpsy, but they were all looking at the floor. The only one who caught my eye was Sereatha, but then, Sereatha is always just right and just so about everything. And there she was, staring back, her pleated skirt hanging just right and her braids as neat as a pin. That nasty old seersucker pinafore Margay made me wear was already crumpled like a wad of paper beside my right knee, and my leg stuck out like a skinny black pencil with the knee all beat up like somebody had been chewing on it. But Sereatha sat straight as a ruler while Mr. Martin yelled like he expected somebody to fall over in a faint and make everything alright again.

"You're all suspended for the rest of the week," he said. "That'll give you time to think about what you've done."

"I didn't do it. Jeremy did it," Sereatha whined. "I don't see why I have to go home."

Mr. Martin turned on her and pointed his finger the way the preacher does when he's giving the Lord's command. "Birds of a feather flock together. You'll all go home."

Then I heard Fern and Margay outside the door and I knew it was just my luck to be sent home first. The other kids gave me low sorrowful puppydog looks, even Sereatha, and I stood up to face the music.

All the way home, they yanked and pulled at me, jerking my arms and hair and dress like they wanted to shape me up the way Mr. Martin had demanded. All the way home they tried to make me feel totally responsible for what that old fool Jeremy had done. They yapped me from the principal's office right into Mama's parlor, and when they weren't flying off at the mouth, they were snatching my clothes or popping me across the head.

"Are you crazy, girl?"

"Ain't you got no sense?"

"Why you let that boy put that thing in his mouth?"

"How long did it take you to think up a dumb thing like that?"

"Have you gone plumb out of your mind?"

And I tried to look half-way smart while they asked me questions I surely couldn't answer. Finally, Uncle Dell and Uncle Roman said it made no sense to sit around jawing about how dumb I had been since they all agreed on that, and Papa said it was maybe because I didn't know any better, that maybe I wasn't learning what I needed to know in that school, especially with Margay having to work all the time. And Mama said, "Yes, Lord, that was the case." And she said she was going to take it personal upon herself to make sure I went straight to school every day, and church every Sunday.

"Keep her butt in this house is what you ought to do," Margay said.

"Well, she got to get some education," Papa said. "Got to go to school so she won't stay dumb all her life." Then he looked at Margay, long and hard, and I saw her clamp her lips tight around an answer.

Then Mama said, "She'll go to school and to church. Somebody's got to pray for Miz Simmons' boy. He must be suffering something terrible right now. Jesus listens to the prayers of the children, so she'll go to church."

Fern said, "Humph . . . that ain't what she needs if you ask me," but she was just talking to be talking because everything had been settled.

Oh, they weren't quite finished with me. I got lectures on how I couldn't do this and how I couldn't do that. Uncle Dell even took me by the hands and looked hard into my eyes when he told me how I'd worried everybody unnecessarily. And Papa warned me once again about playing with kids who were wild. But the Sunday after Jeremy Franklin Simmons ate that mouse, I was plunked down in the first row with the other kids and we all sat there listening to the preacher sweat through a long sermon about how the lambs of God too often stray from the flock. We just hung our heads and tried to look as pitiful as we could. There were only six of us, because Michael is Catholic, and Monica goes to the sanctified church on Saturdays, and Jimmy Dufree won't go to any church at all, but without Jeremy, we all looked like chocolate-colored Raggedy Ann dolls somebody dropped in the first pew of Abyssinia Church, like that picture of Uncle Roman standing in line for the CCC camp that Mama has clipped and framed from the front page of the Argosy newspaper. Every time the preacher started shouting about how one lost lamb made the Lord worry as much as the whole flock, six pair of eyes shifted from side to side and six bodies squirmed against the already shiny seats.

The church ladies behind us started singing out "Yes Lord" and "Amen" so loud, I almost couldn't hear Mildred tell me how the doctors cut a hole in Jeremy's throat so he could breathe while they dug that mouse out of him. And Woodrow Payne said they'd tied Jeremy to the bed and stuck tubes in his body, "even in his ears," and the church ladies said, "We shall be saved," and "Praise the Lord." And I remembered how much trouble Jeremy caused whenever his mother could get him in church, how one Sunday he even put salt in the wine and it tasted so awful, everybody wanted to spit it out but couldn't. Jeremy was the one who told us church wine was really grape juice, and Jeremy was the one who drew a big picture of the devil and pinned it on Deacon Cole's back like a "kick me" sign. But there we were, right there in the front row, singing "Jesus is the Light of the World," and praying for the lost lamb like Jeremy had never done anything wrong.

I waited until the church ladies were in a loud chorus of "Yes Lord" and "Thank You Jesus," then I nudged Bumpsy Pritchard and said, "Get us out of here." With Jeremy gone, I knew we could count on Bumpsy to come up with a plan.

We all stuck together, had even ganged up on some other kids from time to time, but none of us let the others down. Every one of us—Bumpsy, Monica, Rosalind, even Sereatha—practiced bad-mouthing when recess got too dull and we could corner some kid on the playground. We'd sing, "I would if I could but I can't so I ain't," or "I hate to talk about your Mama, she's a good old soul. . . ." then end by teasing that kid on his family's biggest sore point, but if that kid moved into a house on our block, we fought anyone who talked about him. We ham-boned the Dozens, palm against mouth against thigh in a hit-slap-uh-uh-huh that didn't need words. Fern whacked me a good one whenever she caught me hamboning. But we never jumped somebody and beat them up like the kids from Cottage Street. And we weren't like that gang on Newstead Avenue who waited until the strongest kid was home sick before they picked a fight.

Now Jeremy was sick and we were all sitting there like copy-cats of Sereatha Higgins on her good days, like butter wouldn't melt in our mouths. So I nudged Bumpsy again and he started the pinching and kicking, and after a while, folks got tired of saying, "Keep still, child," and "Come over here and sit by me," and "Stop twitching." One by one, somebody from the Ladies Auxiliary would grab us by the neck and march us down the aisle, white gloves on the ends of their black arms like flashlights pinning us on a path to the Sunday School room in the basement where we would learn to behave ourselves. Mildred went first, then I followed Rosalind and Bumpsy. Woodrow Payne told us Sereatha had grabbed him by the knickers and dragged herself out of the seat when Deacon Cole's wife collared him. "I wasn't about to sit there by myself," Sereatha pouted.

Then Bumpsy said, "We don't need no snitch, so you just go on back in there and sit down, Miz Lady Sereatha Big-mouth."

For once, Sereatha stood her ground and they would have had an argument if I hadn't hushed them up. "Cut it out," I said. "We gonna have to get across town and back before they get to this wine down here." I waved my hand toward the table full of little cups of grape juice lined up and ready for all those sinners singing and clapping their hands in the church pews above us.

Bumpsy narrowed his eyes. "What's across town?" He looked at the row of cups, poured evenly right to the top, and licked his lips.

"Boy, look at me!" I shouted. "We going across town to see Jeremy."

That got his attention alright. While the others were buzzing and fretting, even with Mildred tying and untying the strings on her brand new oxfords like she had to practice doing something she already knew by heart, I got them out of there. If I'd bothered to look up the stairs behind me, I would have seen Papa, but as it was, I had enough trouble keeping Bumpsy from the wine table and keeping Woodrow Payne from howling when he tore his Sunday knickers trying to get his fat body through the basement window. Directly across the street, we ran into Jimmy Dufree, hiding in his regular place of waiting for church to let out. And when we got to Monica's, Sereatha went up, all innocent, and asked Miz Frasier if Monica couldn't come to her house for dinner. Monica's mama was so surprised to see old stuck-up Sereatha at her door, she didn't even want to know what time Monica would be home.

It was easy going until we reached Hodiman tracks. Hodiman tracks are like those little lines on the maps in geography lessons when Miss Samples is trying to teach us about the League of Nations and how countries can be broken up and put together by somebody running a line this way or that. We were on one side of the broken line and Jeremy was in the hospital on the other side. It wasn't that we were scared. If we want to be scared, all we have to do is go to Ash Hill on our bikes. When you race down Ash Hill, you have a choice of jiggedy-hicking on loose cinders, skidding into a car, or slamming against a gravestone in the cemetery on the other side of the street. And when the whole neighborhood has just dumped a week's worth of furnace cinders on the hill, you can leave pieces of your skin behind if you fall on some coal that's still glowing. Rosalind has a big scar on her leg from last year. So if we want to really be scared, we wouldn't come down to Hodiman tracks and stand around, looking stupid.

What stopped us was not knowing how badly we wanted to see old stupid Jeremy Franklin Simmons. Crossing Hodiman tracks meant going against the grain of everything we'd been told not to do. On the other side is a city full of Don'ts and Can'ts and white folks to tell you about it. On the other side are places where you lose your name and just become "boy" and "girl" or "chile," and your mama has to say "Yes, ma'am," and your papa has to cross the street to keep from meeting folks he wants to fight. That's the side where money comes in one color—white. Where nothing is broken or beat up, and even the yards look smooth and pretty as the milk Mr. Nichols delivers from the Creamery Dairy every morning, the kind he calls "hog-mogonized." That's the side where everything is made just right, and everybody looks the same, and folks don't care doodley-squat about how much you got to eat or how hard you got to work. Except for the time when Bumpsy had run after Mr. B-B's horse when it broke loose from the cart, or the time when Jeremy had double-dog-dared us, we'd never crossed Hodiman tracks without going on an errand to one of the big stores up-town.

I knelt down and tried to kill time by rolling my socks around both ankles so that one wasn't drooping over my shoe like a boat and the other wasn't half tucked under my heel. Everybody else started fidgeting too, then Rosalind said, "Somebody's hiding behind that tree," and I turned around and saw Papa. I said, "Com'on," and we all raced across Hodiman tracks, screaming like those swarms of wasps we find in the dump shed behind old man Farrow's store every summer.

I swear, Monica took us on a short cut to the hospital and Rosalind knew how to get to the children's floor through the kitchen where her mama used to work, but even so, when we opened the stairwell door and stepped out into the hall, the first person I saw was Papa.

Papa said, "Where are you going, baby girl?"

I turned to run, but there was a wall of kids between me and the door, and all of them were staring up at my grandfather, who seemed to grow at least seven feet taller. Bumpsy's mouth was hanging open, and his nose was already wet. Rosalind's thick glasses blinked in the light like headlamps for a Ford, and Sereatha was twisting that little handkerchief she likes to carry on Sundays.

The only one moving was Jimmy Dufree, and he'd dropped to his knees and was crawling down the hall away from us.

Papa said, "Stop," and Jimmy froze, his butt tooted in the air like a baby with a full diaper load. "I said, where are you going?" Papa repeated.

"We're going to see Jeremy, Papa," I said. Papa kept staring, waiting. "We come to tell him we miss him, Papa," I added. And Mildred said, "Yeah, miss him."

"Get off your knees, James Arthur Dufree. Just no telling what kind of germs on this floor," Papa said.

Bumpsy said, "These white folks gonna let us see Jeremy?"

"This ain't no white hospital, boy," Rosalind said. "Ain't nothing but black folks like us in this hospital. Ain't that right?" she asked Papa.

"They'll let us see Jeremy, won't they, Papa?" I asked.

"How many of you need to tell that boy you miss him? Can't let everybody go in his room at the same time," Papa said.

We were all ready to fight to go in, then a nurse walked by pushing a cart loaded with smelly pans, crumpled towels, and little cups of funny-looking water. "I can wait out here," Jimmy Dufree said. "Me too," Mildred said, and Sereatha and Rosalind nodded "yes." I took a deep breath and stepped right up beside Papa. Monica, Bumpsy and Woodrow Payne followed me. Then, before we had a chance for second thoughts, Papa took three or four steps and pulled us into Jeremy's room.

Jeremy's bed was right in the middle of a line of beds, but his was the only one with all the curtains draped around it. We stumbled along behind Papa, trying to keep up without bumping into each other, and when we got to the spread of curtains, Papa cleared his throat. The curtains barely moved when Miz Simmons slipped through the opening. Standing beside Papa, she seemed not to be taking up any space at all, and I had to blink to remember that this little bitty woman had anything at all to do with old noisy Jeremy Franklin Simmons. Standing in that hospital room with all those other little kids looking like paper doll cut-outs in shoe-box beds, I couldn't get myself to really believe any of us had anything to do with Jeremy. Papa and Mrs. Simmons were talking, but their voices were so low, I couldn't make out what they were saying. Woodrow Payne stood behind me, but he kept shifting from one leg

to the other like Michael Davis does when he has to go to the bathroom, except Woodrow Payne never has to go to the bathroom as
much as Michael Davis does. Then I realized that Woodrow Payne
was moving his mouth, except I couldn't hear what he was saying
either.

I thought I had gone deaf. I could see people moving around.
Nurses walked back and forth, their arms and faces black, but the
rest of them covered in white like their bodies didn't really belong
to them at all. But I couldn't hear their footsteps. Curtains rippled
and lights over the bed went on and off, but there wasn't any noise.
I was sure I had gone deaf until I saw Monica and Bumpsy over by
the bed next to Jeremy's. They leaned over and stared at the kid
who was sleeping in the bed, the kid's face all swollen grey-brown
with little crusts of snot and tears around his mouth and nose.
Then the kid pooted, a quiet rolling fart that sounded like popcorn
in a frying pan. Monica held her nose and backed up against
Bumpsy, who nearly knocked over a tray of water and pills hooked
over the side of the kid's bed. Papa turned and said, "Shh," and
suddenly I could hear everything clear as bells.

"What's the matter with this one?" somebody said behind the
curtain covering Jeremy's bed.

"Tried to eat a rat," somebody else answered.

"Good lord, these nigrahs will eat anything."

"No, I mean this rat was still alive."

"That's even worse. Cannibals."

Papa gathered Miz Simmons in one arm and snatched the
curtains back with the other. The two white men standing over
Jeremy's bed jumped like he'd tried to hit them. "Well, doctor,"
one said, "I guess we've done as much as we can here." The second
one nodded, but the way he looked at Papa glaring at him, you
could tell he wasn't sure he didn't have something else to do.

They clicked their pens in place and tried to brush past us.
Bumpsy kicked one in the ankle so neat and fast, the man couldn't
tell if he'd tripped against the leg of the bed or over his own feet.
Miz Simmons was crying and Papa said, "Come on, children. We
come to visit Jeremy, and we can't stay long," then he led Miz
Simmons behind the curtains.

We turned and watched those doctors walking down the row
of beds, their white coats flapping behind them like capes. When

they got to the door, the one with the worried face gave us one more look. By this time, the four of us were standing in a little group, and when we saw he was watching us, we stuck out our tongues.

Papa twisted me around. "Come in here. Don't be acting like monkeys in front of these white folks," he said. "Come on in here and say *Hi* to this child so he can get some rest."

We went in, but there wasn't much to say Hi to. Jeremy looked waxy like those penny bottles of candy syrup, and Miz Simmons just kept crying. Jeremy smelled like medicine and a bag hanging over his bed kept puffing in and out in time with his breathing, going "skree-ump, skree-ump" like an old piece of roof shingle flapping in the breeze. Monica and Woodrow stood on one side of the bed, and I stood on the other side with Papa and Bumpsy. Miz Simmons let us come up and talk to Jeremy one at a time. I held Jeremy's hand for a few minutes, but it was too hot and dry to hold for very long. And I couldn't hardly see his face for all the stuff they had around it to keep his head still so he wouldn't twist inside the big bandage around his neck.

They didn't have any tubes in his ears, but Woodrow was right about tubes everywhere else. And when Jeremy started coughing, stuff clouded up inside them. Then a nurse came in and told us we had to go away so the doctor could see him again. On the way out, we passed by a doctor rushing toward Jeremy's bed. He was another white man with a worried face, but not one of the ones who'd already been in the room.

"Ain't they got no black doctors in here, Papa?" I asked when we got back to the hallway.

"None that I can tell," he said.

"Is Jeremy gonna be alright?" Woodrow Payne asked.

"If they take care of him," Papa said.

"They better," Bumpsy said.

Then we had to explain to Mildred and the rest of them what we'd seen. By the time we got to the front door, we had four different versions of how many doctors had been next to the bed, and how many kids had farted and how loud, and how many tubes Jeremy had coming out of him, and how many nurses they needed to hold Jeremy down so he could take his medicine. I got mad because nobody would listen to me.

"That ain't the way it happened, is it, Papa? Tell them that ain't the way it happened."

Papa said, "Don't matter so much what happened as long as you know why it happened."

"Well, I know what and why," Bumpsy said. "I know Jeremy ain't gonna be able to yell at us no more. He ain't gonna be able to talk at all."

"Then what is he gonna do?" Sereatha whined.

"Somebody will have to write all his notes to the teacher, cause you know Jeremy can't spell and Miss Samples don't take no bad spelling."

"I ain't gonna write his notes," Mildred said. And Monica said she wouldn't either, but Woodrow said we'd think of something. He said that by the time Jeremy came back to school, we'd have to think of something. And we all nodded yes, and Papa said, "I'm sure you will. Yeah, that's one thing in this world I can be sure of."

Sun, Wind and Water

THE HORSE WAS PINK WITH A BLUE MANE. BLUE hair curled through her fingers as she urged the horse forward. Joyce Ellen balanced on one haunch, her eyes straight ahead. The horse's trot was even, its pacing perfect. A shaft of sunlight framed the clock and the thin, filigree minute hand ticked through a forest of Roman numerals.

"I can ride like a feather," she crooned softly. "My horse is the wind."

The gold bit in its mouth winked, and Joyce Ellen rode into the sun. "Go up, boy. Go up."

As the minute hand reached four, the chimes began. Joyce Ellen counted cadence, pacing the flow of speeding colors against a glowing sun. The sun swayed before her, a red ball growing larger and brighter than she had imagined, its pulsing matching the movement of the minute hand. The horse's pace matched that pulse. Joyce Ellen began to chant, rocking slowly, hanging on for the last stretch of the ride as the clock's pendulum moved faster, so fast she had to hurry. The sun was so far away and time was so swift.

"I'm light as the air," she crooned.

Then a voice cut through the canopy of sun and shadows.

"Joyce Ellen, you talking to yourself again?"

She leaned forward. The horse snorted softly. "Nothing, Ma'Emma. I'm not saying nothing," she mumbled, twisting the blue yarn around her fingers for safe keeping.

"You talking to yourself again. You getting as bad as your grandma."

She pulled away, closing in the forest behind her. Bertie, her mother, would come to fetch her, nag and scold her for being alone

53

too much. Joyce Ellen tried to think of something to say, but the ride had left her short of words.

Bertie looked down at her daughter, shaking her head at the sight of the girl sitting in a twisted bundle on the floor. Joyce Ellen was Ma'Emma's child alright, even looked like her. "Spitting image," some folks said. Parrish said Joyce Ellen looked so much like her grandmother had looked at that age, they could have passed for twins. Bertie had no choice but to agree with her cousin. Joyce Ellen certainly acted like the old woman if nothing else. She watched the girl struggle to untangle herself from a cross-legged position. "I know she's mine, but she's got so little of me in her," Bertie thought.

Joyce Ellen was stocky like her grandmother, the same wood-brown skin, the same oval eyes and large mouth, but she had Bertie's stately nose. "Nigerian," Bertie's mother said, but Parrish said, "Dogon," showing off his degree, and that's where the argument stuck. All Bertie knew was that her daughter's nose was the only thing they had in common, no matter what tribe. The bridge was pronounced, not flat and faintly there like the old woman's, and the nostrils flared like wings. Otherwise, they were an odd pair, like mismatched socks. Bertie was fair, high-yellow with an olive undertone to her pale skin. Her thin wiry body was a contrast to Joyce Ellen's plumpness. People talked about the two of them as if it were impossible for Bertie to have a fat child. "Sin and a shame when her mama's such a pretty woman," they'd say. Loud enough for Bertie to hear, too. Without the pronounced nostrils and kinky, shoulder-length hair, Bertie could have been mistaken for a richly tanned, uptown white girl from a distance. "Carries herself like she owns the place anyhow. Always looking down her nose," people said.

And there was always a small flutter of surprise when the short stocky black child named Joyce Ellen was introduced as Alberta Mayfield's one and only daughter. Although Bertie found herself always reaching out to fix a hemline or smooth a stray hair, she never quite knew how to make it better for the quiet round girl she'd given birth to one cold November day, fourteen years ago. Even moving to the city so Joyce Ellen would know more than life in a country town like Pleasant Hill hadn't helped. Now, she stood in the doorway, sucking on her impatience as the girl fussed with a piece of frayed string.

Joyce Ellen examined the dull glow on her thigh as her mother continued to watch her. Her skin was creamy smooth, not as coarse as her mother's, and her pudginess added extra arcs of light to her dark complexion. She often seemed to change colors as she moved from one end of the room to the other, going from a dull glowing black to a rich fudge brown. Sometimes she would flex her arm just to see the changes in skin tones. She liked watching the creases of fat fold and unfold on the inside of her elbows when she moved her arm back and forth. Now she examined her right thigh, poking it to make changes in tone and also to occupy the time while her mother formed the words for the next command she'd have to follow.

When Bertie shook her head and left the room, Joyce Ellen breathed a sigh and looked at the clock, but it was too late. The minute hand was on seven and she couldn't go back. The shadows had to be just right. She would have to wait until the sun slid across the face of the dial so that only half of the numbers, cut diagonally by the light, glowed like brush fire while the clock chimed its odd hours. That had been her first fascination with it, the chiming on at twenty after and ten to the hours. Ma'Emma had refused to get it fixed once it had started chiming that way the day grandpa died. The clock kept perfect time except for that oddness. Joyce Ellen wondered if she could find the horse again. It came out so seldom these days, not as easily as when she'd been so small, she'd had to look up at the clock by standing on a cushion in the easy chair. Now she had to use chants to get it started. Bertie had told her she listened to Ma'Emma's talk of spirits too much, and Joyce Ellen knew she did, but she couldn't seem to help it. She couldn't really remember when the old woman's stories had become more real and less story, something to be acted out and not just listened to. The stories soothed her until she was no longer Joyce Ellen and nothing else mattered.

Ma'Emma's raspy voice would poke and pull at spirits and spells for as long as anyone would listen. That's why they had moved. Bertie had insisted. Ma'Emma had talked about seeing things in the old house, until finally, Joyce Ellen had seen them too.

Joyce Ellen was still staring at the clock when she heard her grandmother call to her from the kitchen.

"Supper's on, child."

She stumbled up, her left foot almost asleep. She put the blue yarn in her pocket, then rubbed her numbed leg and half bent over, walked toward the kitchen. As she went through the living room door, she struck the edge of a chair and sent it crashing into an end table. The lamp rocked on the table, but the small glass figure of a man and a woman went tumbling to the floor, despite the fact that Joyce Ellen shut her eyes as tightly as they could possibly be shut. Bertie looked back into the living room just as the figurine smashed to bits.

"Oh, Jesus child, be careful. I can't keep nothing round here without you breaking it up. Why you got to be so clumsy?"

Just as Joyce Ellen started to answer, her grandmother interrupted. "Don't you be swearing, Bertie. Lord hates swearing. Devil loves it."

"Mama, Joyce has done it again. I just bought that thing and now she's broken it."

"You can get another, Bertie. What you call that thing anyway? You got a name for it. Call it something and you can find another one. Just watch your mouth."

"She never sees nothing but those spirits of yours, Mama."

"She sees enough. More than you ever saw. Leave the child alone. You com'on eat, Joyce Ellen."

The two women chattered, their voices rising like steam from the pots on the back burners. Joyce Ellen poured the lemonade into three plastic tumblers, then took her seat at the end of the table. Supper was early tonight, so she knew her mother would leave the house before dark. Bertie was never home much, except at supper. She worked days and was almost always out at night, or in bed early. Joyce Ellen didn't see her mother much, which was just as well for the both of them. She wished Bertie didn't know she saw Ma'Emma's spirits. Now Bertie nagged her about that too.

She couldn't remember exactly when she began seeing them, but it must have been more than a year before they'd moved. Even when Joyce Ellen had been trying to keep the spirits a secret from Bertie, even when she'd obeyed her mother and played out by the orchard rather than in the kitchen where she and Ma'Emma could talk, Bertie hadn't let her rest. She even got suspicious of the orchard, Joyce Ellen's place of exile, and told Ma'Emma she'd caught Joyce Ellen talking to the shadows in the trees as if there was really someone out there. Ma'Emma had just smiled and said, "No telling where spirits gone be," but when Joyce Ellen saw the headless man, Bertie decided it was time to leave Pleasant Hill.

Ma'Emma had talked about the headless man, the one who walks around at night looking for his head. She said you might meet him anywhere. Bertie would stalk from the room whenever Ma'Emma began the story, but Joyce Ellen stayed and after a while, she knew exactly how the man would look. One night, on her way to the bathroom, Joyce Ellen had seen a moving shadow. Her room was at the front end of the hall, the bathroom at the opposite end, with Bertie's and Ma'Emma's rooms in between. She'd stayed by the door watching the shadow move toward her room. The shadow passed Bertie's room and stopped at Ma'Emma's. It stayed there by Ma'Emma's door for a moment. It wasn't a man, but it was a man. It was too short for a man, but tall enough to be a man almost. It was wide and kept changing shapes and angles. Joyce Ellen watched as the shadow moved toward her. She wanted to leave, but stood there. She had to get past it to go to the bathroom or let it go past her. She held her breath and soundlessly recited her multiplication tables, the hard ones, the eights and nines, as the shadow moved slowly away from Ma'Emma's door. When it passed by her, she felt a drop of water hit her cheek, then it was gone.

She didn't tell Ma'Emma for a week and she never told Bertie, but somehow, Bertie had known and they had moved.

Ma'Emma said that sometimes spirits tried to send messages through water. Ma'Emma said all spirits come back for something, wanted to bring you something or warn you of something. Sometimes they want to take you away, Ma'Emma said. And Ma'Emma would give her some herb tea and tell her that next time, the spirit might come in a different shape. Next time, it might give her a clear message.

Ma'Emma thought Joyce Ellen might even be able to talk to spirits. "Not many young folks can. Old folks like me, but not many young ones."

Joyce Ellen knew Bertie would want to move again if she found out about the horse, how she still saw it sometimes even though they'd moved into a different house. She sat at the table, rubbing the fresh bruise on her leg and watching her mother. Bertie looked at the plump thigh and grunted. "The one thing she don't need is food, Mama. She needs some sense, but she don't need no food."

"Don't talk like that, Bertie. You be looking for food and it be gone. Folks sneak in and take your food. Real folks, I mean."

"Don't start your spirit stories either, Mama. That's another thing she don't need."

"You hear me talking spirits? I ain't talking spirits. They can do they own talking. I'm talking folks out in the street. You treat food like it's always there and folks think you don't mind being without. They think if you could afford it once, you can buy more. Take anything you got. There's lots of them wouldn't mind eating your food, wearing your clothes or nothing."

"Oh Mama, let's eat. I don't want to hear about it," Bertie snapped.

"No, you just want to eat so you can get out there on the street with them. Leave me and Joyce Ellen sitting here in the dark while you out on the street. No telling what will happen to us, sitting here in the dark. All kinds of things go on in the dark."

"Mama, I'm warning you. No spirits. Nothing goes on in the dark that don't go on in the day. Come on, Joyce. Time to eat. You can clean up that mess in the living room later."

Joyce Ellen began munching on her bread, spreading butter on each bite, spreading it across the bread like sunshine. She could hear her mother chattering about her eating habits, telling Ma'Emma how she grabbed the bread first thing, grabbed the one thing she didn't need to eat. She kept her eyes on her plate.

She was in a field of wheat grass. She caught a glimpse of a rabbit's tail as it hopped out of sight. When she looked around, she saw some small birds in a nest off to the side. She could see the roof of a house. A pony was tied to the gate. There was a light on inside the house, and she headed for it. It was hard walking in the tall grass, each step was a chore. She moved slowly toward the house. It seemed to get warmer as she got closer, a hot sweaty summer day. She wondered who was in the house, a little house with a tiny light shining out like a single raindrop on the windowpane.

"Joyce Ellen, eat your food. It's gonna get cold."

She jumped at the sound of her mother's voice.

"Leave the child alone, Bertie," her grandmother said. "She knows when to eat. Sometimes there's more on your mind than food."

"Mind?" Bertie snapped. "Mama, I wonder where her mind is.

You always filling it up with junk and she's always dreaming. Mind!"

Joyce Ellen continued to slowly munch on the piece of bread. Before she realized it, she had eaten everything on her plate and couldn't remember how any of it had tasted. Bertie finally left the room and Ma'Emma stood up, mumbling as she fumbled with the coffee pot, and groping in the pocket of her housedress for matches. When she leaned over to light the gas burner, the old woman's broad back was like a hillside covered in flowers and ferns. The ferns reminded Joyce Ellen of the potted ones on the windowledge. The kitchen was "L" shaped and rather dark, except in the mornings. Every available space was covered with ferns, herbs, jars of beans, pots, or one of the hundred pot holders her grandmother had knitted, some from the same flowered pattern as the housedress she now wore. It would have been a cheerful kitchen if the wallpaper wasn't dingy grey and Bertie wasn't always bickering.

The big round table seemed to invite everyone to sit and chat with the old woman. The table had been Ma'Emma's best piece of furniture until she and grandpa bought the clock and the big double bed. Ma'Emma had told her how grandpa had cut the wood himself, fashioned the center post out of a single stump. The table was a large oak circle, its top polished and scrubbed so often, it was light tan like Bertie, although its base was as sturdy and dark as Ma'Emma. Joyce Ellen ran her hands across the grain of the wood. The fine lines of the grain flowed across the table like wheat in a field. The tiny house she'd seen was there, in the grains of the wood. The narrow crack down the middle of the table sloped inward like the banks of a dry creek bed.

She was going to take a walk down to the creek when her grandmother said, "Cloudy tonight, Joyce Ellen, but the moon ain't full yet. Night be a good night, a sleeping night if the wind don't come up. Move those clouds across a three-quarter moon, and you don't know what the wind will stir up."

Joyce Ellen left the table and went to the back porch. The sky was streaked with light and a few wispy tendrils of clouds trailed the edges of the sun like faded pieces of ribbon, but there was no real sign of cloudy weather. She tightened the scarf around her head, sat down on the stone stairs and drew her knees up in front of her. The railings of the stairs divided her round black face into neat thin sections. Their house was the tallest one for blocks and they lived on the third floor. Below her, squat wooden houses with cluttered backyards full of old car parts, wash lines, and prairie grass fanned out toward the grain mill. She couldn't actually see the railroad siding, but early mornings, she heard the trains loading up. There was nothing on the other side of the grain mill. Just flat beige-colored grassland rolling away from itself.

Sitting on the back porch, looking out toward the valley, she still found it hard to believe there was a city behind her, a place full of people she didn't know and didn't understand. But she liked the quiet of the porch even though here, at the edge of the city, she saw more people than she ever had when they'd lived in Pleasant Hill. Not that she missed Pleasant Hill. There was the same flat countryside here as she'd seen in Pleasant Hill, but she missed the orchard, her secret place where she could be whatever she wanted to be. Here, all she had was the back porch and the alley below it.

If she lifted her head, Joyce Ellen could see beyond the alley directly and onto the neighboring street. The street was deserted. She was alone and she'd be fourteen in two months. Fourteen, and all she had was Ma'Emma and her spirits. Since they'd moved, she'd tried making friends but it always turned out the same. She never knew what to say, and when she tried, it always came out wrong. Sometimes they simply did not speak when she passed, little clusters of girls who seemed to let their eyes slide over each other but never her; little giggly groups who let her walk by, then burst into laughter as if someone had told a bad joke. Sometimes it was an elbow nudging her out of the lunch line, or no one to pass her paper up front when the teacher called the end of an exercise. And when the school photographer came and she couldn't smile without showing the spaces between her teeth, there were bound to be names. "Hey gatemouth," they'd call. "You left your barn door open." So she'd wander back home to Ma'Emma and Ma'Emma's spirits.

Joyce Ellen watched the blue sky fade into evening light. The steps were turning colder but the air was still warm and a little damp. She thought about going into the house, but going in meant more of Ma'Emma and her spirits. No one else really listened to the old woman, yet everyone, but Bertie, humored her. Cousin Parrish was worse than anyone else, teasing Ma'Emma and making her repeat her stories although he didn't believe them either. He told Joyce Ellen that he just listened because it made her grandmother happy, but he thought talking about spirits all the time was foolish. He thought the old woman was just lonely. Joyce Ellen listened to Parrish and the others, Uncle Isaac, Tommy Langston and Uncle George, talk about going over to Rippleton just to stand outside the movie show or sit inside Ike Fletcher's two-gun poker parlor while the old men swapped stories about their days as sleeping car porters on the railroad. But not one of them, except Parrish, had dared move out of Pleasant Hill, and Parrish had only lasted long enough in Kansas City to finish college. Now he spent as much time swapping tales with the old men as he ever had. But those tales never made as much sense to Joyce Ellen as her Ma'Emma's stories. Nobody believed in Ma'Emma's spirits. Joyce Ellen guessed she was the only one who really did.

She'd decided to go back into the house when she saw the boy coming around the corner. She couldn't see his face at first, just the dark blue cap fitting snugly over a mass of crisp kinky hair. Then he looked up and caught a glimpse of her, stood there staring at her with a flat plastic radio glued to his ear. She could see the light dance along the thin spiral wire of the radio antenna, the red pea-shaped ball on top of the antenna bounce rhythmically from front to back, again and again. He put his right hand over his eyes to shield them from the direct rays of the fading sunlight while his left hand kept the radio anchored to his ear.

As Joyce Ellen stared at him through the porch railings, she felt a sudden rush of wind force its way through the wooden slats and ruffle through the scarf around her head. The boy moved his right hand to his hat, clutching it as the gust of wind threatened to blow it off. She guessed him to be about sixteen or so, and despite the radio planted against his left ear, she guessed that he was probably returning from some important errand. A blue and gold-striped tie hung loosely aroound the open collar of his shirt and his jeans were still too stiff to find the exact curves of his body. He smiled at her, danced a few steps, then moved toward the bottom of the stairs. When the screen door opened, he stopped. Her grandmother looked down at the boy, then turned away, shielding her eyes against the afternoon light as she examined the sky.

The old woman began to mumble, waving her free hand in the

direction of the western rim of the skyline. The boy looked at her grandmother for a second, then smiled again and turned on his heels, heading away from the porch, the red ball bouncing back and forth a few inches above his hat. Joyce Ellen tried shutting out the buzz of her grandmother's ramblings.

She watched him move down the length of the alley, then turn into the yard of the house on the corner. He climbed the back stairs and when he reached the top, he looked back at her. She seemed to be able to see his face better now, although he was farther away and the light played tricks with shadows from the stairway. But she could see him smile just before he turned to enter the house, the angle of light making his round face made even rounder and leaving his broad flat nose as shiny as a pecan. The thin wire of the antenna swayed back and forth like a tall stalk of wheat grass in the center of a golden field, lifting and falling like its movement had all the time in the world. She looked at the house a second longer as the door closed behind the boy. The last rasp of sun flashed on the glass pane in the upper part of the door. A light went on inside. Then she remembered that house had been vacant all summer.

Her grandmother spoke directly to her. "Child, you come on in now. Get ready for school tomorrow. The wind's coming up and no telling what it might stir. You better come on in now."

Joyce Ellen sat still. The fading sun turned her skin into a dull wood-brown color. She practiced breathing evenly, wrapping herself in every second of her thirteen, nearly fourteen years. Her grandmother spoke again.

"Come on in, baby. First day of school tomorrow. Besides, I got some folks to call and I need you to dial for me. All of them numbers always mixes me up so."

Joyce Ellen turned and smiled at Ma'Emma. The old woman's face was checkered by the shadows from the screen door, and Joyce Ellen could see that she was watching the skyline carefully. Joyce Ellen stood up and went to the door, ducking under her grandmother's arm as she stepped back into the house. "Ok, Ma'Emma. I'll come in now. Do your calling, if you want me to."

She walked into the familiar warmth of the kitchen.

The old woman took one last look at the pale sunlight, then said, "Look child, the wind is already stirring."

Farm Day

THERE WAS ALWAYS WATER TO BOIL AND BABIES to feed. Suka could never seem to get it all finished in one day. Even as a child at her grandmother's, she had never been able to keep up the pace the old lady set.

She would remember being sent to get the small splintery wood bits for the fire at hog killing time. Her older brothers would quickly clean the shallow pit from the last fire so that she and Gordon could fill it. Then grandpa would go after the pig. It always seemed that she had only brought in a few bundles of wood before he'd reached the pig pen. When the squeals started, she'd head for the house. Gordon, her youngest brother, would fume and kick up a fuss as soon as he realized he would have to get the rest of the wood by himself. But she always managed to get out of the yard before grandpa got started. Her grandmother would yell at her from the kitchen window as she approached the back of the house.

"Mary Ellen, Mary Ellen, you git back dere. Git dat wood so's papa can git de pig started."

She'd nod her head and kick the loose dirt with her bare feet. Her black toes would turn sandier as the dirt scattered in little puffs, like the smoke from grandpa's pipe in the evenings. The dirt would settle on her toes in fine grains and the cracks and edges of her toenails would turn the color of half-done baking powder biscuits.

She'd nod to her grandma, her head down, making little patterns in the dust with her feet. She'd walk slowly toward the house, nodding.

"Mary Ellen, you git back dere, you heahya? Gramma's gonna take a strop to you."

When she reached the door, she'd look up.

63

"I'm hep you shell peas, Gramma."

She'd sit at the big table, the smooth worn tree stump of a table, and concentrate hard on the shell peas. When the boys got the tub onto the fire, the squeals would grow louder. She'd know her grandpa was in the pen, tapping the sides of the pigs, checking on the one that was ready, fat and firm. Her grandma would mumble at the sink.

"Don't know what I'ma do wid you, gal. We gotta eat. Can't eat lessen we got food."

Her grandma would shake her head and hum a church tune, punctuating the tune now and then with a sad message about how some children just weren't meant to behave.

She could never remember how much time it really took to get the big pot bubbling, but the increase of squeals and grunts always meant grandpa had found his pig. The boys would join in, chasing the pig, adding to the noise. She would examine each pea pod, the faded red and grey shell and the knobby edge of the pod. She'd run her fingers along the knobs, wondering how they could be smooth with all those bumps, then wondering why the pod wasn't all red or all grey, not a mix of the two. Then she'd turn the pod to the splitting side and slice it open with her fingernail, letting the small peas slide down the wall of their cell and into the cork bowl.

There was always a mound of peas on the big table at killing time. Peas always seemed to be ready to shell at hog killing time. Grandma sang at the window, her song growing more mellow and softer as the squeals grew louder. Grandma would wash the dirt from the turnips and the onions and sing. She would fill the crock bowl with peas. Sometimes the snap of the pea as her fingernail found the splitting spine would join the sharp squeal of the pig when her grandpa jabbed him before they bled in the big tub.

She'd seen this once. She'd seen the blood running into the tub, her brothers dancing around, talking about how much meat they'd get from this pig. She'd seen the pig's eyes grow dull and she'd seen them grow hard when grandpa finally put the body in the boiling tub for skinning. She'd seen it only once. After that, she'd always managed to help grandma shell peas. When the only noise she could hear was the gurgling of the pot and grandpa's poking stick hitting the edge as he jabbed the rim to keep the pig clear of the sides, grandma would bring her singing down to a low hum. It would buzz deep in her throat and she would walk over to the table, wipe her hands on her big apron, and stroke the many braids of her granddaughter's hair.

"You got to learn to move faster, child. Keeping a body moving keeps meat on the table."

She had never really learned. Now she was called Suka, Pepesuka or Suka, because she fluttered like a flapping cloth. She fluttered like the gown she wore and the headdress that made her resemble an African tribal queen. Suka realized she'd been standing in front of the bathtub poking at the soaking diapers for at least five minutes. She shook her head, wiped her hands on a towel and headed for the kitchen.

The children were playing with the pots again. She took a metal spoon from Uzima's mouth. Her youngest looked up, protesting slightly. Suka tousled the mass of thick hair covering Uzima's head.

"Little flower, Uzima. My little flower. Mama's flower."

Kadimu was loudly banging a pot on the floor and Suka thought how appropriate the name Kadimu was for her first born. She smiled at her son's energy, then clicked her tongue at both of them as she checked the pots on the stove to see if they were cooling. She'd have to empty the water into the five gallon jugs when it was cool. The pots were still too warm. She sighed. She really wanted a drink of water, but she was a good Muslim and could wait until the boiled water was cooler and free of the germs the city put into the water system that supplied Black folks.

She checked her cupboards. There were enough soy beans for lunch, but she'd have to grind up some more if she wanted to make bread tonight. She checked the cupboards carefully, noting the number of half-filled jars and number of full jars.

"I'll have to use some of those bits and pieces. Make a stew."

She remembered being told to use everything. Benjamin was proud of her thrift. He talked about it gloriously at Temple meetings. She checked the big kitchen clock. Another two hours before Benjamin came home. He wouldn't bring home bean pies tonight. He and Mjinga were out at the farm today. He would be too tired to stop for pies. The farm was thirty miles outside of the city and Mjinga's old truck made the ride hard. It was hard work. Benjamin would finish his day's work for Allah for one more week. She decided on stew.

Reaching over Uzima, she took the pot from her older son's hands. It was a heavy pot and no amount of banging put dents in it. It had been a gift of Halali's when she and Benjamin were married. Halali had been only a messenger then. Now, he had moved up and it was said that he would visit the northern mosque next spring.

She washed the pot carefully and began bringing out the half-filled jars. There were fewer carrots and raisins than she had imagined. She could make up the difference with spice, particularly celery and paprika. Benjamin liked a well-seasoned pot. She was pleased with herself.

Grandma had always been pleased when the skin was ready to be stripped from the hog. They would lift the carcass from the tub, grandpa and the boys, and grandma would stand there with her hands beneath her apron, nodding approvingly. Then she'd tell them to let the tub cool.

"Dirt settles to the bottom. Fat's on the top."

Grandma let the boys skim off the top layer of fat. That part was always filled with bits of hair and ever so small pieces of hide. Then she would take the big ladle and remove the rest of the fat. It would go into the soap bucket.

After grandpa cut the hide, they would help grandma strip the remaining layers of fat from the meat. This, they added to the blood tub for sausage.

Suka shook her head. It had been messy work. She no longer ate the greasy hot sausages. No pork at all, in fact. Pork was impure. She'd had no problems giving it up.

After she finished preparing the food for the stew, she set it aside and began pouring the water into containers. It was cooler now. Almost ready to drink. She'd filled three of the five gallon jugs when she heard the door. She sighed.

"One more to go and someone's come calling."

She pulled the apron from her gown and checked her hairline with her fingers. She hoped she was presentable and didn't have bits of hair sticking out. Benjamin would not approve. Halali had told him once to remind her of her appearance. She walked toward the door, worrying the edges of her clothing into neat straight lines.

Mlizi greeted her in Muslim fashion. "Salaam." Suka returned the greeting.

She and Mlizi walked back toward the kitchen. Mlizi was Mjinga's wife. She had a long face, but very expressive eyes. The blue cloth framing her face made her eyes important and gave her a striking appearance. Mlizi asked about her health in a soft voice. Suka glanced at Mlizi's bulging stomach.

"How is your health, sister?"

They both laughed. Mlizi patted her full figure.

"I am fine, Sister. Our son will arrive any day now."

It was her first child. She and Mjinga had come from Chicago just after their marriage. Mjinga was learning the print trade from Benjamin. Mlizi did weaving and until this last month, she had supplied most of the Sisters with beautiful fabric of Islamic design. Now she was preparing for her baby.

"I've been thinking about my grandmother all morning," Suka told her.

"Is she a Sister?"

"No. She passed away. Before I left home. She was Baptist. Very Baptist."

"Oh. A follower of the white man's ways."

"She knew no other."

"That has been the plan. Keep us ignorant. Keep us down. Aren't you adding too much celery, Sister?"

"No, Benjamin likes it."

"Why were you thinking of your grandmother?"

"I remembered how she was always trying to get me to hurry. I never did learn to get everything done in one day."

"Praise Allah, Sister. We all have those troubles. Let me help. I can finish the stew."

The two women began working. Uzima had fallen asleep on the floor. Suka picked up the child and caried her into the smaller bedroom. Kadimu toddled behind, his thumb soothing him. He crawled in beside his sister. On the other side of the room, the baby, her second son, slept soundly. When Suka returned to the kitchen, Mlizi was dicing the chicken.

"I have decided to call my son Kazi, for work. I have found myself more at ease with work these days, so he will be Kazi."

"And what if it is a girl, Sister?" Mlizi laughed.

"I'll have to think more about that. Mjinga wants a boy. My mother tells me: Barbara, you take what you get."

Suka laughed too. "Mothers are like that," she said.

Then she went into the bathroom and started on the diapers. She pushed them up and down, squishing until they were sudsy, then pushed the water out, bundling them on the floor before draining the tub for rinsing.

Mlizi joined her.

"They have not found the mad dogs that killed poor Ugine?"

"No. And Gordon has disappeared too." Mlizi frowned. She watched Suka work the diapers, the frown deepening on her face.

Gordon, Suka's baby brother, had become Muslim first and introduced Suka to it. It was only natural that Gordon should be the one to show her the way. She and Gordon had always been together until he'd left grandpa's farm. The two of them had been sent to pick dandelions and catch evil-looking catfish at Baker's Creek. Gordon had pushed her from a tree, breaking the little toe on her right foot. She hadn't cared when her older brothers had left home. She'd cried for weeks after Gordon left. She remembered how Gordon had sang, *his song*, he called it.

"If I live, Sanga-ree . . . don't get killed, Sanga-ree . . . I'm going back, Sanga-ree . . . Jacksonville . . ."

They had become Muslims. They had found purpose and peace. She had found Benjamin. Yet Gordon had not been satisfied. He was restless for action. He wanted to clean up the streets, clean up the minds of the young, rebuild the junkies and whores and trashpickers and winos. And he didn't want to wait. He was a good man, a clean Black man. Now he was missing and his friend, Ugine, was dead. Assassins! She frowned as she flushed water over the sudsy tub.

"Do you think Gordon is safe?" Mlizi asked.

"I don't know. Benjamin is worried. There is talk about Gordon."

"I know. I heard it too. But I said nothing, Sister."

"Gordon wouldn't do anything wrong. He knows the evil that is around us."

"Yes, but will everyone believe he knows? He spoke against Nommo in the meeting."

"It is only because Gordon wants so much for our people."

"Perhaps it is not up to Gordon to make that decision."

Suka did not answer. She began filling the tub with water. Mlizi dashed for the kitchen.

"Chicken's burning!" she cried.

Suka let her fingers drift in the water. She wondered if the talk Mlizi heard had come from Halali. He had not visited since Gordon disappeared, and although he had never been friendly with Nommo, he was becoming important, powerful. Halali with his sense of right. Where was he? She stirred the water and began dropping in the bundled diapers. They made plopping sounds, the soap spreading from them in bubbly circles. Then she started to add the blueing. It poured from the bottle in a thick stream, hitting the bottom of the tub before rising to the top and spreading, discoloring the water. She thought it strange that such a thickly colored liquid could cleanse. She heard the door open and placed the cap on the bottle, balancing it on the edge of the tub.

As she left the bathroom, she heard Benjamin's voice.

"Benjamin?"

"Yeah, Suka. Mjinga is here too."

She walked into the room. "You're early."

"We didn't go to the farm today."

Suka's eyes opened a bit wider, but she said nothing. Both men looked tired.

"I'll talk to you about it later," Benjamin added.

They sat on the sofa. Suka looked at Mjinga. His thick glasses made him seem out of focus, opaque. His face was almost indistinct behind his glasses. He looked foggy, like his name, Mjinga, suggested. Suka's husband sat next to him. His muscular chest square beneath his coveralls. He always looked so handsome in his dark suit and tie. She really didn't like seeing him in coveralls, but it was farm day and everyone had to pitch in their share for the Temple. Still, even in work clothes, she felt good just looking at him. His head was beautifully round, shaved clean and the brilliant deep-rich color of ironwood. That was her first awareness of mornings. The feel of that strong clean head beside her on the pillow. She always thought each morning, "Praise Allah for sending me a strong man."

Benjamin looked at her again. Both he and Mjinga seemed to be waiting. Mjinga had dropped his head over his folded hands, his elbows resting on his spread knees. But Mjinga's ready smile wasn't there and Benjamin had not given her his usual affectionate hug. Benjamin cleared his throat. She knew the men wanted to be alone and talk. Mjinga raised his head and smiled at his wife who was standing in the doorway. Mlizi smiled, rubbing the mound of her belly.

Suka nodded to Mlizi, then hurried back to the bathroom to shut off the running water before she returned to the kitchen. She and Mlizi then worked to finish the meal. They didn't talk, but worked rapidly. She took charge of the bread and Mlizi finished the stew before slicing fruit.

The voices of their husbands rose and fell, but they couldn't really understand what was being said. Suka remembered over-hearing her grandfather in the kitchen on Saturday nights. His brother would join him and they would share corn whiskey and conversation until the fire had died completely.

She must have been thinking about that time when they entered. Her hands were covered with a sticky mixture of brown wheat flour and soy bean paste when she heard the first shot. Mlizi screamed. Suka heard Mjinga yell.

"Run, Mlizi. Run!"

Then there was another shot.

Mlizi blocked her way to the living room. Then she turned, pulling Suka.

"The back door! Quickly!"

Suka shook her off. "My babies!" She turned for the bedroom.

"No, Suka. Run! Run!"

Mlizi was halfway out of the back door, her blue gown extended behind her, fluttering. Suka held her hand up to her mouth, forcing back a scream, then headed for the bedroom. Uzima was crying, babbling in half words. And the baby and Kadimu howled in that scream that said they already knew the meaning of fear. The taste of wheat flour and soy beans was heavy on Suka's lips as she stumbled toward the bedroom.

The tall man cut off her path before she reached the room.

"Where's Gordon?"

She looked at him. She began rubbing the wheat flour from her fingers. She could feel the stickiness of it still clinging to the corners of her mouth.

"My babies. My babies."

He forced her into the bathroom, backing her up, away from the bedroom. He asked her the same question again.

She looked at the tub and back at the tall man.

He pointed the gun to her head. She could hear the others moving about the house, pulling things out of place. Kadimu screamed her name this time, and she could hear Uzima and the baby crying hoarsely.

The tall man pushed her against the edge of the tub. Suka extended her hand to the wall on the other side of the tub to keep her balance. She knocked the bottle of blueing into the water and the loose cap floated. The blue liquid left the bottle in gulps, spreading in dark blue circles, then mixing with the water. The diapers floated in the colored water like globs of fat. Then the gun went off.

Jesus and Fat Tuesday

PLAISANCE HAD STOMPED PAST THE DOUBLE *Receiving* doors and down the hall when the cops brought Maggie Boujean into ARC. We'd only been on duty for half an hour when Maggie arrived, and aside from a soldier they'd snatched off a Greyhound bound for Gulf Port, a D-and-D who had messed over a whole bus load of passengers and was still sleeping after being pulled in during the afternoon shift, Maggie was the first casualty on the ward that night. Before she arrived, I figured to have an easy night of it, so I'd let Plaisance make the waiting room his center stage. Then the cops burst through the doors, noisy as usual—sometimes noisier than the drunks they dragged in behind them. Not that Maggie Boujean needed any additional racket, but all the hoo-haa the cops made trying to get her out of the car and into the lobby had forced Plaisance to cut his conversation short.

He had been in the middle of one of his man-to-man talks with me; that is, I was the dude listening and he was the fool talking. The problem with Plaisance was that he believed all that shit folks told him about Blacks and Cajuns being great lovers, so every time I turned around, he was trying to get me to slip him the skinny on what women needed so he could score. Like the other day when he said, "Touti, I was doing this piece when she put the squeeze on me so tight, I think my balls they gonna fall off. This happened to you sometime, Touti?" I said, "Man, how come you always got to be asking me some shit about screwing? Black folks don't want to be talking about screwing all the time, man."

Now and again, I'd let him talk me into cruising with him. It didn't make any difference that most times when we'd tried hustling together, women had all but laughed in our faces. Plaisance wasn't a quitter. Mostly I kept to myself. But if he wasn't talking tail, he was talking fast money and how it must be that I know where the two of us could make some of it. That was the one thing he had in common with my mother. She was a woman who didn't want nobody to bring her no bad news. Didn't matter if her bad news was somebody else's good news, she still didn't want to hear it. So when half of Pointe Coupee Parish struck it rich with oil, and we didn't own enough land to even sink a dry hole, my mama wouldn't let us mention the VasCo Corporation in the house. *Don't make no difference if we can't smell money, Toulouse. That money be in the ground. Ain't nobody gone give you nothing. What you want, you got to take it, boy. It's right here in Pointe Coupee, Touti. Right here in front of your nose. You got to make the good times roll. Listen to you mama, Touti.*

Next to my mother, Plaisance was the only person I knew who thought it was a God-given duty to talk some sense into me. The night Maggie Boujean showed up at the ARC, Plaisance's "good sense" had to do with trying to make me turn slick so we could hit it big during Mardi Gras. He'd been working on that idea for nearly two weeks, and he had a week left before New Orleans went on its annual ape-shit spree. I wasn't buying, but that didn't stop Plaisance. To him, New Orleans was Mardi Gras, and Mardi Gras was a good way to make money off a bunch of fools trying to be hot shots with nothing in their pockets but chicken scratch. He claimed it was easy pickings if you got bold enough. That was surely another thing he had in common with my mama. *Standing there smiling won't even catch you a toothache,* she'd tell me. But I hadn't left Pointe Coupee Parish to dance jim-jack on some New Orleans street corner. A good job was good enough until I could figure my own ways and means.

Still, I let him talk. His noise was no skin off my nose. And before Maggie arrived, all the noise had belonged to Plaisance. I would have had no luck trying to tell him I'd already heard most of the nonsense he was spouting, so I had just been letting him eat up some time until he got tired. Mostly, I didn't trouble myself with his words; I simply watched his face, contented myself with noting how he fit his lips around the words he made. *Lip service,* Mama had called it. *You can tell a lot about folks that way.* I had figured out what kind of dude Plaisance was before he opened his mouth. Three years I'd been working with him, and I wasn't impressed one diddley-damn with what I'd seen in that time. His face full of bad skin gave me all the history I needed to tell me why he resented having been born on that skinny stretch of Delta he called home. Now, the way he told it, he was out, in the big city, but I knew he spent most of his time scared that he'd have to go back.

"They always ready for to take you home, Touti," he'd say. Didn't matter how many times I told him he had to have something to go back to, he simply didn't see the world my way. He viewed working in the alcoholic recovery ward as a sign of failure. That had been his pitch before the cops busted through the door.

"They gone keep you here till the Bayou been sucked back to the sea, man. Folks like us—Cajun folks, Black folks, even big time Creoles—we all the same to them. Me and you, we got nothing. They make money, Touti, but all we gone get is white hairs." He'd patted his belly. "Mardi Gras coming. We make it our day, eh Tooti? We get a scam, eh? They make Lent come Fat Tuesday, and we make like fat cats come Lent."

I'd let him have his fill of saying that shit, then tried to change the subject away from that same argument I'd heard back home. Even after VasCo pulled in three wells in two months, folks around my neighborhood had ragged about getting the short end of the stick. Even after they could stop picking pecans and start stuffing croker sacks with hard cash, they were still scared some white man was going to come along and rip them off. That's the problem with being born black and poor in a country that expects you to stay black and poor. Folks see your color long before they see your money. I had to shake my head to keep from thinking about it, but if I closed my eyes, Plaisance's ragging didn't sound much different from what I'd always heard. *Make something of yourself, boy.* The same-old, same-old, just a change of names, I thought.

Plaisance had been on my case all night, and right when the cops shoved open the doors, he'd pumped his fist into the air and said, "You don't watch it, Touti, they hump you like some ol' stray dog. Take your stuff from you when your back is turned." He was still pumping air when the cops burst in. They stared, but Plaisance flashed his brown-toothed grin and left the lobby. And while I listened to the protesting stomp of Plaisance's departing feet, Maggie

Boujean, bleary-eyed and clothed like a bat out of hell, came lurching into my life.

And she started on me as soon as she reached the desk. "Jesus done been here and gone," she slurred. Then both patrolmen let her slip to the floor, the two of them so eager to release her into my custody, they simultaneously reached for the admitting papers.

"Been here and GONE," she repeated in a louder voice. One of the officers attempted to pull her upright, and Maggie thanked him by spewing a thin stream of bile onto his shirt. The cop yelled, "SHIT!" and let her go, while I looked anxiously toward the *Receiving* doors that seconds before had held big-butt Plaisance, the only person who was bound by job description to clean up behind Maggie. At least I could make him clean up unless his objections to doing dirty work forced me to grab bucket and mop rather than hear one more explanation of, "This one Cajun they got to pay twice fore spring till he work so hard."

I quickly walked around the desk and lifted Maggie to her feet. "Let me get you a chair," I coaxed. The cop wiped his shirt as I steered clear of the brown spittle that trailed off the end of Maggie's left arm, but he made no attempt to help me raise her off the floor. Not that I needed his help.

"Where's the doctor?" he asked.

Maggie heaved again and I tilted her bony shoulders away from me, wincing as the motion hurled vomit against the connecting rim of the counter and the floor. This would certainly bring some bit of unwelcome philosophy from Plaisance, I thought. I turned my head as the liquid spread in a thin line along the Rubbermaid rim of the baseboard—an expensive donation from some feeble-minded politician in lieu of more staff, and by Plaisance's calculation, the hardest place to clean in the entire damn hospital. Yeah. I was destined to hear a few of Plaisance's choice words.

"Can't you get a doctor?" the cop insisted.

"Doctor ain't here," I told him. "This time of night, all you got is orderlies. This time of night, any doctor with sense is home in bed."

Maggie slid from the chair and whacked her head against the counter before I could catch her.

"It's a sin what a body can do to itself," the cop muttered. His buddy, the one who had escaped Maggie's reconstituted booze, grunted an eager, "UN-huh," then asked me how to spell *delirium*. I plopped Maggie into the seat a final time, and signed Dr. Ann Garcia's name to the forms, blessing the good doctor with the insight of never once, in ten years of my employment, having checked to see where I placed her signature. Then I wordlessly handed them their route copies of the admittance papers. As the cops left, I overheard one of them say, "Either that nigger is a dummy or he's got a stick up his ass. Put a white coat on some colored folks and they forget their place." I knew my place enough to keep Maggie from throwing up all over me, I thought as I buttoned my lab jacket.

"Eh, Touti. How they make us work now, eh?"

I silently swore this would be the last time I'd let Plaisance sneak up on me. I usually had to swear that at least twice a week. "Don't call me Touti," I said.

"Big Toot," he laughed. "When we gonna bust out of here? We get somebody with dice, eh? With cards? I know your people roll the snake eyes like that." He snapped his fingers.

I said, "Buzz off, man," and stretched Maggie across two chairs. "Just get that crap cleaned off the floor, Plaisance. I'm gonna check the ward for bed space."

"You think we need to call Garcia?" he asked. "They don't like it if we take this old bag's clothes off and we got no female interning."

"Don't sweat it," I told him. "Let Dr. Garcia stay at home. This old bag can sleep with her clothes on. By the looks of her, she's used to it."

Maggie was snoring almost before the blanket settled around her. And she would have been comfortably situated in the ward if the next half-hour had run smoothly, but ten minutes after the first two cops disappeared, another team brought in a kid yelling and screaming about bats and vampires, and we never got a chance to put Maggie in a room. Both Plaisance and I had our hands full tying the kid down and mopping up after him. The newcomer was a thin faced boy about twenty-two, and so pretty, he could have been a girl, except his silk slacks were tight and full in all the right places, and he had enough muscles to carry his own weight with any man; that is, if he stayed sober and off the streets long enough. He had the kind of body some movie type could turn into a hot property and fast money. I looked at the tightness of his biceps as he pulled both me and Plaisance off balance and decided he was probably into fancy weights and jogging. He was the kind of kid who could bust a French Quarter party and make the host apologize for the trouble he'd gone through to get in.

"Just be cool," I said as he arched his back and tried to buck free of us. "The party's over, kid." I almost had him down when he grabbed my arm and pulled himself up until his face was inches away from mine. His lips moved, wordlessly, but his eyes were closed. Suddenly his eyes opened, flat and unfocused, and he began a howl that I swore was going to last longer than any man could hold his breath. His pupils were so wide, all I could see in the panic of his eyes was my own reflection. "Just be cool, kid. Go to sleep," I said, then ducked as he took a swipe at me.

"Cajun," Plaisance grunted. "Somebody been giving him thin drinks." Then he sniffed the kid's breath and looked at the lower rim of his eyes. "Little bit of smack too, eh? Uptown," he snarled as the boy fought us again. Plaisance straddled the kid's legs and removed his shoes. "Italian leather," he said and grunted again.

Even his toes had been manicured. "Mardi Gras gonna be good to him if he sobers up," I laughed. "He's so bad, betcha they match those shoes and don't put nothing but Italian olives in that booze they feeding him. Nothing but the best for this custom model."

Plaisance gave me a look he reserved for doctors and middle-class drunks. I decided to make myself scarce.

I was in no mood to show Plaisance the connection between one thought and another. That would take more time than we had left on the shift. He deliberately wouldn't understand what olives had to do with a good looking Cajun drunk any more than he really understood what Mardi Gras had to do with Lent. Like most white folks, he got thick-skinned if he had to hear the truth from the black side of the fence. If I pinned him to the wall on some of that hokey crap about black folks that he'd learned in school, he'd beg off talking. "So much thinking make it hurt," he'd say, then let his eyes turn into little hard black dots and he'd look like one of those bull-mouthed river-bottom fish stacked face-up in the open market.

What saved Plaisance from being really ugly was his Clark Gable mustache. You know, that kind of slick, bad dude-gambler's dust mop that looked like it was painted on. The way he kept it shaped, some folks overlooked that mess of thick black hair on his head . . . and chest, and arms, and neck. Plaisance was just one hairy dude. Ape-man, I called him when we hosed down after the shift. Without his clothes, you could really say that Plaisance was into hair shirts. And the hair on his head was clumped up like lumps of overcooked spaghetti. Thinking about his hair made me rub my own head. When my fingers got tangled, I decided I'd better get a haircut soon. Hair and gut. We were a pair, alright. Both of us fat and unable to sleep nights—that's why we made such a good ward team—but Plaisance's mustache made him look smarter than he was. Underneath all that Hollywood front, he was dumb and stubborn. I had a better chance of watching the wind whip up his greasy hair than I did of seeing him change his opinion. And he always thought he could wear me down by talking.

In a pinch, I could throw him off guard. I'd tell him his problem was that he didn't understand jazz. I'd say, "Plaisance, jazz is something you got to listen to. Lookit, it ain't what they play, it's what they don't play that makes the music rock. You know . . . not just some loud keyboard shit, but how they let you wait for the next sound, then don't play what you expect. You got to fill in for yourself. You got to learn to wait, to ride with it. Slip in and over what you hear." But Plaisance said he wanted regular music, that old country thump-thump Delta banjo music. "So you know where you going and where you been," he'd say.

I was back at the desk when I heard Plaisance leaving the boy's room. The ward grew quiet again. It was surely a slow night. I thought about the jazz concert that was coming up that next weekend and hitched my belt a notch tighter. I'd been on duty for nearly two hours. Six more shifts and four hours on this desk before I could lose myself in Freddie Hubbard's sounds. I reached for papers I had to fill out before the night was over. If I'd had Plaisance's view of the world, I'd have been able to disappear in a trail of bad words and reappear only when the situation reached disaster, but as it was, my timing had never been under my control. I'd just settled down to work at the desk when Maggie woke up.

Some patients I never really get to know, and some I know too well—drunk or sober, whether I want to know them or not. Maggie Boujean selected the chair with the busted bottom and fixed me with her eyes, two bleary headlights centered in a face that was so boozy yellow, her skin looked like a beeswax mask, or an old onion peel. But her expression suggested she knew too much about me already. I tried fixing my own face with a look that said I was bored with drunks who had nothing better to do than test my good manners. I found myself wishing for a mustache like Plaisance's, or maybe even a beard, anything to hide from Maggie's shrimp-eyed stare.

"I seen Jesus tonight," she announced.

"We got a kid in there seeing vampires. Maybe you ought to talk to him," I said.

She leaned forward and began to speak slowly, shaping every word as if by being deliberate, she could fool me into thinking she was also sober. "I-said-*Jesus,*" she repeated. "In-Heavenly-light," she said. Then she leaned back, smiling as if she'd just discovered sentences, and satisfied that she had kept a string of sounds from tumbling into the wrong words.

I shook my head. I wasn't fooled. Her voice was soft and quiet. Too soft. I'd never known a woman to go soft in voice unless she had something directly in mind. I watched her trying to keep her expression attached to the loose flesh of her face, then her features lost some of their alcoholic fuzziness and turned accusing, like a cop about to give a ticket when a warning would have served the same purpose. Or like she was thinking of some Marie Laveau voodoo spell to put on me.

"I seen Jesus," she chanted. "Seen him."

I waited.

"Standing in front of his flying saucer and it all golden with light."

I'd been suckered again! Years of working on this job, and I'd been suckered like a catfish baited on cornbread, like a tourist buying an original Basin Street tambourine. Then I heard Plaisance behind me.

"If I could see Jesus . . ." he sang, "could see him walk . . ."

I hoped that by not turning around, he'd think I wasn't listening, but Plaisance was still warmed by the idea of calming down that Cajun kid, so he walked over and put his arm on my shoulder. "Could see Jesus make all the good folks talk . . ."

I found a reason to pick a wad of paper off the floor. Next to having him sneak around all the time, my second problem with Plaisance was his need to always touch me—grab my hand, slap my shoulder, or pat my ass. He claimed it was in his blood, but Cajun or not, folks don't have to get that close all the time.

"She needs a ward bed," I told him before he could start singing again.

"She get the best one, eh Touti?" He grinned as if we'd been waiting the whole night for Maggie Boujean.

"Don't make no never mind if it's the best one or not. Just get one," I said.

". . . could nat'chully make folks down here walk," Plaisance sang, then slapped the floor with his mop and whanged through the swinging doors. "I see you in a minute, Big Toot," he said.

Maggie watched me take a deep breath. "I had a husband like that," she laughed. "Stubborn and no-carrified. Had to paint him white."

"*White?*" I knew I'd heard the word, but I repeated it anyway. It was like looking for a sock or something you'd lost that was supposed to be only in one place. You figure if you keep looking in that place, you'll change what you see and find that sucker. I figured if I said the word again, I could keep Maggie from making some kind of stupid racist remark. "*White?*" I said again.

"I told him," she grinned. "I said: mess with me one more time and I'll make sure you get your just rewards. Woulda painted him red, but didn't have no red paint."

Well shit, I thought, that ain't exactly racist. Not yet anyway. But I still wasn't winning. "Red?" I whispered.

"Yeah," she said, like she was telling me what any fool would know about red. "Well what the hell," she said. "Don't you think red would have been better, seeing as how my old man wasn't going nowhere but down there with Lucifer nohow? But I couldn't find me no red, so . . . white it was."

For a moment, I actually had tried to follow her, then I realized I'd been leaned into the deadly combination. "Booze and logic," Dr. Garcia would say. "Put them together and the whole world goes to shit." I glared at Maggie, but I finally managed to close my mouth and point my finger at her the way my mother used to do when I had fat-mouthed once too often. There are only two ways you can talk to a drunk: you can either play charades and say the magic word or you silence them with death threats. Maggie understood my threat right away, and leaned back in her chair. I knew my night would not return to normal until I got her into a ward, but I could hear that dime-a-dance Cajun kid screaming into the alcohol that was stuck in his system, and I knew that right now, Plaisance would be too busy to find Maggie a bed. I started shuffling papers, looking official while I brought myself under control.

I pulled a blank chart from the files and settled down to pass the time. "If they're talking in here, they can't be drinking out there in the street," Dr. Garcia would say. "That's our job. Keeping them off the street and getting them sober." I watched Maggie as I straightened the papers in the clipboard. Garcia must have gotten her patience from growing up in Casper, Wyoming, because what I read in Maggie's New Orleans eyes told me sober hadn't been a part of her vocabulary for a long time.

"You're my best intern, Toulouse. You know how to listen," Dr. Garcia would say.

I told myself that one day, I was going to have to explain to that lady doctor that all I knew to do was not say anything. That wasn't the same as listening. That wasn't the same as that blue-eyed patience she used when folks opened up to her. What I had was what most Southern folks have, especially black folks. I'd had time to learn how to close my eyes on what was really happening and let all kinds of secrets slip by me. But with Maggie sitting there, I picked up my pen and readied myself with the questions the good doctor had taught me to use.

"You fill out your papers yet?" I asked.

Maggie looked stupid. "Did you slip me some when I come in here?"

"I got some forms here," I said, holding up the clipboard. "I got some questions to ask."

Maggie smiled. "Ain't met many colored folks ask me nothing, but I don't mind if you ask me some. Pretty black man like you could ask me anything."

I stroked my chin and thought again of growing a mustache. "Well, I got some questions for you."

"I'm ready," Maggie said, and that was the last time I had to urge her on. Once she got the hang of it, no official forms could have held the answers she gave to any one question.

She was a farm girl, if you could call sandbag Bayou country, farmland. Took care of chickens, she said. "When I gathered eggs, I'd cluck. CHEE-chick-chick-CHEE. Could cluck them eggs right out of their asses," she laughed.

Maggie's laugh damn near rocked the walls. I cocked my ear to make sure the boy in the ward was finally going under, but the only sound I heard was the faint scratch of cicadas snapping away at the sweet May night that seeped under the outside doors. And I could smell Plaisance's evening meal heating up on the burners in the back room—cayenne peppers and bay in day-old fish stock. Somewhere, near the south end of the ward, I heard Plaisance's mop slapping as he dipped it from his bucket of pine-blue water and flung it against the corridor's walls. But nothing seemed to be reacting to Maggie's laughter. I eased back to the questionnaire, and chose another one of those red tape standards, the bit about next of kin and permanent address. Maggie took it to heart.

Her father beat her, she told me. Came back to the farm every night with his string of fish and his gut ready for drinking. He'd raped her too, she added. More than once, and afterwards, if I could believe her, took her to church to say confession. "Got the booze from my mama," she said. "But didn't get nothing from my old pappy but shit. Still, I'm luckier than some. Seen a lot worse off than me. You know that's the truth, don't you?"

I grunted. More because I'd learned to grunt no matter what the question. I grunted and let her talk. Sometimes I listened; sometimes I didn't. I already knew the story and a dozen versions like it, but when my attention wandered, she'd fix me with her eyes.

It was Maggie's shifting gaze that let me know someone had entered the waiting room.

For a second, I didn't understand Maggie's signal. I thought she was punctuating some seamy part of her story about her daddy, or her old man and how she'd sent him painted on his way to hell and glory. Then I heard a voice, and though I could not understand the words, I turned. I was still trapped in Maggie's world of dirt farmers and home brew, but I began to focus until finally, I realized the woman staring back at me was my sister, Lacey.

"Weasel," I said, as if I'd been calling out to her every day for the last ten years. "You're here," I said, as if I'd unlatched a door and all the shit I thought I'd stored away had started falling toward me. I hadn't heard the ward doors open, hadn't heard her footsteps or any change in the way the air smelled. She was just there, staring at me. Her face made the memories of all those years I had in my head seem like something that had happened yesterday. It was like looking into my own face—a little smoother, a little older than my thirty-four years, but mine—the same dark brown skin, the same long nose and heavy eyebrows. Mama's face. The face of Pointe Coupee Parish.

I would have been less surprised to see Dr. Garcia standing there in housecoat, haircurlers, and hiking boots, carrying a fishing rod baited with one of her famous hand-tied flies. I would have even accepted Plaisance's latest woman leaning on the arm of a rednecked sheriff, or better yet, his woman come to tell the truth about all those Saturday nights he'd claimed. But no, I faced my own dear sister, standing there looking like swamp bait with her hair as ratty as an unmade bed, and her clothes rumpled from sitting on a Greyhound. And if I knew my sister at all, her knees and hands rough from doing day work. Lacey had been born old and bent into habit, and like Mama, she'd kept to it, pulling her hour wages no matter how many wells VasCo struck for folks lucky enough to own land. *The luck of the draw,* Mama had laughed when the money passed us by. *Lincoln gave colored folks forty acres and a mule. All I got was the goddamn mule,* she'd said, laughing at me. The only time she hadn't laughed was when I'd left home. With that thought, I went from Mama to money to all the reasons I'd put ten years between me and my family. "Weasel," I said again, this time, whispering her name as if the sound would make her disappear.

I looked down at the clipboard. None of the questions covered this, so I placed it carefully on the counter, and hitched up my pants. Nothing could have brought Lacey here except Mama. I knew I hadn't summoned her up, had not called her by letter or Vieux Carré voodoo spirit. So surely the only way she'd arrived to see me was because of Mama. Here was my sister come to track down the renegade, the no account runaway son. I looked up. Looking into Lacey's face was harder than sidestepping a drunk who was bursting through the fog of a minus bloodsugar count. Except, I wasn't nearly ready to see through the fog that covered Lacey's eyes.

"Ain't you got enough trouble without coming here?" I asked.

"Mama's dead," she said in a flat voice.

"She's where?" I asked, and we both heard the stupidity in that question.

"Mama's dead," Lacey repeated.

"Dead?"

"Mama's dead so you can come home now, Toulouse," she added.

I shrugged and straightened up the papers in the clipboard again. For a second, Lacey was silent, but when she opened her mouth to speak, I spread out my arms. I had to say something, but I needed to remember more than what you say when a drunk goes off on you. Still the best I could do was, "Home is where you hang your hat. Home is where people want to see you when you get there. Home . . ." My mouth dried up.

"Folks need to get home," Maggie interrupted.

"Who's that?" Lacey asked.

Lacey's voice was still flat, as if she were ready to fill it with accusations. I leaped at the chance to divert her attention. "That's Maggie," I told her. "Maggie Boujean, lately of the ARC." I said it as if Maggie were more family than Lacey, as if saying Maggie's name might keep me from saying the wrong name, keep the ARC in focus, keep Lacey from telling me again what she'd just said.

When Lacey said Maggie's name, she added a soft curl to her voice. "Maggie Boujean, eh. Your new lady friend, brother? Something you want to tell me about?"

It was the last question that stopped me, the tone of it, the way she made her voice turn into Mama's in just a few words. *I ain't gone never act like Mama,* she'd once told me. But then, she'd also said, *Mama's dead,* saying *Mama* as if she expected me to still know who that was, and *dead . . .*

Ten dogs for every boy like you, Mama had laughed. I was ten years old, in the tree outside her bedroom window. *Come on in here, boy,* she'd said. *You can stay out there all night and tomorrow, and that dog ain't never gonna come back. It's dead. Say it. Say that dog done died, and come on in here.* I'd put my head down, gulping air, holding onto the tree as if it would keep me alive. *Come on down from there, you hear me? Come on down. A black man ain't got that much time to be making up his mind, so you get on down from that tree.* My head was full of drowning but my mother stretched out her arms to help me to safety. At the bottom of the tree, there was Lacey.

"What you gone do?" Lacey asked. She was talking louder now. Almost shouting to cover Maggie's sobbing.

I stared at both of them. Women. I shook my head.

"I got two boys out there somewheres," Maggie sputtered. "Cutest damn babies you ever saw."

I knew drunks cried over everything and nothing at all. Half of what you did in D-tox was waiting out a drunk's need to cry. But Maggie had been sitting there, talking so easily, looking so much a part of ARC, like a piece of equipment, her crying seemed out of place. "Don't," I pleaded.

"Damn it, man," Lacey snapped. "I said your mama's dead and you begging this white woman not to cry. Don't you understand me?"

"Mama sent me away. Told me not to come back," I said.

"Well, she's dead now," Lacey said, and Maggie cried, "Dead. Dead."

"Told me I wasn't nothing to speak of. Said I couldn't hold my own. Wanted to stay in my room too much. Let folks tell me what to do. Said I was scared. Said . . ."

"Will you shut the hell up!" Lacey shouted.

"My babies," Maggie wept. "My babies. Send them letters when I can. Gone now. Gone . . ."

Lacey and I stared at each other and Maggie began to seriously howl. At least, somebody was crying, I thought.

"You tell me right now what you gonna do," Lacey demanded.

She waited, but I couldn't bring myself to form the right words. Now Maggie was blubbering about God and her family and how a woman's got to do what she'd got to do to keep going in this world. I remembered my mama talking, loud and full of herself—my daredevil of a mother, my double-dog-dare-you and I'm-disappointed mother. Always pushing but always there to help, even when I didn't need it. Reciting *Hiawatha* to me and Lacey when we couldn't get past some bull shit story about the antebellum South for a seventh grade test. She'd memorized the first part and all we did was to fall asleep giggling about our half-Indian neighbors. And Mama doing the Charleston on Saturday nights in the living room, just before the fire burned out, her big frame loose with the movement of dancing and drinking, and some dude come in from the mill on False River with a pocket full of money and a weekend to spend it. I thought of her catching the snake I needed for fifth grade show-and-tell. Catching it in a pickle jar and sealing the jar tight until the snake turned pale in the moonshine gin, thin and papery like the vegetables she canned one summer and left too long on the back porch. My daredevil mother. My don't-need-you mother.

"Bus for Pointe Coupee leaves at seven. You tell me what you gonna do, brother." Lacey waited. "You got family back home, like it or not," she added.

Between them two women, that boy don't need no father.

"Don't seem I got much to speak of by way of family now," I said.

"Faith ain't nothing for a woman," Maggie muttered. "Look at the Bible. Turned the wife into a pillar of salt just cause the lady had curiosity. What kinda God turns people to salt cause they got the balls to look for something?"

"I guess I better tell them you ain't coming home," Lacey said.

I still couldn't get my mouth to work.

Maggie snorted. "Who's to say? Specially since the husband was the one who told the wife not to look back. Well, hell, don't that make sense? Course she had to look back. What kinda wife would let her old man tell her what to see?"

Lacey looked around the waiting room, then narrowed her eyes at me. "You still playing that same old game, huh? Stuck in this rat hole with some fools cause you can't flash no dollar bills. I thought when you left home, you was gonna get rich overnight. Thought you was gonna be some black Horatio Alger. Some big superstar with Motown albums and suede underwear."

"What you talking about? That's Mama's talk."

Lacey shrugged. "Could be, but I still see you stuck in this dump, poor as ever." She looked at the way my belly bulged against my belt buckle. "Thought you was gonna be the next Fats Waller, gonna do the boogie-woogie piano like Big Maceo."

"I'm working here," I said. "Got me a job and don't have to BE nothing but working. You see me working here, don't you?"

"I didn't ask you about no job. I'm asking you about all that big time dreaming you did back home. You remember all that dreaming about the good life, don't you? Told me it was the American way."

"I got nothing to say."

Lacey pursed her lips. "That's always been your trouble, brother. You always got nothing to say and won't listen to folks who try to talk some sense into you."

"Why I got to listen? Wasn't nowhere for me to go, back home. Always on top of me. Acting like I got to make up for what they ain't never had. I told her: You ain't responsible for my happiness. I told her: I got to make my own way. But she was always on me, asking for something. I couldn't hear myself think for listening to her mouth. And half the time, I didn't even know what she wanted from me." I stopped. My own voice was beginning to fill up too much of my head.

"Mama never asked you for nothing, Toulouse. She never asked cause she knew she was never gonna get it."

"Men always leaving women to do by themself," Maggie cried.

"Shut up," Lacey told her. Then she turned on me. "You ain't changed, brother. Everybody's fault but yours. I just come to see for myself. I knew you'd find out she was dead sooner or later, but I just wanted to see if you had any forgiving in you. Should've saved myself the trip, Toulouse. You still holed up like always." She looked around the room. "Seems fitting for you. A place to sack out and crazy folks to waste your time. But don't you worry none. Pointe Coupee can bury Mama without you. Ain't no reason for you to come home now."

I sorted forms, and the noise of the papers almost drowned out Maggie's crying.

If Plaisance hadn't entered the room at that moment, I wouldn't have known Lacey was near the door. "Somebody go home now, eh Touti?" Whatever Lacey saw in Plaisance made her lips tight. He tried brushing aside her look. "You stay," he told her. "We make him show you a good time. Find us some easy money, eh?"

"I had all the good times I need," Lacey said, and turned again, but she stood there for a moment when I called out to her.

"Weasel, I can try to make it home next week," I said.

She shrugged. "Don't bother on my account," she said, then she walked into the sweet-smelling spring night. This time she shoved the doors open wide and the antiseptic air of the ARC fought with the night flowers for a while before the doors choked off their scents. Then the latches clicked and the outside world no longer existed. I breathed again.

Plaisance was laughing. When he saw my expression, he stopped. *Half a mind,* Mama had said, *Half a mind makes half a mouth.*

I nodded toward Maggie. "Get her into a ward, Plaisance."

"Touti, how come you never ask this boy, eh? Shee-et! For you, Cajun just work." Then he motioned Maggie toward the south ward.

"What kinda God won't let you turn back?" Maggie asked. "What kinda God turn you to salt?"

More Than a Notion

W HEN THE WHITE MEN CAME, THEY PRETEND-
ed to be friendly, but Mama spent most of the time ignor-
ing them. She didn't usher them into the front room where she
took important company and she didn't invite them into the
kitchen where she took folks she wanted to make feel at home. She
sat at the far end of the middle room windows knitting a piece of
string around and between her fingers, her profile etched against
the leaded glass panes. Uncle Roman sat on the opposite side of the
windows, and between Mama and Uncle Roman, the ashy black
pot bellied stove stood clean and ready to be used the next winter.

But it was late summer, close to Labor Day, and the stove had
not been fired since last May during the freak hail storm. Papa had
been home in May and it was Papa, coming in after dusk, his mustache full of melting crystals of ice, who'd fired up the stove to keep
the chill out of the house, his teeth grinding into his cigar as he
cursed and poked and prodded until he got things just right, while
Uncle Brother stood by the door, useless as ever, watching his
father, my grandfather, arrange the chunks of kindling and coal
inside the wide black belly of the stove. I never understood just
what purpose Uncle Brother served, why Mama and Papa and all
of his sisters seemed to value him so. All I'd ever seen him do was
brood.

Uncle Brother always seemed to be brooding. Even on bright
sunny days, you could find him huddled in the dull grey light at the
far corner of the room, his features muted and blurred by the dark
shadows rooted behind his eyes and his lower jaw working spas-
modically on some nameless bit of food like a cow worrying its cud.
Some families have children who have trouble seeing or can't hear

91

too well. Some families have children who have something wrong with their arms or legs, or children who have trouble thinking or holding up their end of a conversation. We have Uncle Brother who can chew and rechew food that the rest of us have forgotten we ever ate. Uncle Brother's stomach doesn't close all the way, Mama says, so all he needs to do is bring the food back up and start all over again. Sometimes you can't see him do it; sometimes you don't even hear the soft burp when he pulls the food back into his mouth, the sound muffled like an air bubble rising to the top of a muddy sink hole, but sooner or later you notice the movement of his jaw, the mindless grinding as he chews and chews.

"Brother, you stop that," my mother yells. "Eat your food like everybody else. Ain't right for human folks to be eating stuff two or three times."

"Brother can't help it," Aunt Fern will say. "He's just built different."

"Built like a cow," Aunt Maddie laughs, her mouth always ready for a sour answer.

If Papa's in the room, nobody dares make fun of Uncle Brother. Papa makes everybody keep their place. If Papa's in the room, I can get away with just about anything I want to do, but the whole family wishes there was some way to make Uncle Brother stop eating his food two or three times.

But that day in August when those two stone-faced white men came to our house, nobody paid much attention to Uncle Brother's cudding, as Papa called it. Mama was sitting by the dining room windows that morning, sitting near Uncle Roman, Papa's brother, sitting the way she'd been when I'd gone to bed the night before. And that morning, Papa was dead.

That day, I woke up in the four poster without Margay yelling for me not to get too comfortable. I'd been sleeping in the four poster for nearly a year, since the time the spider bit me and left a blister on my back. "A water bag big enough for a witch's brew," Papa had said. He'd said not to take any more chances, so Mama had put me in the four poster and no matter how much Margay protested, that's where I slept. Mind you, Papa had been "dozing" on the davenport for five or six years before I was born, but that was considered temporary and my place in the four poster, as Margay reminded me each morning, was as temporary as Papa's dozing. "Don't lay there looking for quail on toast," she'd say, or "Don't drop your anchor, miss lady. You moving soon."

Of course, if it had been a regular morning, nothing could have kept Margay from jogging me awake with another of her old sayings, snapping open the day like a can of sardines. But that morning was different. Even the shadows, the very smells in the air, were different. When Papa was around, the house smelled of peppermint and heavy smoke from his last cigar mingled with an odor that Mama, Margay or Aunt Fern can't even come close to. They're filled with the traces of what women are. Food, babies and perfume. Bits and pieces of sewing thread and furniture polish, hair oil, spicy soap, last night's supper, or maybe even some man they've rubbed against. Women have smells that float around them like clouds, but a man is a mass of separate smells that push against each other like muscles, an itchy, kind of loose stuff, like tangled beards, or the quiet rumble of deep voices that put you to sleep at night if they're feeling good or wake you up suddenly in the middle of the night if the world is pressing in on them.

That morning, I woke up trying to squeeze out the sandpaper noises and talcum powder odors of Margay and her sisters, and conjure up the smooth checkerboard sounds, the tweedy scents Papa left in the house as he chunked firewood into the potbellied stove in the winter or opened the dining room windows to let in the fresh air of summer. All morning, I had heard my mother and her sisters passing the bedroom door, stirring up the air with their noise as if my being in bed made it harder for them to face this day.

For a while, I had snuggled under the covers and listened to the footsteps coming and going, the sounds of neighbors bringing with them sympathy and good food until the house was filled with smells of collard greens and oxtail stew, red beans and rice, yams, and gumbo, skillet bread and all manner of puddings and cakes. Neighbors coming and going as my mother set everything in place for Papa's wake. By the time I'd managed to pull myself out of bed, most of the neighbors had been to see Mama at least once, and all of them had promised to make sure the wake would be "a proper putting away of Mr. Smalls." And like all good black folks, they were determined that Papa would have a wake everybody could remember.

There was so much food and so many good smells filling the

house when the white men showed up, they looked puzzled, staring into the kitchen where all the bowls and roasting pans sent up vapors of odors, staring at the table where covered dishes and jugs of sweet cider stood ready for all the folks that would show up for the wake. They looked as if they had accidentally stumbled into the wrong house and couldn't think of a reason to leave. My mother and her sisters brought them into the dining room, then abandoned them so they were caught between Mama and Uncle Roman on one side, and the women guarding the front door on the other side. When the men arrived, the neighbors, as if by signal, found they had things to do in their own houses, so suddenly, the family was alone in the middle room waiting to see what those men had to say.

The men had not come to tell us Papa was dead. We already knew that. And they had not come to give us sympathy. Papa would be the first to say that white men, especially the men who worked at the brewery or on the railroad with Uncle Dell, Fern's husband, would never give you sympathy or anything else that was necessary. When the men first came in, they didn't seem to know which of us to talk to. They stood in the dining room, hemming and hawing and beating around the bush, as Papa would say, like they expected us to rush out in the street, shouting and singing old-timey gospel songs.

The longer they stood there, the gloomier everyone became. Our house is dark and shadowy most days—on the low side of sunset, as Papa put it—but when those two men walked in, the dull light seemed to grow thicker. Since the house is built like a skinny shoebox, both the hallway and stairs leading up from the street are made cave brown by the heavy walnut paneling and the thick bannisters tunneling up from the front door. We don't have a yard. As a matter of fact, the only folks on the block that have yards, little bitty postage stamps of weeds, mud and scraggly flowers, are Miz Amery, Miz Lucy, and Miz Simmons. Our house is a walk-up, where the front door ends in a closet-sized porch with four cracked marble steps butting right onto the sidewalk. So anybody coming into the house falls into a pool of darkness right on the other side of the door. But most people try not to bring it up the stairs with them.

Those men seemed to divide the room in half. They stood there, rumpled and white, while my family filled the space on either side of them, separated but somehow connected as if there were an invisible link hooking us all together, as if someone had tried to draw the same face over and over, and finally had come up with a bunch of folks that had more or less the same slant of nose or angle of jaw or shape of head done in slightly different shades of brown. Even though Aunt Maddie is tough as an alligator with her wide hips, box ankles, and moon face, she just looks like a bigger version of Aunt Fern and Margay. Aunt Fern is the prettiest. Papa always said she should have been a dancer, like Lucille Armstrong or one of those other Cotton Club show girls from Harlem. Aunt Fern is all legs and quick-silver movements. My mother is rounder than Aunt Fern and not as hard-edged as Aunt Maddie who doesn't like anybody since she had to leave her no-account husband in Texas. But my mother can make folks nervous, maybe because she has beige eyes, like Uncle Brother, and folks think she's looking straight through them. Me? I look a like a little bit of all of them, but I've got some of my own father's features because my eyes are bigger and my hair is thicker, not like the washboard crinkly hair Mama and Papa's children have. Still, when we're all gathered in the same room, we look like one of those faded brown pictures of church folks Mama has hidden on the top shelf of the chiffonier where she has hidden Papa's gun and a feather boa Aunt Maddie claims she got from that West Indian she married down in Texas, the one thing she brought back when Papa had to rescue her.

Then I realized that I was so busy thinking about Papa and the family, I'd almost forgotten those white men.

They didn't seem to know where to begin saying whatever it was they'd come to say. They called Mama "Miz Ethel," and they stared at everybody, including me and Uncle Brother. But the more they tried to include all of us, the less it worked.

"Just speak your piece," Mama told them, spitting it out like she really didn't want to hear it, but the sooner they said what they had to say, the sooner they'd leave.

"I don't spoze you 'member me, Miz Ethel," one man said. "I was at the picnic last month. The one for the brewery," he added as if Mama went to picnics all the time.

"Yeah," the other one joined in. "We thought we should come by to see y'all." He bounced from side to side like some little kid who was ready to go to the bathroom. Then I noticed one of his legs was shorter than the other, and the shorter one ended in a clubfoot.

I didn't recognize the one who said he'd seen Mama at the picnic, the one who called himself Staffer, but I recognized the other one, the one Papa had called Mitch. Once, when I went to the brewery with Papa, I saw Mitch talking to the wagon master's wife. Papa had introduced me to them and the wagon master's wife had looked down her nose, then told Papa to take her dog for a walk. The dog was one of those little Mexican dogs with pointy little teeth that snip-snipped at everything and everyone. All Papa had to do was jerk the leash and that dog nearly flew into the air, and since Papa was six feet tall, that dog walked on air most of the time we had it out. We'd been walking for a while before Papa said anything.

"I'm not paid to walk dogs."

"What are you paid to do, Papa?" I'd asked.

"Not to walk dogs."

"You're paid NOT to walk dogs?"

"I'm paid to survive, that's what."

I felt so dumb, I never asked him what he did again. Papa had a blunt way of saying things sometimes that made the words settle around you like a wet wool coat, all heavy and smelly, but it's the only thing between you and the rain. "Sometimes, it's best not to say nothing," Papa had told me.

Those men standing in our house that day in August didn't seem to have anything to say, but they surely used a lot of words to say nothing.

"We don't want to cause y'all no trouble," Mitch added. Aunt Maddie cleared her throat and he stopped, then said, "We was right sorry to hear about . . ." and stopped again.

"Her husband?" Aunt Maddie interrupted. "You sorry to hear about her husband."

"Ain't like this wasn't his home," Margay snapped.

"You surely is sorry."

"A sorry lot."

"We all like Smalls down at the brewery," Staffer smiled, but when Mama grunted, he stood there with his mouth hanging open, then looked to his partner. Mitch started talking really fast. "It was an accident," he squeaked. "See we had this delivery to make . . ."

Staffer made a funny, jerky kind of movement that silenced Mitch. "What he means, Miz Ethel," Staffer began. "What he means is that we had to make a run . . ."

"To Colfax. You know that's a dry county so . . ."

This time, Staffer held out his hand and I could see Mitch swallow whatever was going to come next. A look passed between them that said more than the words Mitch had spoken already, but Mama wasn't ready to let the matter drop. At least, not right away.

"My husband wasn't a religious man, but he wasn't no fool," she said.

"Oh no, ma'am," Staffer said. "He was spozed to go . . . I mean, it was a regular trip and all . . . We didn't want no harm to come to Smalls."

Mitch nodded, and Aunt Maddie muttered, "Um-hum" and "I know," like she expected those white men would understand she was saying more than the sounds she made. I almost laughed out loud. It seemed strange that white folks could think black folks were ready to say just what they believe, when black folks aren't ready to tell other black folks just what they believe.

Since yesterday, when we'd first received the news of Papa's death, I'd heard four or five stories about how he'd died. Mama had whispered, "He just passed away," like she expected him to reappear any second. My mother, Margay, claimed it was milk poisoning. "When he ate that food down there on that job, no telling what was in it," she'd said. I couldn't understand why Papa would drink milk when he could get all the beer he wanted, and I couldn't understand it especially since I knew he didn't even like milk. But I listened to that story along with everyone else's.

"Tell me they carried his body clear up the railroad tracks and set him in a chair so it would look like he was sleeping," Miz Avery told Aunt Fern. Miz Avery's husband worked on the railroad too, so she and Aunt Fern were always talking about the train yards, and Miz Avery's husband had already sent a message up the line to bring Uncle Dell home from his Chicago run in time for Papa's wake.

"I told him about working round those big draft horses," Miz Owida Granberry said. She's the Sunday school teacher, and thinks it's her business to warn everybody about the trials and tribulations of the world no matter what the day of the week. "Them horses is in-bred and mean-tempered. I warned him many's a time."

And old man Farrow, down at the nickel-and-dime grocery store, told us he'd seen the body at the undertaker's. "Had this little hole in his chest, Miz Ethel," he'd said in his thick Jewish accent. "Gevalt! Such a little hole for such a big man." Then he'd patted me on the head and handed me a quarter, like he used to do when Papa would take me into the store to buy birthday candy. I put the quarter in Mama's milk money jar, and filed away his story of the icepick hole as something to watch for at the wake.

I even heard Uncle Roman give his reasons as to why Papa died, and Uncle Roman rarely offered reasons for anything. But all of the family agreed with him when he said, "Amos never did want us to know just what he was doing on that job. I reckon we know why now."

By the time those men came to our house, I'd heard just as many stories as we had relatives. And now the men had come in with a new story, watching us closely as they sputtered their way through their version of Papa's death, watching us as if waiting for the first "Hallelujah," and "Amen Lord" that would make them feel comfortable about coming to Papa's house once he was dead.

They came in carrying a box of old clothes and things they said belonged to Papa, things he'd left in the gatehouse at the brewery where he slept when he had to "help out" at night. Mitch said two other men had gotten killed that night. "One was a district boss," he said, as if that would make us feel better about Papa's death. Staffer said Papa had some back pay coming, mumbling the words like he didn't want to give us anything. The whole time he talked, he folded and folded a bent-up hat, and Mitch, bucking the knee of his shorter leg, nodded and nodded his ok. They talked about Papa's clothes and money owed him as if they had accidentally discovered some old clothes, loose money and our house on the same day.

"That money and them clothes ain't gonna bring my husband back," Mama said flatly. "So just why is it that y'all come here?"

"We kind of curious to know if the po-lice been asking round," Mitch said.

"I wouldn't have nothing to tell them," Mama said.

Mitch cleared his throat, then added. "Well, we ain't got much to tell you bout what happened either, Miz Ethel. But seeing how loyal your husband was, and all. I mean, how he kept the other boys in line . . ."

"I don't want to hear it," Mama said.

"Smalls was just like family to us," Staffer said. "We want to help best we can. We want everything to turn out for the best."

Aunt Maddie humphed.

"Best?" Aunt Fern demanded. "Does that mean better? Better that what, may I ask?"

Once she got started, her sisters fell into place, the three of them butting against those men like the Billy Goats Gruff.

"You act like Papa planned all this."

"Papa would never have let you in his house anyway."

"You just upsetting Mama. What do you want? Wouldn't even talk to us yesterday."

When the women ran out of steam, the white men had turned red. But while they were gathering up more words, Uncle Brother spoke up. "We just want what we're entitled to," he said. "My father didn't beg no man and we won't either."

I decided I should say something too, but I'd no sooner started with "Papa says . . ." when Aunt Fern nudged me with her foot. I'd though it was safe to sit on the floor beside her, but now I saw no place in that room was safe that morning. I scrunched my knees up under my chin and tucked my skirt around my legs. Papa had told me that sometimes, it's best to be square with the world and keep your mouth shut. "Then folks think you know something when you don't know nothing at all. And it bothers them." Papa bothered a lot of folks.

Papa worked at the brewery but didn't carry a lunch pail like all the other men in our neighborhood. Papa carried a gun that he kept cleaned and ready to slip in his shoulder holster sometimes when he went to work. Papa went to work whenever he was needed, whenever they wanted him to "help out," as he told it. Went to work wearing old pants and a shirt, and sometimes came home, days later, wearing a suit. But Papa never talked about a pay check or a time clock or a union hall, like Uncle Dell was always doing. And Papa was the only one to sit down and tell me what happened to my own father, how he'd got cut up so bad during a railroad strike, he'd bled to death before anyone found him.

As a matter of fact, Papa was always trying to make heads or tails out of some story he'd overheard or one the family had twisted up so much, nobody could remember the truth. But Papa always skirted any questions about the brewery, and there was always talk about just what kind of work Papa did for the brewerey.

"Papa needs to quit that place."

"Them white folks is something else."

"Um-unn, them folks is a crying shame."

"Man's got to make a living."

"Now WHO you telling?"

I could feel the air popping with all the words my family had stored up behind their pursed lips. It was as if they had had a spell, a fit like Miz Lucy Bates' brother, Max, who lives across the street, and who, mostly on days when it was hot, twisted and foamed at the mouth while all the little children on the block danced up and down, screaming, "Look at Crazy Max. Crazy Max is having another fit." The white men seemed to be having some kind of fit too, jiggling and fidgeting like they'd arrived at the principal's office, late for school and no excuse. Like they were about to sit down in a seat somebody had already messed up.

The man with the bent-up hat cleared his throat and said, "We already talked to Carrie, Miz Ethel," and I thought: *I declare, y'all surely have a way of saying the wrong thing to this family!*

To begin with, the man had called Aunt Carrie just plain Carrie, in the same breath as he'd called Mama Miz Ethel. Aunt Maddie took two steps forward and two steps back, the way I'd seen Sugar Ray Robinson do in a film about boxing. And Uncle Roman wiped his mouth with his handkerchief, taking time with the movement so he could watch the men. Most everybody else was watching how Uncle Roman would react to Aunt Carrie's name.

Aunt Carrie is Uncle Roman's ex-wife and not in good standing with the family. We all knew Papa visited her on a regular basis, and I knew Papa gave her money to make ends meet, because, as he said, "Folks think all a black woman can do is housework and welfare." But if those men had talked to Aunt Carrie, there was a good chance that they'd talked to Lucien, Uncle Roman's son.

Since a year ago last April, when Lucien had left his mother's house and disappeared into the pool halls in East St. Louis and Cicero, Uncle Roman had acted like he was hard of hearing anytime anyone mentioned Lucien's name. Even Papa had grown tired of Lucien. Nobody liked the way Lucien had walked out of his mother's house, even though Papa knew where Lucien was and what he was doing. But Lucien-poor-child, had already gone to jail once when he'd been caught gambling up near Centralia, and now that Uncle Roman wouldn't speak to him, Lucien-poor-child, didn't have mother nor father to talk some sense into him. Nobody was concerned about those men knowing Aunt Carrie— "That woman would party with old man Death," as Aunt Maddie would say—but the idea that if they'd talked to her, they'd probably talked to Lucien before they'd come to see Mama was an out and out insult. And right on cue, Staffer said they'd also talked to Lucien while they were at Aunt Carrie's house.

For the first time since the men arrived, Uncle Roman made a move as if to get up from his chair, but Mama's stare pinned him to the seat. Margay moved closer to Mama, and Fern cleared her throat before rushing past Uncle Brother and into the kitchen, then changed her mind and marched back into the room again. And Uncle Brother started twisting his hands together as if he were wringing out an invisible rag. I must admit, I was as nervous as everyone else over how Uncle Roman would react. Mentioning Lucien was the same as finding an old sore on a knee or elbow that hadn't quite scabbed over. Anything that brushed up against the spot might rip the skin again.

Lucien was not much older than me, four years to be exact, but he was trifling, and his slovenly ways had made his own father disown him. More than once, Papa had tried to talk some sense into Lucien. Papa never thought of anyone as an outcast, so Papa and Uncle Roman had fought over what was right or not right to do about Lucien. Uncle Roman had refused to discuss his son with anyone but Papa. When they started talking, Uncle Roman would get mad, but he knew my grandfather, his brother would not let him speak right out against his own son, so when he got upset, he just sucked in air like he was holding a piece of dry lemon in his mouth.

"Ain't enough to be born from the same seed," Papa would say. "You got to take an interest in what it brings you."

Uncle Roman had turned his back on Lucien anyway, and now, Uncle Roman stared straight ahead, his mouth shut tight and his chin up the way Papa used to do when he was waiting for everyone to be quiet. But those white men didn't know they were supposed to be quiet too.

"Lucien says he understands what has to be done," Mitch added, talking about Lucien as if he were a grown-up man, or better yet, as if Papa could still protect him.

"Damn Lucien!" Uncle Roman snapped when Mitch started to speak again. I held my breath. "Lucien better keep his black butt on the other side of town," Uncle Roman blurted out.

If I'd been Catholic, it would have been time to make the sign of the cross so that my mama and her sisters would take pity on Uncle Roman.

"Roman, watch your mouth!"

"You crazy? Talking that stuff in front of white folks."

"Don't be acting no fool, Roman. That poor child is your son."

"What you saying, Roman? That's family talk. Lucien's family."

"Damn Lucien," Uncle Roman repeated, and all the women tried to shush him up by reminding him that Lucien-poor-child couldn't help the way he was.

Now they were all arguing and trying to get Mama to agree with one of them, but she'd turned her head toward the window and was knitting that piece of string around her fingers again. The men tried to get a word in edgewise, but in my family, arguing is as common as bad weather in winter. While the family bickered with Uncle Roman, Mitch, the one with the club foot, spoke directly to Mama. He kept it up, plugging away at her silence with Carrie this and Carrie that, then Lucien, Lucien, Lucien. But he was trapped in a web of noise, a sticky mess of our family lines where one end twisted and curled around half-a-dozen other loose ends, like that piece of string Mama was worrying.

Staffer cleared his throat. "Ain't like we can exactly replace Smalls, Miz Ethel," he said to Mama, "but we can break the boy in real easy. We can have him on his own in no time."

Uncle Roman jumped up and shouted, "You can take Lucien to the river and drown him for all I care."

Staffer looked puzzled. "We ain't talking bout Lucien working for us. We talking bout the boy here." He pointed to Uncle Brother.

That did it! Uncle Roman said, "Un-huh," and sat down,

thump, back into his chair. Aunt Fern let out her breath in a "Humph!" but Margay whispered, "Who they say they want?" And we were all aware of Mama shifting her position so she could study the men.

"He ain't no boy," I said, figuring somebody had to stick up for Uncle Brother.

"That's right," Aunt Maddie added, "and this ain't no slavery time, so don't come here to do no trading."

"Brother don't need to go nowhere."

"We could use his help around here."

"If Amos had wanted that boy at the brewery, he'da took him there himself."

"Now that Papa's gone . . ."

"Let Brother decide," Mama said in a flat voice.

"Papa did all he could, Mama," Margay began. "If Papa . . ."

Mama turned on her. "You heard me."

"But Papa could've . . ."

"Could've what? Just what could Amos do this boy can't?"

Everybody looked at Uncle Brother. I don't know about the rest of them, but the first thing I remembered was the time Uncle Brother brought home a wife from California. Everybody was talking about marriage and divorce that year, because that was the year Aunt Carrie and Uncle Roman split up. And that was the year Papa had gone to fetch Aunt Maddie in Texas, where she was stuck with that West Indian husband of hers after she caught him slipping out to see some white woman who was giving him money on the sly. That was the year they said, "Some no-good woman from California done tricked poor Brother into marrying her."

By the time Uncle Brother arrived, I was set to see that woman from California. I stood by the stove with Papa, who was chewing on his cigar and listening to his daughters hiss and spit about a woman they hadn't seen yet. Mama had made me help her air out the living room, fluff up the lace curtains, clean soot from the window sills and open the windows so a bit of light could bounce off the leaded glass panes. That let me know Mama thought of Uncle Brother's wife as company, but just as important as the insurance man or the preacher.

"Family is family," Papa had said, so we were standing ready when the ten-cent jitney brought Uncle Brother and his wife home from the train station. We shouldn't have spent all that time getting the house ready, because, as it was, the woman from California didn't last six months before she caught the train back to the coast. But while she was with us, I paid more attention to Uncle Brother than I ever had. Now, I couldn't remember any other time when I had thought of Uncle Brother as interesting. That is, until Staffer said he wanted Uncle Brother to work at the brewery.

Everyone kept staring at Uncle Brother. I guess you could think of him as handsome if he could make his stomach act right, but that day, Uncle Brother just kept burping and burping, a soft smooth sound like a baby makes just before it drops off to sleep. I said, "What kind of work you gonna do, Uncle Brother?" and Fern reached down and pinched my upper arm so hard, I wanted to bite her hand.

"Let Brother find out what he wants to do," Mama said.

"Brother ain't well," Margay told the men.

"They got doctors to fix his stomach," Uncle Roman said flatly.

But Margay said, "You can't expect him to do what Papa did."

"Beats living off women," Fern muttered, and although we all knew she was thinking about that West Indian, Mitch took what she said to mean she was on his side.

"'Pears to me, you got no choice," he said. "If the boy here wants to come work for us, we be glad to show him around. Ain't easy to find a good boy these days."

Mitch had the words out of his mouth before Staffer could stop him, but we saw Staffer try, so we let Mitch's talk of "good boy" ride for the time being. For the time being, it was enough to see how Staffer made Mitch nervous just by staring at him. Mitch flexed the knee of his bad leg to ease the weight of his club foot.

I tried thinking of Uncle Brother taking Papa's place, but no matter how I looked at it, it just didn't seem right. Uncle Brother's cat eyes, that big hooked nose, and his habit of cudding made him look like he was about to spring on something, then changed his mind at the last minute. I almost wished the men had been talking about Lucien after all. Lucien looks more like Papa than he does like Uncle Roman. Uncle Roman is compact, but Papa always carried himself tall, like he was about to pose for a picture. Always looked important, even without his pipe or cigar, and his dark skin stood out in a room full of Mama's pale relatives like a velvet rib-

bon on a pair of coveralls. Something about Papa just never quite
fit with regular folks. Papa was that way and Lucien is like that too.
He holds himself the way Papa did, stands with his legs slightly
apart and his calves pushing against his pants. And although
Lucien doesn't have mutton chop sideburns like Papa, it's still easy
to think of him taking Papa's place.

Staffer squinted at Uncle Brother. "Miz Ethel, you don't have to
say yes right now. He can come down if'n he wants to. We just
thought that since Lucien . . ."

"I can work good as anybody," Uncle Brother mumbled.

"Mama, you best talk to this boy," Maddie snapped.

Margay and Aunt Fern muttered something, then everybody fell
silent again. Maybe it was because Uncle Brother walked over to
the windows, or maybe it was that Uncle Roman stood up again
and seemed ready to walk right through the stove to get to Mama,
but whatever it was, we waited and for once, the white men had
enough sense to wait too.

Mama took her time. She had always been quiet, so much so,
even Papa sometimes was impatient with her. "If silence was
money, that woman would be rich," he'd laugh. Most of the time,
we could tell how Mama felt by the way she moved around the
kitchen. The more upset she was, the more she kneaded dough or
beat tough meat with a mallet. If she was really upset, she'd go into
the parlor, slide the doors closed and practice her choir songs. I'd
come home from school and hear her singing as if the entire choir
from the Abyssinia Church was behind her and she had to drown
out their noise.

Mama never talked about what it was that made her sing any
more than she talked about her other troubles, but since the news
of Papa's death, Mama had sat by the window, and we had no way
of telling what she was thinking.

Uncle Brother walked over to her, then leaned down and took
her hand. He held it near his face, brushing it across his lips
and cheeks as if she were blind and needed to be reminded of who
he was.

"You got to do better than that, chile," she told him.

"What am I gonna say, Mama?"

Mama looked at Uncle Brother for a minute, then turned back
to the window. "There's that Pritchard boy," she said, pointing to

the street. "Running around with that old mangy dog like Miz Simmons' boy used to. Sometimes it 'pears like Bumpsy Pritchard ain't got sense nor kin. Miz Pritchard just don't seem to make him mind her one bit since her husband gone and died."

I could see Bumpsy turning the corner at the end of the block, his coat unbottoned and his shirttail flapping in the breeze, that spotted grey no-breed dog nipping at his heels.

"Don't seem right that a woman has got to tell a child what to do all the time," Mama added. "Too many colored folks waiting round for somebody to tell them what to do."

"Mama, make them tell us why Papa died," Maddie whined.

Mama pointed to Jimmy Dufree who was hurling a paper sack full of coal dust and ashes at Bumpsy's retreating figure. "There goes another one of them boys. Ain't got the sense he was born with either."

Both Mitch and Staffer leaned forward, and I had to force myself not to laugh when Mitch jerked as if Jimmy Dufree's trash bomb was going to hit him, and not Bumpsy. Staffer had his hands stuck in his pockets and was jiggling coins like he was counting them in the dark. His oily hair seemed to bounce with the rhythm of the coins in his pockets, and as he leaned into the light from the window, a hank of hair fell away from the rest and landed across his forehead like an old piece of balloon rubber, the strands stuck together and slick as those dishes of slimy okra Mama likes so much.

Then Staffer made a noise in his throat, like those scratchy sounds squirrels make when they scramble across the roof in the winter.

"We don't want to be keeping you," Uncle Brother said. "I can come by and pick up any back pay you owed Papa. Maybe I can talk to you bout working . . ."

"Mama!" Aunt Maddie interrupted. "You can't let Brother go just cause some men come here . . ."

Uncle Brother walked over to Maddie and shouted at her as if his face weren't just a few inches from hers. "Don't you LISTEN at all? This ain't no time to be talking. "

Everyone fell quiet. "I reckon we can get going now," Staffer said, but he said it more to fill up the silence left by Uncle Brother's outburst. Still, we all knew their visit had ended. Whatever they needed to say, had been said.

"Be back directly," Uncle Brother said to Mama, then he ushered Mitch and Staffer out of the room and down the stairs.

"It don't seem right," Margay muttered.

"Black folks been walking the line between right and wrong since they took us off the ships from Africa," Mama told her.

"They just come in here and we act polite, like we forgot how Papa died. Don't seem right," Margay protested.

"Talking to them like they could understand," Aunt Maddie added.

Margay grunted and Humphed, then looked at me as if she'd just noticed I was in the room. "Ain't you got some work to do, Josephine?"

"That kitchen needs cleaning up," Aunt Fern said. "You best get to it."

"She don't pay no attention," Aunt Maddie complained as Margay jerked me to my feet.

"Get a move on."

"Don't be sitting there. We got a lot to do before the wake."

"Mama, Miz Lucy's gone come over and start setting up the chairs," Aunt Fern said. "And Miz Simmons promised us some roast chicken."

"This whole house got to be cleaned," Aunt Maddie announced.

I must have looked as if I didn't know which way to turn first, because Uncle Roman covered his face with his hands, then sank back in his chair and groaned, "Leave the child alone. Lord, leave her be. Ain't but so much a body can take in one day."

"They alright, Roman," Mama said. Then she turned to me. "Jo- Jo?"

"I'm ok, Mama," I answered. "Papa said . . ."

I started, and although I swallowed the rest of the words, I knew whatever Papa had said would hang heavy in our house for years. All of us would remember him the way you hear somebody singing a few lines of a song, and the whole thing comes back to you in a rush.

"Papa said . . ." Maddie cried, then walked into the kitchen, slamming shut one of the cupboard doors almost before she had fully entered the room.

"Papa said . . ." she muttered again, and I heard the front door click shut as Uncle Brother closed it behind the white men.

Sister Detroit

THIS IS THE STORY OF THE DETROIT HOG WHICH fell into the hands of a righteous Sister. Just seeing this hog on the street would not have drawn anyone's attention to it particularly, especially if all the other hogs in the six square mile area between Prospect and Troost were considered. And surely, Buel Ray Gatewood wasn't the first man in the neighborhood to graduate from high school, and two years later, with a job and a wife, buy a fully equipped, luxurious, special edition Detroit Auto-Mo-bill. "More car, Mo-bill" was a neighborhood slogan.

When Buel Gatewood bought his Gran Turismo Hawk, folks around Troost Avenue and Prospect Boulevard hadn't learned how to talk about Vietnam yet. After all, Bubba Wentworth had just returned from Korea, and the V.A. had helped him get a job at Swift Packing House. Grace Moton was just recovering from having to bury her brother, who'd been shot in a border skirmish at the Berlin Wall. "Ain't much of a wall if it can't stop bullets," Grace had wept. And Nicholas Clayton had taken his sissy self off to some white school in the West just to test all of that Supreme Court business about integration.

But Buel Gatewood had plunked down a goodly portion of several paychecks in full certainty that with his deluxe edition, $3400 Hawk, he would own the best wheels on the block for some time to come. There was one thing for certain about that notion: he was going to have the biggest car payments on the block for at least five years.

Still, there was no doubt that Buel's Hawk was tough enough. It was all grille and heavy chrome borders, black like a gangster's car, but road-ready for a sporty-otee like Buel. "Any car got the name of Hawk is bound to be good," Buel had said. "That's the name of that wind that blows off the lake in Chicago. Hawk! That wind says: look out, I'm the Hawk and I'm coming to get you. Now I got me a Hawk, so Look Out!"

In that car, Buel could outgun DeJohn Washington's '54 Coupe de Ville, and outshine the Merc Meteor his brother, Calvin, owned. And, despite its retractable hard top, he simply dismissed the Ford V8 Roger Payton had bought on the grounds that only somebody working in a gas station could afford a gas guzzler. "I don't go around talking bout other folks' mistakes." he'd said, but according to Buel, almost everything about Roger and the others was a mistake. Unlike Calvin, Buel had a high school diploma and didn't have to tend bar at Rooster's Tavern. And he didn't have to haul cow shit at Swift Packing, like DeJohn, or nickel-and-dime in a gas station alongside Roger. He had a good paying job with Arbor Industrial Services, and once he bought his Hawk, he'd settled into outrunning the competition. That competition completely surrounded Buel and his Turismo Hawk.

That year, the Detroit exhibition of cars featured *The Wheels of Freedom,* a display of Detroit's best, all locked in park and placed bumper to bumper on a disc-shaped turntable. It amazed the public to see all that shiny metal swirling past them. That crowd should have come to Buel's neighborhood, where cars dazzled owners and passersby alike. The traffic moving down Brush Creek Boulevard, Blue Parkway, or The Paseo alone would have been enough to put Detroit on the map, but with the added interstate traffic between Kansas and Missouri, between the city and the suburbs, between the haves and have-nots, the need to have bigger and better wheels kept folks buying cars: Mustangs, Barracudas, Cougars, Mercs, Caddies or Falcons, speed-ohs or rattle-traps, FOB factory or custom-cut to the owner's specs.

Cars were a part of the neighborhood, the status symbol of having arrived into your own, with wheels. Cars were the black man's stock portfolio, his rolling real estate, his assets realized. What roads the city didn't provide by way of streets, it made convenient with expressways that cut through the length of the town, leaving a trail of cheap motels, used car lots, and strip joints at one end, and Swift's Packing House and the bridge to the Kansas side at the other end. Any of the roads from the center of town allowed easy access to a state highway, but the convenience was counted only by those who needed to flee the city or cross the state line.

Real estate developers in the select sections of the inner city that were being upgraded for white residents called those expressways "The River of Lights." Folks around Buel's neighborhood called them "The Track," and tried turning their backs on the whole business unless they were unlucky enough to have a reason to skip town.

Sometimes, Buel and his friends had vague dreams of eating up roadway in a hot machine of their choice, but Nicholas had been the only one to find a fast exit West, and when he'd left the city, he'd just vanished as far as Buel and the rest of the Technical High School class of '62 were concerned. Nicholas might have vanished, but Brush Creek, Swope Parkway, and Pershing Road were always there. And when cars from the neighborhood around Troost and Prospect passed each other on the road, their owners would honk their horns in recognition.

If someone had taken a photo of Buel, DeJohn, Roger, and Calvin back in 1964, they could have spotted the contentment on those four faces. In those days, everything they set out to do seemed easy, especially when they stayed within the boundaries of the world they knew, places they could reach on one tank of gas. They couldn't imagine, did not bother to imagine, anything pushing them farther than that point. That would come later. For now, it was enough to wait for Sunday afternoon, when Buel or one of the others would say, "Let's show Nab some tail feathers and floorboard these hogs."

On a good day, when the heat and humidity were in agreement, when there was no snow blowing off the Kansas plains, or winds whipping north toward Chicago, the men took to the roads, their cars spit-clean from the fish-eye taillights and split-wing trim to the sleek roofs and grillework. Their only worry was the occasional cop on the Nab and ready to grab them as they sped past a billboard or crossed the state line at rocket speed. When Miss Swift raised her skirts over the Intercity Viaduct and they smelled the rancid odors of dirty meat, they knew they were heading West. And when the messages on billboard after billboard along Highway 40 were shattered by blinking neon like black lights on a disco floor, they were heading East.

But for the women, those cars were the excuses that helped their men stay as fickle as the tornadoes that occasionally passed through the heart of town, the winds that sometimes danced through living rooms and took everything a family had managed to scrape out of a pinch-penny job, and sometimes turned corners down the centers of streets as if they were following traffic patterns. For the women, those cars were merely another way to haul them from the house to a day job—"the hook between Miss Ann and the killing floor," as Autherine Franklin would say—because, for the women, the cars were to be looked at and paid for, but never driven.

Anna Ruth Gatewood remembered the family gossip about her Aunt Charzell, who had driven a Packard to Oklahoma City in 1927 all by herself. "The only way she did it was she dressed like a man and she was so light, she could pass for some old honkey anyway." But Anna Ruth's family had fallen on hard times, and there were no Packards available for the women when the men could barely hang onto a job long enough to support one car.

Even when some old fool, like Dennis Frasier, went on pension and bought a new car, keeping the old car for a runabout and the new one for churchgoing, women weren't likely to take the wheel. All of them had excuses for not being able to drive: Luann Frasier claimed she was too old; Nona Payton said her babies made her too nervous; and Autherine Franklin told everyone she was too tired to do anything after spending all day scrubbing Miss Ann's floors out in the suburbs.

When Buel bought his Hawk GT, Anna Ruth told everyone that Buel had never said "boo" to her about buying a car, and if he had, she would have taken driving lessons before he'd signed the papers.

"He just showed up with it," she said. "Drove up to the house, big as cuff, and walked up the path like he'd just hopped off the Prospect bus and come home from work, as usual."

According to Anna Ruth, Buel had sat down on the sofa, picked up the paper and folded it back to the Sports page the way he always did. But about a quarter of an hour after he'd been in the house, Anna Ruth came to the window to see what the commotion on the street was all about.

What she saw was a jet-black Studebaker Hawk surrounded by half the neighbors on College Street.

At first, Anna Ruth didn't connect the car with Buel. All she saw was the top of the car, a bright swatch of black metal, a glob of shiny color that looked like the smear of tar road crews poured in the ruts along Brush Creek Boulevard every spring. At first, she couldn't even determine what kind of car it was.

"Looked like some kind of funeral car," she said later. "First word that come into my head when I seen that car was *death*. If I was gonna buy a car and spend all that money, I'd have bought me a pink one, something bright and pretty like them cotton candy cones they sell over at Swope Park in the summer. But that thing looked like somebody had been laid out and the undertaker had come calling."

"Girl, if he was my husband," Autherine Franklin said, "I'd make him give me the keys to that car. That's why I don't have no intention of marrying that no-good DeJohn Washington. Can't never depend on men for nothing."

Anna Ruth almost told Autherine that men was all she'd ever depended on, but she held her tongue. Everybody knew Autherine was fast and loose, and that was why she and DeJohn didn't get married. But if anyone said anything to Autherine about it, she'd be ready to go upside their heads, and since Autherine was her best friend, next to Nona Payton, Anna Ruth had better sense than to pick a fight over nothing.

"I was thinking about going over to the YWCA," Nona said. "Tell me they got driving lessons over there for anybody to take."

"Girl, Roger ain't gonna let you spend no money learning how to drive," Autherine and Anna Ruth said at the same time.

Then they both leaned back and laughed at the sharpness of their perceptions. It was comforting to see some part of the world clearly, and the three of them had been friends for so long, they clearly saw each other's worlds, even if they could not see their own.

What was happening to change their own worlds did not make itself known until Buel had owned his car for nearly a year. But in that time, he and Anna Ruth more or less settled into a routine, an edgy kind of quarrelling mixed with hard-loving that told the world they were still newlyweds. Each morning, Anna Ruth still took the Prospect bus to the Plaza and her stockroom job in Ladies' Apparel. And each morning, Buel drove his Hawk one block north of Arbor Industrials, where he parked and walked the rest of the way for fear one of his bosses might see the car and think he was trying to be a big shot.

"I ain't got the patience to be teaching you to drive," Buel told Anna Ruth. "Ain't no reason for a woman to be driving. Women too nervous. Besides, you got me to do your driving for you," he laughed, and stroked her ass to make her forget the idea of his car.

No matter how many times they argued the logic of her learning to drive, or how many times Anna Ruth offered to help with the weekly Simoniz, the only time she sat in that Studebaker was on Sundays. And even then, she only got a ride to church. Getting home was her problem, because Sundays, Buel and his buddies went to Rooster's to listen to whatever game was being broadcast on the radio. Anna Ruth knew the seasons by sports more than she did by weather: football in the fall, basketball in late winter, track in the spring, and baseball all summer. In a pinch, the guys even listened to golf or tennis, anything to keep their standing arrangement of Rooster's after church, then onto the Interstate or Highway 40 and one of the bag-and-bottle clubs until late Sunday night. Except for an occasional family gathering at one of their parents' houses, little had interfered with the boys' routine in the two years since they'd left high school.

None of Anna Ruth's complaints could keep Buel away from Rooster's after church.

Buel said, "Anna Ruth, you ought to feel good when I drive up to the church and help you out of this baby right there in front of the preacher."

"I'd feel a lot better if I was driving this baby by my lonesome," she said.

And Nona said, "Ain't that just like a man? Thinking that just cause he can drive you to church, you got to feel happy bout him driving off and leaving you alone at night."

"How you think they kept all them slaves in line?" Autherine asked. "Told them God meant for them to be slaves, that's how. Fed them a whole bunch of crap about God and church. That's why I don't like going to nobody's church. When I really want to talk to God, I just get down on my knees and commence to speaking."

"Honey, when you get down on your knees, you talking to Ajax and Spic-and-Span," Nona laughed.

"Nona Pettigrew Payton, we been friends since the second

grade," Autherine snapped, "but if you don't watch your mouth, I'm gone make you one dead friend."

"Just hush," Anna Ruth said, "You know you don't mean that. Now just hush, both of you. I swear, seems I spent half my life listening to you two snapping at each other."

Autherine was ready to take the argument one step farther, but Nona paid attention to what Anna Ruth had said.

"Aw girl, com'on," Nona said to Autherine. "You know I didn't mean nothing. Let's walk over to Bishop's and get a fish sandwich we can turn red with some Louisiana Hot Sauce."

"Ohh, now you talking," Autherine shouted, and linked arms with both Anna Ruth and Nona.

Still dressed in their Sunday best, they left church and headed toward Bishop's.

At one point, their path took them down a two-block stretch of Brush Creek Boulevard. The trees lining the four-lane street rustled with the wind, and debris, caught in the back-wash, swirled down the creek bed that separated the traffic patterns into two lanes on either side of a concrete abutment. The creek itself was concrete, paved over years ago by the Pendergast political machine, which owned the local concrete plant. Now, it resembled a spillway for a dam site, except it was flat, like the rest of the landscape, with sections of sewer pipe cut in half and laid open along a winding stretch through the middle of the city. And it was either full or empty. In dry seasons, a trickle of water oozed through the mud that crept up in the middle where the concrete sections didn't quite meet. But the creek offered the neighborhood sudden flash floods during the wet seasons. In those times, crossing the boulevard could be perilous and more than one person had suddenly been faced with the prospect of drowning while the rest of the city stayed high and dry.

Still, the creek had its advantages, meager as they may have been. It separated the rush of traffic up and down the busy boulevard, and the trees stirred the wind so that gas fumes did not linger the way they did along Blue Parkway, The Paseo, and other thoroughfares. And in the winter, when the snows froze into ice, neighborhood kids used the creek as a playground, while the hot summer air left the trees heavy with fragrance and wild flowers bloomed in the cracks edging the creek.

It was rough walking those two blocks, but Anna Ruth and her friends knew what kind of jaunty flash they made, laughing and high-stepping their way to Bishop's. Some days, they walked to a chorus of car horns honking their owners' approval at the sight of three foxy ladies. Autherine had more interest in pointing out who was behind the wheel of a passing Bonneville, or a two-toned Barracuda, or a fish-tailed Plymouth. Anna Ruth was busy counting the number of women manuevering their old man's Oldsmobile or Falcon or Fleetwing. Only Nona was interested in how much money had been wasted engineering the Brush Creek project.

But Nona had always been the curious one of the group. As a child, she'd been more interested in playing Monopoly than pickup sticks, or jacks. And in high school, she'd taken a course in drafting along with her Executive Secretary program. Even now, she was enrolled in night school in an effort to upgrade her job with the most successful black dentist in the city from receptionist to bookkeeping. Nona liked to read better than she liked to dance, and Nona had a library card that she used at least once a month. So, Nona had been labelled the brains of the group.

"You so stuck up, you got no business over here in Tech," Autherine had told her one spring day after typing class. "You ought to be at Richmond where you could be wearing them football sweaters and going to the prom."

But Richmond wouldn't take Roger Payton, and more than anything else in the world, Nona Pettigrew wanted to be with Roger Payton. It was probably Nona who had put the idea of marriage into Anna Ruth Simpson's head. Anna Ruth had liked Buel well enough, but she hadn't thought much beyond her next date with him. Nona had plans for Roger Payton, and when she consulted Autherine and Anna Ruth on the best way to make Roger aware of those plans, the fever of marriage struck Anna Ruth as well. The three of them had giggled and plotted, and three months after Roger and Buel graduated, there had been a double wedding with Autherine and DeJohn acting as witnesses for both couples.

Once they were married, Anna Ruth had settled into not thinking past any given day again, but Nona simply worked around Roger's midwestern ideas of what a wife should be and enrolled in night school. By the summer of 1964, she was working her way toward convincing herself that she needed a driver's education course as well as those bookkeeping courses she took while Roger was on duty nights at the gas station, and by spring, she would have enrolled if the country hadn't been faced with Johnson's Tonkin Gulf Resolution.

Suddenly the U.S. was fighting in Vietnam and Roger Payton was one of the first men in the neighborhood to be drafted. Within six months, all of them were in uniform, and in the six square mile area between Prospect and Troost, families were learning to pronounce the names of places that even President Johnson had trouble wrapping around his tongue: Phan Rang, Chu Yang Sin, Quang Ngai, Dong Hoi.

Like everyone else, the women had been totally unprepared for the impact of Vietnam, but of them all, Autherine seemed hardest hit by the news of her man called to war. She saw it as a plot against black folks, and even after she helped DeJohn pack his clothes and sell his car, she preached against his participation in some white man's war games.

"Going to church and going to war is all black folks is allowed," she shouted. "We ought to form our own state. Let them white folks fight it out amongst themselves."

And as she wept and ranted, refusing to go to church any more, refusing to go to movies or even press her hair in her protest against white injustice, Anna Ruth and Nona saw the revolutionary she would become within the next three years. But by the beginning of 1965, Nona and Anna Ruth became more troubled over the decrease in letters they received from their husbands.

Now, walking along Brush Creek was a problem, no matter what the season. They ignored the cars that honked at them and tried to imagine what kind of scenery the men could see in that place called Vietnam, a small speck on the map that Nona had helped them locate one day in the library. Now, each of them found ways to occupy their time, especially the nights, and Nona, free to take any classes she wished without hiding them from Roger, finally enrolled in a driver's ed course.

"I aim to tell him," she said to Autherine. "I aim to tell Roger all about that driving course next time I hear from him, but I don't want to be throwing him no surprises until I'm sure he got the other letters I sent him. I ain't heard from him since last September, and here it is January."

"I got a letter from Buel in November. Said he was being transferred to Roger and DeJohn's company. But I ain't heard from him since."

"DeJohn don't write much, but I should've been hearing from him bout now. Last thing I heard, they was moving them farther North."

"Well, if I know the boys, they got themselves some hootch and up there painting the town," Anna Ruth laughed.

The others laughed with her, but no one believed what she'd said. The news was filled with stories of war casualties; B.L. Jefferson's boy had been killed on a destroyer in the South China Sea; and the Andersons, over on Bales Street, had lost a son and two nephews. And everyone was beginning to have news of another name added to the list of those missing in action. In June, the names Roger Payton, Buel Ray Gatewood, and Calvin Gatewood were added to that list. And in June, DeJohn's mother told Autherine she'd received a letter from the War Department telling her that DeJohn had been fatally wounded and was listed as a casualty.

"Those cocksuckers can't even say *dead*," she screamed. "Just some shit about casualities and missing. Like we gonna turn a corner and find them standing there grinning. This is *some* shit. I want you to know, this is *some* shit."

"I just can't believe Roger's dead," Nona said. "Roger wouldn't just go off and die on me."

"Honey, Roger didn't die on *you*," Autherine snarled. "He died on Uncle Sam. He died fighting for some white man. He died same as DeJohn and Buel and Calvin."

"I don't believe Buel is dead," Anna Ruth said in a flat voice. "I just don't believe it."

"And Roger can't be dead," Nona wept. "Look. He didn't even sell his car." She pointed to the Ford parked at the curb in front of her house. "He left the car right there. I mean, you can't see him going off and leaving that car."

"I don't see nothing but that car," Autherine said. "I don't see nothing but that car out there rotting in the rain. Ain't nobody in it. Roger ain't in his car, and Buel ain't in his. They might as well have sold them. Might as well have done what DeJohn did, and sold that shit. And if you got any sense, that's what you'll do."

"I'm not gonna sell that car until Roger comes home and tells me in person to sell it."

"Then, that car's gonna be sitting there till hell freezes over," Autherine snapped.

But Nona finished her driving course, and on Sundays, when Autherine didn't have a Black Panthers meeting, Nona would take her for a ride, the two of them zipping along Blue Parkway, the Paseo, the Interstate Viaduct, and Highway 40 in Roger Payton's Ford Skyliner. Loneliness for Nona became those Sunday rides where she tried to duplicate the outings Roger had taken, Buel and the others trailing him. Only Nona had Autherine spouting Black Nationalist doctrines in the passenger's seat beside her. Anna Ruth refused to come with them.

Anna Ruth said her Sundays were too busy. She had to make sure Buel's Hawk received its weekly Simoniz, she told them. And she had to attend meetings at the church where she helped the auxiliary track down government addresses so the ladies could write to the War Department and ask them to send their men home.

On Sundays, Nona and Autherine drove by Anna Ruth's house on College Street, but every Sunday, Anna Ruth was too busy to join them. Through that whole summer, Anna Ruth seemed too busy to have any time for them at all. By fall, Nona and Autherine noticed how Anna Ruth didn't wait for the weekend to Simoniz Buel's car. Often, they would see her washing the white-walls, polishing the chrome, or waxing that car on Wednesdays or Fridays or Saturdays, only to do the whole job again on Sundays. And more and more, Anna Ruth retreated into a kind of unquiet muteness that was more like a scream than a silence.

And in early December, four months after the Watts Riots, when the winds blowing off the prairie seemed loaded with little crystals of ice, and the bare limbs of trees along Brush Creek Boulevard crackled in the thin air, Anna Ruth snapped and took the wheel of Buel Ray Gatewood's Gran Turismo Hawk.

It seemed so natural, sliding into the driver's seat. For months, she'd brushed the upholstery and floor with a clothes brush to keep the dust from eating the fabric. For months, she'd polished the steering wheel, the wrap-around windshield and dash. And from time to time, on orders from Buel, she'd started the engine and let the car idle. But on that day, she'd slipped it into drive, popped the brakes, and eased away from the curb.

She was on Brush Creek before Nab spotted her. At three o'clock, when the cop pulled her over, she'd put the car in neutral and waited patiently.

It surprised her a bit that she didn't feel frightened. It wasn't as if she knew what she was going to say, but she hadn't felt that heart-pounding rush she remembered feeling the day she'd worked Buel around to asking her to marry him, or the first time, a few days later, when she'd slept with him. In her rearview mirror, she watched the cop lock his cycle in park, and waited until he tapped on the glass before she cranked down the window.

"It's my husband's car. He's in the Army in Nam," she told him when he asked for her driver's license. "He's missing in action so I'm taking care of his car till he gets back."

The cop never blinked an eye. "I'm gonna have to take your keys," he said. "Why don't you just park this heap close to the curb and let me have your keys."

"This ain't no heap," Anna Ruth snapped. "It's a Gran Turismo Hawk and it belongs to my husband. He's in Nam. Missing in action . . ."

"We got 200,000 boys in Vietnam, and not a one of them took his car. You got no driver's permit for this thing, so you park it. This car is impounded."

The cop walked to the rear of the car to take down the license number, and Anna Ruth leaned over to start the engine. She gunned it, giving the 255 horsepower full rein.

"Easy there, girl," the cop said. "Don't get fancy on me. Just slide on into that curb."

Anna Ruth slipped it out of neutral into drive, then while she was still inhaling, into reverse. The engine responded as if it had been starving for attention. In one fluid, sudden movement, Anna Ruth took out the cop's motorcycle, and if that Nab hadn't stepped back, she'd have nailed him too. Then she slammed it into gear and raced down Brush Creek. She was four blocks away before the cop stopped slapping his hat against his knee and yelling, "Goddammit! Goddammit!"

Passersby gawked, and some, heading toward Bishop's or Maxine's Bar-b-que, called to friends to see the sight. "Nab got creamed!" they shouted, and the news spread up and down the street like brush fire. Unfortunately, Anna Ruth had left the cop's radio intact.

But that was not her concern at the moment. When the cop finally realized he could call for help, Anna Ruth was careening off parked cars along the boulevard. Her foot seemed frozen on the accelerator, and when she entered The Paseo, she skidded into a spin at the icy intersection, circling twice before she headed north, leaving five crippled cars stuck in the middle of the street behind her. The police call reached patrol cars at 3:18 pm. By 3:20, she was spotted on The Paseo, and two cars gave chase.

Somewhere along that thoroughfare, Anna Ruth came into her own, and the occasional clatter of metal when she sideswiped a parked car, or grazed a driver too slow to move out of her path, no longer made her gasp. When she saw Nab behind her, she left The Paseo at Plymouth and returned to it later off Linwood. The snow plows had been working in her favor. In fact, the weather was in her favor. It was a gloomy day, but cold and clear, so cold, no one was out that Sunday unless they had to be. So cold, slush hadn't formed on the roadway and the ashes left by the plow crews were still on top of the ice. Despite the damage she'd caused, for the most part, the path ahead of her was clear. But behind her, there was a stream of police cars.

She had decided to head for the Interstate Viaduct and the Kansas side, but Nab began to descend in all directions and she had to criss-cross her own path across The Paseo and back. Once, when she was parallel to The Paseo on Troost, she saw two cop cars coming toward her. The units behind her knew they had her cornered, but Anna Ruth jerked the wheel and in one wild open circle of a swing, headed in the opposite direction, weaving between and around the cars that had been trailing her. Three cars ran into each other to avoid a head-on with Anna Ruth's Hawk.

As the cop driving the second car pulled himself from the wreck, he looked at Anna Ruth's retreating taillights and shook his head in begrudging admiration. "Goddamn that bitch can drive," he said.

But whatever luck Anna Ruth had found in encountering very little traffic on newly plowed streets was about to run out. By all accounts, the police had brought in twelve units by the time she reached the last lap of her odyssey. By all accounts, Anna Ruth had travelled the length of the Paseo from Brush Creek to the Viaduct intersection and back by the time Nab had cut off her escape route. And just as she reentered the neighborhood, just before a line of squad cars flanked the street and forced her onto the lawn of the Technical High School, she'd left behind her a trail of more than twenty damaged cars.

But in those last two miles, Anna Ruth had gathered a cheering section. Folks in the area between Troost and Prospect lined the street, yelling directions that would place her out of Nab's path. And sometimes, folks blocked Nab's path by shoving junk cars that had been abandoned in the neighborhood in front of the cops. Young boys threw rocks, practicing for the riots that were soon to come to the city. And old men, rising from their Sunday afternoon slumber, marked the day as a turning point.

Nona caught up with Autherine just as Anna Ruth swerved off Brush Creek onto Euclid. Autherine had been helping make posters for a Panthers' meeting in the basement of the school, and when Nona banged on the door and called to her, she was just warming up to an argument with a fellow Panther about the causes of revolution. The news of Anna Ruth's rebellion erased her need to convince the man.

The two women were running down the front stairs of the school when Anna Ruth turned onto the block. At the opposite end, the police had parked several paddy wagons. Behind her, a phalanx of patrol cars, sirens blasting and lights flashing, raced toward her in full bore.

Perhaps she would have made it if old man Frasier had not have been backing out of his driveway at that moment. Frasier had heard all the noise, and his neighbor, Charleston Davis, told him some crazy woman was tearing up Brush Creek. That was a sight the old man felt determined not to miss. He could not have known Anna Ruth had detoured off Brush Creek and was aiming for a new route north along Blue Parkway. He eased the big Pontiac out of his driveway and directly into Anna Ruth's path.

Even from the stairs, Nona and Autherine could see Anna Ruth didn't have much of a choice between old man Frasier or the school's snow-impacted lawn.

"Damn! I bout made Kansas, Nona," Anna Ruth whispered after the police had pulled her out of the wrecked Studebaker. "Half-way there and driving by myself."

Nona shushed her and cradling her head, rocked her until the ambulance attendants got the stretcher ready.

"Buel's gonna be mad at me," Anna Ruth said. "Buel's gonna come home and find out I wrecked his car, and he's gonna have my ass."

"Don't worry about it, baby," Nona told her. "By the time Buel gets here, we gonna have everything fixed."

Autherine watched the cops trying to handcuff Anna Ruth even as the medics were placing her on the stretcher. "This is *some* shit!" Autherine shouted. "*Some* shit!"

Exercises

IT WAS HIGHLY UNLIKELY THAT ODENA MOTLEY
and Joyce Ellen Mayfield could solve each other's problems,
but Joyce Ellen had to find a room and Odena needed company,
someone to fill the silent corners of that big three-story house. Her
grandson, Leon, was nested in the upper reaches of the house, but
Odena took no pleasure in climbing the stairs only to find Leon,
sprawled as usual, in the middle of a smelly island of comic books,
mail-order catalogues and dirty clothes.

She was preparing herself for death, or as she put it, a much-
needed rest, and the business of making herself as tired as possible
before she took to her bed that final time did not include trudging
up three flights of stairs only to confront Leon's silence.

She needed company, and Joyce Ellen Mayfield didn't seem to
know exactly what she needed. So Miss Dena sized up Joyce Ellen
and decided she wouldn't be as pushy as the young woman boarder
she'd had last year, the one who'd listened to operas all day Sundays and littered her kitchen with cracker crumbs and bologna
skins every day of the week. Of course, anyone was better than
Leon, yet Miss Dena laid her plans carefully, as carefully and craft-
ily as she'd woven all the events in her life for the past ninety-odd
years. And, at first, like most people who crossed Miss Dena's
path, Joyce Ellen only saw the bleary eyes floating in their pale blue
pools of ripening cataracts, the sparse chicken-plucked patches of
frizzly grey hair and the parched black skin stretched tightly over
Miss Dena's bones like the thin crust of an overcooked turkey hen.
This frailness was Miss Dena's shield.

"Me and the Reverend used to take tea in this room every afternoon. That lamp over there. . . ." She extended a bent black twig

125

of a finger in the general direction of a spindly-legged table, and Joyce Ellen dutifully followed the quavering end of that bony finger until she spotted the velvet-shaded lamp, half-hidden by two oddly shaped statues and a dozen other knick-knacks. ". . . now the Reverend, he never did like that lamp," Miss Dena continued. "Said it didn't give much light, but he always took his tea right there at that table. Don't suppose you care for tea?" she asked.

"Coffee helps me stay awake."

"That school keep you pretty busy, I guess. Can't let it keep you too busy." She cocked her head to one side and tucked her hands under her armpits, beating her elbows against her waist as if she were cranking herself up to move. She looked more birdlike than ever, and Joyce Ellen hid her smile by bending over in a closer examination of the crocheted lace doily pinned to the chair beside her.

"Got to leave yourself a little time to socialize," Miss Dena continued. "Them white folks run you crazy. I hear tell it's one of the best schools in the country for doctoring, but I remember a time when colored folks couldn't. . . ."

Joyce Ellen's sharp intake of breath cut Miss Dena midsentence. "Is it a large room?" Joyce Ellen asked.

Miss Dena's elbows stopped moving, and for a moment Joyce Ellen believed that the center of that room rested in the protruding mass of Miss Dena's watery eyes. Then Miss Dena dropped her arms and walked toward the door, balancing her weight on the balls of her feet with a rotating motion that was surprisingly reminiscent of a long-distance runner or a star center on the basketball court.

But she took the steps one at a time, clinging to the bannisters as if the effort itself might send her tumbling at any moment. Joyce Ellen followed at a distance comfortable enough to catch her.

"I clean up here twice a week," she said. "Don't spect you'll have much time to do that, not with all them books they make you study. It won't be no trouble for me, though. Doctor says: 'Miss Dena Motley, you best stop climbing them stairs,' but I been cleaning this house pretty near sixty years now. Me and the Reverend moved here long before the war." She stopped and peered down at Joyce Ellen. "First war, not that other one." Then she inhaled and moved forward again. "Lost my son in that second war. Baby Leon's been with me ever since. His mother died, you know."

"Do you have a light in the stairway? Some of my classes let out rather late, and I usually study on campus at night."

"I clean everything. Scrub and wax the floors, change the beds. Don't make no mind if there's roomers here or not. I got five rooms up here and six downstairs. Clean them all. Light switch is right there, and there's another one at the foot of the stairs. Been a snake, it would've bit you," she mumbled, then added as she opened the door at the end of the hall, "Baby Leon's room is up at the top of those next stairs. This one here is yours."

Joyce Ellen followed her into the room and stood there, buffeted on one side by the sudden urge to run, and on the other by a warm feeling of coming home at last.

The room was large and irregularly shaped. The west wall seemed to have been extended or added as an afterthought, its buff-colored wallpaper newer and less elaborate than the pale yellow Grecian design on the other walls. And yet, because the room was filled with the same heavy wood and bulky upholstered furniture as the downstairs area, everything seemed to fit. Perhaps because it was all a collection of Miss Dena's past, all of it slightly faded, slightly dusty and choked with an odd assortment of paraphernalia.

"I'll take it," Joyce Ellen said, but the sound of her voice was lost in a series of muffled explosions—a thump and a wheezing crash followed by a long screech as something scraped across something else.

"That's my baby, Leon," Miss Dena told her. "If he ain't out in that workshop of his, he's hiding away in his room making just as much noise as he does when he's out back. You'll get use to it."

Three weeks later, Joyce Ellen still jumped whenever she heard those abrupt sounds. And in three weeks, she'd only caught glimpses of Leon—a grey-black shadow at the top of the stairs when she returned from campus at night, a murky pale-brown face in the upstairs window when she turned the corner at the bottom of the hill, a half-smile just as he closed the door to his workshop in the backyard, a silhouette in the leaded-glass window of Miss Dena's living room. She never saw him leave the house, but occasionally she heard him return.

Leon always slammed the heavy oak front door with a force that signalled his arrival, his defiance of Miss Dena's sensitive hearing. Joyce Ellen had been under the impression that old folks, especially anyone as ancient as Miss Dena, suffered a multitude of infirmities, including deafness. Even before she'd thought of entering medical school, her own grandmother had confirmed this belief, shouting in a thick Midwestern accent made even thicker by a loss of hearing and never understanding half of what was said to her. Ma'Emma filled her medicine chest with all kinds of nonsense, all of which she said had been handed down to her from some long-lost Mayfield who'd been taken as a slave from Africa. Miss Dena also had bags and jars of this and that to cure mysterious ailments, but none of them had to do with deafness. The old woman could hear a pin drop in the next room.

Perhaps it was Ma'Emma's juju remedies that had finally persuaded Joyce Ellen to study medicine, because surely it had not been her own mother's constant nagging. At any rate, it was definitely Miss Dena's unnerving habit of posting herself as a sentry, coupled with Leon's defiant arrivals and barrages of swearing against some invasion Miss Dena had made on his personal belongings that prompted Joyce Ellen to enter the house as quietly as possible.

She always left the campus not knowing exactly where she was going. That clinical menagerie of textbooks, laboratories, white starched coats and anatomical charts filled every available space in her head. It was a cold building, shrouded by a cold Pennsylvania sky, and sometimes Joyce Ellen could only vaguely remember the hot Kansas sun and home.

For at least three blocks, she redissected some part of cadaver A7-359-320 and, until she caught a glimpse of her face in one of the shops along the avenue near the University, she thought of herself as just as colorless and lifeless as the anatomical sketches in the CIBA collection. For those few blocks, she was efficiently everything her mother ever wanted her to be and, as much as possible, as clinical as her professors expected her to be. Then she saw her reflection—her broad black nose, oily and shiny as the skin of an eggplant, her broad mouth with its large teeth and the way she pulled her upper lip down to hide the wide spaces between them, her hair pressed into greasy shafts that stood stiffly away from a nape of kinky curls she hadn't had the time or inclination to press carefully. One look at her reflection and she knew where she had been if not where she was going.

Her routine was simple. A quick stop at Provicio's Market and the long walk up six steep hills to Miss Dena's. Check the house when she reached the bottom of the last hill. The light was sure to be on in Miss Dena's living room. Slip past the double glass doors at the foot of the stairs and toss her books and coat onto the chenille-covered bed. Then stand in the middle of the room, stretching and bending away the cramped space of library carrels and lab stools made for six-foot men with long legs.

She was standing in the middle of the room when Leon entered. The patchwork picture of him she'd collected over the last three weeks did not resemble the handsome, rust-colored man a few feet away from her. Miss Dena called him Baby Leon, and Joyce Ellen had heard a certain petulance in his voice when he berated Miss Dena, but the Leon she saw staring at her was tall and slender with broad shoulders and firm, masculine hands. Only the eyes betrayed him.

Joyce Ellen squirmed and shifted her gaze to the corner of the room where one of Miss Dena's many side-tables offered a cluttered view of several New York World's Fair souvenirs, a stack of neurology textbooks, and the obligatory velvet lampshades.

"I thought I'd shut that door," she said.

Leon's eyes wavered for a moment. "You did," he said finally. "I just wanted to see you."

"Well, now you have."

Leon's eyes seemed to go torpid, like a rabbit at bay.

"Now that you're here, sit down," Joyce Ellen sighed. She was finally a part of the house, a link between its lower reaches and the outskirts on the third floor.

Miss Dena had been dropping hints for the last two weeks. "What my baby needs is someone to help him along. They kicked him out of that school. He didn't do anything wrong, mind you. They just kicked him out. Colored folks sure have a hard way to go. If he could just finish highschool. . . ."

Joyce Ellen wondered how many of those lectures Leon had heard. She knew her own by heart—how her mother's voice glorified God one minute and condemned her to an ugly hell of streetwalkers the next, all in the name of getting an education. She had no desire to be a party to Miss Dena's version, but she had no friends at the University and Leon seemed lonely. His eyes told her that.

Leon walked over to the study nook she'd set up under the bay window. "Nana tells me you're going to be a doctor," he said. He thumbed through several books, then leaned forward and stared at a multiple overlay of sections of the brain. "You got to know all this stuff?"

"Frontal, parietal, occipital and temporal," Joyce Ellen chanted.

Leon's shoulders stiffened slightly. "You sound like a school teacher," he said. "Say it so I can understand it."

"It's not that simple," Joyce Ellen said.

Leon studied the flecks of silver paint on his hands, and Joyce Ellen suddenly noticed how those same bright flecks dotted his arms and shirt.

"Try it," he offered.

"Well," Joyce Ellen began, "it's a map of cerebellar function . . . the brain, right? That first transparency is the first layer of the brain. Then each successive layer is a deeper section. Layer after layer descending down to the core."

"All of those little spidery things on top is a layer?" he asked.

Joyce Ellen plopped on the bed. "Those are the arteries," she answered dryly, but when she saw him frown, she added, "Feeder lines that supply the brain tissue with oxygen. The frontal lobe is supplied by those arteries in the anterior section, the parietal . . ." Then she stopped.

Leon continued to flip the pages and the transparencies hissed against each other like the whisper of nylon stockings. Joyce Ellen traced the knobby pattern on the chenille bedspread.

Then Leon broke the silence. "You mean like a motor? Like in airplanes, right? When I make a model engine . . . you know? They got vanes. Uh, kinda like these fans. Yeah, there's a series of vanes that compresses the air . . . uh, air enters the chambers for, uh, fuel." He frowned, studied the spots of paint on his hands, then spoke again. "Fuel is injected in . . . into the combustion chamber . . . and the compressed air is ignited by . . . the, uh, the . . . ignitor. Arteries are like fuel lines, huh?"

Joyce Ellen stared at him. "I guess so."

"See," he laughed. "It's pretty simple. Just takes a little time. I got plenty of time. Tell you what, you can show me all of your fra-prietal things and I can show you my engines. In my workshop," he added.

"Frontal and parietal," Joyce Ellen interrupted flatly.

"What? Oh, OK. Whatever . . ."

He closed the book and walked to the door, picking at a few pimples clustered beside his left ear, then running his fingers across his kinky, close-cut hair. The movement completely hid his face as he walked past her.

Joyce Ellen softened her voice. "Sounds like a good idea," she told him. "We can both learn," she added, but he was gone, shutting the door without a word. Then she heard him walking up the stairs to his room.

Whenever he was downstairs, Joyce Ellen was sure he could be heard all over the neighborhood, but as soon as he left Miss Dena's end of the house, he seemed to float to the third floor. Those occasional explosions, those unexplained bursts of noise were the only evidence of his existence, outside of his quarrels with Miss Dena. And those muffled sounds occurred without warning, without pattern.

In the months that followed, Joyce Ellen's contacts with Leon increased, but she was still unable to predict when she would see him. She began to talk to him about school, and one day he asked, "Think you can get me into that library?"

The question came shuffling out, and when Joyce Ellen looked up he had turned his head away from her. But his long fingers continued to twist a length of string into a series of complicated knots. Joyce Ellen smiled. "I usually study around two in the afternoon before I come home," she said. "You can meet me. Just ask anybody. They'll tell you how to get there." Then she gave him her carrel number.

But three days later, she found him standing by the entryway turnstile, gazing into the room as if he'd wandered into the building by mistake.

"Everybody looked so busy, I didn't want to bother them," he mumbled.

She led him through the maze of reading rooms and reference stacks to the third floor where her carrel was located. Then she took him through the map room and the periodical section. The engineering wing was off to the west side of the building. "That's your turf," she pointed.

Leon nodded, and although she never saw him walk down the

corridor, she noticed that he always approached her third-floor cell from that side of the building. When he saw her, his smile eased the weight of the Latinized names and complicated diagrams that threatened to suffocate her until she feared her body would be as grotesque and distorted as the medical drawings of homunculus figures she studied. Somewhere in the space of a few months, her days began to pivot around the few hours she shared with Leon. Although Miss Dena never said anything, Joyce Ellen saw her shadowy figure in the window each time Leon walked her home. And when she met Miss Dena on the stairs or in the kitchen, her eyes were liquidy bright with unspoken questions. Now, if Joyce Ellen didn't see Leon on campus, she visited him in the upper reaches of Miss Dena's house. To Joyce Ellen, it seemed that Miss Dena took special care to be as far away from the upper floors as possible at those times.

His room was a cave, a hollow prehistoric cavern with stalagmite piles of objects jutting up from the floor. Shards of wallpaper hung from the ceiling and wafted in the breeze. Unlike Miss Dena's part of the house, the room didn't seem to have any definite period of past life. It had always been there, building and collecting disheveled mounds of clutter. And yet, that room was as much a part of the house as Miss Dena's living room with its velvet lamps, cushioned settees and gospel hymn books embossed with family names.

Joyce Ellen could never seem to fix on any one section of the room. The bed was a tumbled grey mass of sheets and rumpled pillows. Dirty clothes and magazines littered the room and the walls were covered with posters, most of them torn and punctuated with suction cup darts. Some of the darts were stuck against the ceiling and eventually, their weight stripped the dry cracked wallpaper from its base like the pendulum on a tired clock.

Those thumping, scraping sounds, Joyce Ellen thought.

"Experiments in stress and motion," Leon said.

She enjoyed their talks, was even humored by the little aggravations Leon used against Miss Dena, yet she still wanted to avoid the tightening circle of that house. Joyce Ellen realized Leon was not unlike the black kids in her neighborhood, the ones who had called her "gate mouth" and had torn the pages out of her favorite books, yet he was different, different from those crusty black boys she'd seen lurching around the entrance of the Stadium Theatre or walking the fringes of Schenley Park. Whatever protest Leon felt, all that had not been squelched or ridiculed by his street buddies, he now used to help him keep his balance in Miss Dena's house.

"Nana ain't feeling too well tonight, so I'm going to stay home," he'd say, and before the evening was over, he'd come to her room on the pretense of asking about a book or to offer her a cup of sweet honey tea while he drank a beer. Sometimes they'd play Chinese checkers or he'd copy structural charts, his drawings of the anatomy as fine-lined and complicated as any textbook's. Sometimes he'd teach her to recognize the rhythms of one of the jazz artists from the many record albums he had in his collection. Through it all, Joyce Ellen tried to avoid becoming the link between Leon and Miss Dena.

Now, more often than not, he was waiting to walk her home from school. One day, somewhere between Provicio's and the foot of the Hill, Leon suddenly pulled her to him. For a moment they stood there, stiffly facing each other like duplicates of the mannequins in Bonnie's Apparel Shoppe on the other side of the street. Joyce Ellen giggled—a sound so utterly uncharacteristic, so completely unlike her usual husky, hurried voice—she wasn't quite sure of what to do with it, whether to let it build or drift like the shreds of paper that floated in the wind currents at the sidewalk's edge. She let it vanish but checked nervously to see if anyone else had heard the sound.

Leon frowned, but his fingers clutched her forearms even tighter. "Will you be my girl?" he asked, his voice surprisingly even and firm.

Joyce Ellen had not known what to expect, but the question was so abrupt, so old-fashioned, this time, she laughed—an electrical cackle that exploded from her throat without warning. She imagined she had been visibly transformed, had magically changed from debutante to witch, from giggling teenager to brassy harridan. She quickly swallowed the echo. "Be serious, Leon. What would that get us?"

"I could go back to school," he muttered.

Joyce Ellen tried to shrug out of his reach, but Leon drew her closer. "You don't have to break my arms for an answer," she told him.

When Joyce Ellen struggled against him for that brief moment, the rhythms of the street changed slightly. One old woman, entering a store at the end of the block, cast a weary look in their direction, then her face regained its neutral mask and she hurried into the doorway. Three or four teenage boys lost a beat in their hand-slapping routine, but adjusted the rhythm and moved on down the street, looking over their shoulders once or twice to see if they would indeed be allowed the privilege of watching someone else fight. An old man shook his head and crossed the street against the traffic to avoid passing the spot where Joyce Ellen and Leon stood. Joyce Ellen tried to relax.

"Well," Leon insisted. "Will you be my girl?"

"Oh, come on," Joyce Ellen pleaded. "Look at us? What will your friends say when they see you with me?" she asked. Then she nodded toward their reflections in the rippled surface of the store-front windows.

Immediately, she suppressed the urge to giggle again. She remembered scenes like this from high school, but she had never been the reluctant—no, the willing girl, the one pursued, cornered in the hall and pinned to a locker by some hulking high school football hero. Or outside of the school, near the corner hamburger stand, or under the trees at the edge of the football field. The girl who always had some leather-jacketed boy buzzing frantically in her ear. The girl who always seemed to be detached, uninterested, but leaning toward that broad chest and into those lean arms. And now, here in this grey cold town where she'd learned no longer to think of those scenes, she was a part of one. She laughed and nodded once more at their figures reflected in the windows.

Leon released her and turned away. As Joyce Ellen rubbed her numbed arms, he muttered, "What friends?"

They began to walk slowly toward the Hill. For a while, they both watched their reflections move against the sloppy surfaces of the window panes—Joyce Ellen's thick short strides bobbing in double time to Leon's lanky shuffle. Joyce Ellen's roundness fading and rolling into the uneven surface of one glass frame to the next, while Leon's muscular image flowed beside hers, his seeming to move without any effort.

"You need someone your own age," Joyce Ellen said finally.

"Hey, pretty, I want you."

Joyce Ellen moved a step away from him. "Don't call me that!" she snapped.

He took her hand, clutching it so that she could not pull out of his grip. "I calls them as I sees them," he laughed.

"It won't work," Joyce Ellen mumbled.

"Then you're thinking about it?"

"I didn't say that," she added hastily.

Leon stopped again, but this time when he pulled her against him, the movement was gentle. "I want you to think about it," he told her. "I'll go back to school. For you, I'll go back." When she shook her head, he added, "Hey, pretty, it's no big deal. If it'll make you happy, I'm happy. Why you got to be so hard-headed? I see you all the time anyway . . ." He paused. "You seeing somebody else?" She shook her head again. "SO?" he snorted. "It's no big thing. Right? You think about it. OK?"

Joyce Ellen watched his face, but his eyes did not waver. In the sun, his reddish-brown hair was even redder, and his skin was tinted a deep copper. The eyes held her. And for the first time, she noticed specks of grey tinting the brown irises, little dots of color that reminded her of the speckly hen's eggs she'd once gathered from Ma'Emma's prize chickens when the family still lived in Pleasant Hill.

"There's nothing to think about," she said. "It's simple. I'm too old and . . ."

Before she could finish, Leon began to sing, "And I'm too young, shoo-boo-be-doo."

"Oh, hush," Joyce Ellen grumbled.

"Don't like that one?" Leon asked. "How about: Oh will the circle be unbroken by and by, Lord, by and by?"

They both knew this was one of Miss Dena's favorite songs, and laughing, they sang a few choruses of it. But Joyce Ellen was troubled. She had her own circles, and Leon's presence, no matter what she felt for him, would only bind her to another life in which she'd appear to be out of place. If she gave him an answer, she'd become a real part of Miss Dena's house. And she was already tied to the cramped space of her mother's house. Joyce Ellen knew her mother's ever-increasing dependency had widened with the death of Ma'Emma. That's when her mother had started going to church. But there simply weren't enough First Baptist Church functions to keep Alberta Mayfield from busily arranging her daughter's life. And her mother's match-making would only end in embarrassment as Miss So-and-so's son sidled up to light-skinned girls like Autherine Franklin or fun-loving girls like Frieda Jefferson.

Now there was Leon, and she was four years older than his nineteen years and she could no sooner avoid his smile than she could avoid Miss Dena.

"You ought to have more than coffee. Breakfast makes your day," Miss Dena told her.

Joyce Ellen nodded, gulping coffee and hoping she could escape the kitchen before Miss Dena added one of those flat pieces of fish she had every morning to the pan of hot olive oil already overheating on the burner. Every morning, Joyce Ellen fought the nausea of evil-smelling cooking oil and preserved fish. Some mornings, her coffee was too hot to allow her to escape the sight of a wet white fillet dropping into the pan like a glob of solid chicken fat. Even Ma'Emma's chitterlings seemed, by memory, sweeter than those jelly-coated slices of fish.

On several mornings, she'd had the misfortune to linger long enough to see the fish begin to simmer in the pan. At first, it sat there, stubbornly cold and wet, a white eye in the middle of an oil slick. Then it began to fry, moving in the pan as if pushing the oil away from it. Slowly a border appeared. A quarter-inch ring surrounding the fish and, somehow, etched in green. An awful green aura adding its sickly aroma to the already rancid smells filling the kitchen.

When she questioned Miss Dena about the fish, she had, as usual, been confronted with a reply that at first had nothing to do with the question. Any simple request, any query or comment directed at Miss Dena always resulted in a lengthy story of hardship or an equally long discourse on Miss Dena's philosophy of life. Miss Dena gobbled words, grabbed them out of mid-air and chewed on them. No response Joyce Ellen had to offer was ever long enough. Miss Dena delayed her until she fled to the second floor, hitting the stairs with almost the same force as Leon.

She'd only hoped to find out what type of fish it was, and, if time permitted, aim for the extra added bonus of why the green ring appeared whenever it was cooked.

"The Reverend had the strangest eating habits," Miss Dena began. "Started them about the time he started preaching at the Free Methodist Pentecostal Church. Maybe even before that. Kept them right up until he walked in the way of the Lord."

Then Miss Dena moved her through the Reverend's eating habits to his bad habit of falling asleep when she was talking to him, and right on through to his extravagant habit of spending all the money any of his churches had to offer and a goodly sum of whatever the most devoted church ladies could bestow upon him.

Joyce Ellen tried to bring the subject back to the fish, and for a brief moment, Miss Dena complied.

"Doctor told me I couldn't eat no more meat. Eighty years I been eating meat and then he said, 'Miss Dena Motley, you best give up meat. Fish and eggs, that's all. Fish and eggs.' "

She peered up at Joyce Ellen. Miss Dena was just under five feet tall and she looked like the child of some sea creature. The wrinkles in her dry black skin seemed to be waffled like scales, and the lines around her eyes and ears were deep enough for gill slits. Joyce Ellen remembered how Ma'Emma had withered during the last few months of her illness, her eyes protruding as she'd watched Joyce Ellen with the same exopthalmic stare Miss Dena had. But unlike Ma'Emma, Miss Dena's bug-eyed gaze probed Joyce Ellen for a reaction to whatever babbling her mind made her mouth say.

"Do you know how many eggs it takes to make you sick of them for life?" Miss Dena asked. "I ate eggs for four or five years. Can't stand the sight of them no more, and I won't eat river fish. No telling what's in that river. I wish I could eat cheese. Now the Reverend was a great cheese eater."

She was off again. This time with such a vengeance, she insisted on pulling out an overstuffed volume of pictures that represented the last half of Reverend Motley's adult life. Joyce Ellen sat beside Miss Dena on the itchy horsehair love-seat and in the dusky light of the living room, watched the Motleys grow from a cookie-brown old-style picture taker's daguerrotype of a family of seven, actively a part of the social life of black folks in Pittsburgh's Hill District, to a crisp black-and-white Polaroid of Miss Dena and Leon, stuck at opposite ends of that house on Bryn Mawr Road.

Joyce Ellen fought the impulse to rush through the years past Reverend Motley's many churches, past the family weddings and ceremonies, the deaths of Miss Dena's three children, and onto the subject of brine-soaked fish. Then Miss Dena removed any hope of discovering the nature of that foul-smelling breakfast dish by digging into the cherrywood china cabinet to find "the Reverend's last natural act in this house."

Joyce Ellen had learned never to take Miss Dena literally, but the phrase "last natural act" set her on edge. Her imagination flipped past images that flickered like old reels of movies. Miss Dena poked and lifted various tissue-wrapped objects she'd pulled from the lower reaches of the china cabinet. Joyce Ellen rejected the images she gathered faster than Miss Dena pushed aside those small dusty bundles she'd so carefully saved.

Then she found it. A bulky package wrapped in several layers of wrinkled paper. "Did this myself," Miss Dena told her. "Took most of three weeks. I knew he wasn't coming back, so I kept it. Started this before the funeral. Used three candles before I covered the whole thing, but look at here. . . . You can see his teeth marks clear as day."

Joyce Ellen stared at the wax-coated, charcoal-green lump Miss Dena held out for her inspection. It was pock-marked with little holes like a clump of bituminous coal pulled from one of the old mine shafts in the surrounding Pennsylvania hills. But it had been preserved, waxed over like a piece of wedding cake or a flower from a first date. Three sides were smooth, but one side was bubbly and slightly ridged. That was the side Miss Dena's bony finger jabbed as she explained how the Reverend always placed everything in his mouth just so before taking a careful, definite bite of it.

"I told you how he just loved cheese. Always kept two or three kinds around the house. Liederkranz, cause that old German he used to work for never bought anything else. But the Reverend liked bleu and strong cheddar, so I spect it was just his nature. Those were his favorites alright. Gave this to him myself. Real good cheddar. Last thing he ever ate. Walked out of this house with that piece of cheese still rolling around in his stomach. Walked right into the way of the Lord."

Joyce Ellen felt her mind go numb. "I have to get some air," she said.

And repeated it as she dropped the photo album and ran. Joyce Ellen was out of the kitchen door before Miss Dena could protest, and when she reached the back yard, she heard a roaring whoosh of noise in the workshop. The path to the workshop took only a few seconds.

She stepped through the open door into a room filled with a thick white vapor.

"Hey," Leon shouted, "I knew you'd come to see me." But in her confusion over what Miss Dena had just shown her, Joyce Ellen could not immediately find him.

A pattern of hooks dotted the walls on three sides, and the strips and pieces of metal hanging from those hooks reflected a blue acetylene flame as if hundreds of fireflies were trapped on their irregular surfaces. Leon held the torch toward the wingtip of a sleek, model-sized airplane, his face partially hidden by a set of grey goggles.

"Close the door," he shouted, then steadied himself against the work table.

Joyce Ellen blinked her eyes. For a minute, she thought she was back at the laboratory at the University—the same clean lines, the same methodical placement of oddly shaped tools, graphs tracing systems and diagramming complex patterns that were duplicated and reduced to describe Leon's experiments with the same labyrinthine confusion as any anatomical chart. But this room was alive with smoke and the ominous hiss of Leon's torch. This funnel of a room with its low ceiling was a netherworld, more of an afterlife than even the University lab. This was the area Miss Dena referred to as "a clear waste of my son's pension check."

Then Joyce Ellen remembered that paraffin-covered hunk of cheese. "She killed him," Joyce Ellen muttered to no one in particular.

Leon shut off the torch, lifted his mask and started towards her. The vapors had begun to clear, but as he moved across the room a misty cloud swirled around him. Joyce Ellen lurched and grabbed the end of the table for support.

"Watch it," Leon yelled as she screamed in pain. "That tubing is still hot."

He grabbed her hand and examined the palm. "She killed him," Joyce Ellen repeated as Leon gently kissed the scorched crease in the palm of her hand.

"Who? Killed who?" Leon asked. "Looks like you haven't

burned it much, but that damn tubing stays hot for five minutes sometimes. Especially this end." Then he gestured the length of the room. "It gets cooler by the time it reaches the other side."

Four parallel lines of light grey tubing travelled along one wall, then curved at right angles down the back wall where they ended in a patch of cotton batten plastered against the fiberboard panelling.

"Didn't even get it from ignition to propulsion this time," Leon added.

Joyce Ellen moved back, then stopped when she heard Miss Dena shout her name. Leon reached behind her and closed the door.

"The cheese," Joyce Ellen mumbled. "She showed me the cheese."

Leon went back to the model of the jet plane he'd been repairing. He held it up to the light, shook his head, then placed it in the trapezoidal sling at the end of the metal tubing.

"You know, don't you? You know what she's done."

He dabbed paint on the patched portion of the wing and examined the plane again. "What's there to know?" he asked.

"How can you stay here knowing what she's done?" Joyce Ellen yelled. "The Reverend!"

"Hey, that happened before I was born. Anyway, where am I going to go?"

"Anywhere away from here. From this . . ." Her hand made a sweeping arc, moving from the doorway to the far wall before the gesture ended in the general direction of the house. Leon's eyes followed the path of her gesture.

"Give it up," he smiled. Then he repositioned the plane, wiggling it against the stantions of the sling. "It's just another family story. Most everybody's got at least one family story," he added. He gave her a teasing look, like the ones he used whenever he surprised her with an ice cream bar or a Coke on those nights she studied late.

The heavy fumes in the workshop began to irritate Joyce Ellen's nose, and she moved to the other side of the room. The floor was rough-cut planking which had obviously been repaired and leveled off since the floors in the house, as in the rest of the houses in the District, sloped under the pressure of the hill. Joyce Ellen stared at the wavy, hairlike lines in the floorboards.

"I don't understand you," she muttered.

Leon's "sheeh" was a soft rush of a sound, like air eased out of balloon. "What's to understand?" he snorted. "Remember what you told me about the appendix? You said it was just something tagged on, some part that didn't have any purpose anymore. You said as long as it doesn't hurt, don't sweat it." He grinned. "Some things can't be explained. Right?"

He picked up a bottle of liquid and shook it until a milky substance was diffused through it. "I hope I've got this fuel mixture right this time," he muttered, but when he heard Joyce Ellen groan, he continued. "Hey, look, it happened a long time ago. Nana's ninety-three years old, and she thinks she had something to do with the way the Reverend died. Maybe because they fought all the time, I don't know. What I do know is that they left the house together that night and his body was found in the Ohio River three days later. Whatever she thinks she did won't change that fact one bit. Only the Reverend knows what happened, and he ain't talking." Leon laughed. "Least he wasn't talking when they pulled him out of that river. Found him where the Monongahela meets the Allegheny to form the O-hi-o." Leon laughed again.

"How can you make fun of it?" Joyce Ellen asked. "Even if she didn't kill him, do you think it makes me feel any better to know she must be in agony believing she did? And you just bait her, tease her and pretend it's all a great joke."

"Cops thought it was a joke. Another black man floating in the river . . . HA HA. Why don't you try telling somebody? Place a bet on how many of them will think that old man got wiped out. Don't nobody care about some old black man with a bad heart. Besides, Nana didn't do nothing. It's all in her head, so forget it."

"Get serious," Joyce Ellen snapped. "You can't just toss people away."

"Look who's talking," he said, then imitated her voice. "Leon, I'm too OLD for you, don't you know?"

Joyce Ellen turned away. "That's not it. I just can't see you hiding out here all day. You've got talent but you won't use it. That's sad."

Leon held the plane up to the light. "OK, I'll make you happy. I'll join the Ne-gro Air Force. See this? It's my bird. It can fly right out of this town." He walked over to her. "It can follow you, little bit. Just say the word. I mix the fuel myself. One day . . . VA-ROOM, watch out for my tail fire."

He pointed to the shelf over the window where a squadron of model planes glowed like bright new quarters above the shiny lines of the tubular runway. He had made scale models of wooden bi-planes, miniatures of crop-dusters, thin gliders and fighter planes—one or two of them like the needle-nosed model he now placed in the starting position of the tubing.

"A waste," Joyce Ellen mumbled. She swung around and stud-ied the charts on the wall. After a minute or two, she spotted sev-eral faded newspaper clippings sandwiched between a floorplan for a control tower, endurance charts for metal stress and the diagram of a fuel-injection system.

GANG WAR RESULTS IN DEATH, one headline read. YOUTH LEADER ARRESTED was printed below a picture of Leon, while TRUANT FIREBOMBS SCHOOL was the caption below a face she did not recognize. The same face was captured un-der another headline—YOUTH SHOT DURING PROTEST RALLY.

She looked at Leon. His broad shoulders and the line of his back curved away from the workbench like a question mark. His hands were firm and steady as he measured liquid into a beaker. Joyce El-len saw him as the man he could have been. He wasn't a part of the black family history captured in Miss Dena's picture album, and despite the headlines, he wasn't even a part of the city, a part of the seed pods of tenements that housed so many people in this factory of a town. He was just there.

When she was a little girl in Pleasant Hill, her mother would send her to the orchard to keep her from hearing too many of Ma'Emma's hoodoo stories. After a while, she began to use the or-chard as a way to get away from her mother, and later, a way to es-cape being teased by other children. Out in that orchard, she hadn't minded being black and lonely. But she was no longer a lit-tle girl. Pleasant Hill was a long time ago, even before all those years in Kansas City, and ages before Pittsburgh and Leon. She'd made her choices, and no canopied orchard would protect her from the world. She turned back to the newspaper clippings, but the print was so faded she couldn't read the names.

"Who is this?" she asked.

Leon finished filling the beaker with the cloudy fuel mixture, then looked over his shoulder. "Oh, that's a blood named Thomas Lyons. Thought he could change things. They called him a revolutionary, so he took to the streets. Mostly he didn't like going home." He paused. "Hey, pretty, this bird is ready to fly. Want to help?"

Joyce Ellen shook her head. "No, I'm leaving. I don't want to see your exercise in futility."

"I watch yours," Leon grinned. "Why don't you watch mine?"

Joyce Ellen closed the door firmly behind her. Miss Dena was standing in the kitchen when she reached the house.

"You alright?" she asked. Her eyes bullied Joyce Ellen for an answer and she blocked the path through the kitchen, standing in the little circle of light from the open door like a frog on its private lily pad.

Before Joyce Ellen could find the right words, the workshop erupted. It was not the usual explosion, and they both knew it. Joyce Ellen turned on her heel and saw smoke curling out of a hole in the back wall of the workshop.

"Stay there!" she yelled at Miss Dena, then tore across the path.

At first, the door would not budge, but when she finally got it to move, it swung free so quickly, she almost fell. She could hear Miss Dena following her, and she yelled once more, "Stay there!"

The room seemed to be alive with colors. Grey, blue and white smoke billowed like clouds in a storm. A thin stream of black fumes hung over the workbench. It took her only a few seconds to find Leon.

First his moans, then his hands glued to his face. She pried them away. His features were indistinct, and for a moment she thought one side of his face had exploded with the rest of the workshop. But she got him to his feet, past Miss Dena and into the kitchen where she lowered him to the floor. Behind her, the workshop rumbled with small new explosions.

"Call the hospital," she shouted. Miss Dena brushed past her and headed for the hallway telephone.

Leon was trying to sit up. "Be still," she said. "We've called the ambulance."

"It just took off," he muttered. "All by itself. Just took off. The wing came off. I bent over and it came off . . ." He propped himself up against the refrigerator. "Oh shit! My nose! Is it there?"

Joyce Ellen dropped to her knees and took his hands away from his face. After a second or two, she could see the jagged hole where the wingtip of the plane had ripped into the left nostril.

"It's there," she told him. "A little messy, but it's there. Can you see?"

"Hey, pretty, I can see you," he whispered. "You gonna take care of me, doctor?" He tried to smile, then groaned as she covered his wound with a dishtowel she'd pulled from the cabinet. "Don't let Nana see me," he pleaded. "Don't let her see me. What am I going to do? God . . . God . . ." The towel was red with fresh blood.

"Hush, hush," Joyce Ellen said. "I'll take care of Miss Dena. I'll be here. I'll take care of it."

She rocked him and crooned, holding him close. Then she kissed him gently, not caring that the blood was smeared on her face, not caring that he was nineteen and the world had already shoved him into a corner.

Leon pulled her closer to him.

His arms were a canopy and Joyce Ellen nestled there. Miss Dena watched them from the doorway.

A House Full of Maude

I

WHAT TO REMEMBER ABOUT THE HOUSE ON Ashland and Taylor? Maude's house with its darkness, the wet brown bricks that seemed to shimmer, to suck in light so that the house was more of a gape at the end of the block than a building. The ever present wetness—winter and summer—a mossy velvet covering that seemed to grow, to move in an effort to absorb every inch of brick. And the bricks themselves, shiny with the stuff—a residue that permeated everything, ate its way through the outer surface and into the mortar, the plaster, the wallboards of the house. The yard carried the smell of mold. Moisture seemed to muffle sounds coming from the house or off the street, and Maude's brand new DeSoto, as round and black as Maude herself, clotted one end of the driveway.

The house couldn't be seen from the south end of Taylor. That end was divided into exacting little post-war plots of bungalows and cottages. And every one of them held a woman who was determined to put her stamp on the property. Upright solid black women like my mama, who would have you believe dirt was a personal enemy and so, the house was a major threat. Their yards held back the power of the house. Each one displaying some peculiar array of potted plants, or cheap weather vanes and brassy street numbers. Each yard with its own degree of tastelessness, the next more awful than the one before until by the time you reached the house, those overly decorated cottages blurred into one gaudy string of cheap baubles. Each one a little bit of country and a little bit of what the women saw on the Ozzie and Harriet show they watched every evening on their postage-stamp television sets when they weren't watching Ed Sullivan, or listening to the gospel sounds of

Rev. Staples and dreaming of pulling that old man out of Memphis and into their parlors. The house intruded its dark presence onto the end of this flashy line-up of neighbors. The house was somber, secretive and so much bigger than anything else on the street, it blunted Taylor Avenue into a cul-de-sac passageway someone had named Ashland Place but was, in actuality, an alleyway, a shaft of paved road rammed between the house and the patch of city park that completed the north end of the block. And the house, nested in a semi-circle of cottonwood and willow trees, pushed forward by a jumble of narrow rooms and add-on storage porches, seemed to be straining to reach the street. Leaning forward as if to step past the thatch of trees and into the sunlight where it would fling open its windows and all its raunchy secrets would swirl down the street and scare the hell out of its churchified neighbors.

The first time I passed the house, it sent a trail of Maude's laughter through a window, and the sound wound itself around me and held me rooted to the spot. I was wearing a despicable little seersucker dress, all fuzzy dots and pastels, and the laughter tugged at the material, seeping under the sleeves until my armpits were wet, then flicked the hem so that the warm summer air billowed under my skirt and embraced my legs. The laughter buzzed in my ears, its sound so clear it seemed to hold words I could almost understand. Laughter that made me step back, then laugh a little myself. A woman's laughter. Laughter that owned the world. Laughter that knew something I wanted to know.

II

Violet Nashberry was fourteen years old—technically. At least Violet had been alive a mere fourteen years, but Violet had lived more than her years and looked it. She believed in living. A month in one week, three weeks in one night. Whatever she needed, she took without question. The house accepted her, drew her past its inner ring as if she'd always been there. When she settled into the left wing of the house, when her mother had finally stopped leaping out of the shadows of the trees and snatching the poor girl into the street in an attempt to drag her home, the house had settled in, night cries of its creaking floorboards smoothed into low moans. Violet took the first corner room on the Ashland Place side of the house. It jutted away from the main structure, rounded in the arc of its former sun-porch shape. That suited her fancy, gave her a sense of not really being there. Bay windows tempted her to escape and enter without using the front door. But the house welcomed her fugitive habits. When she entered from the street, she turned into the center path between the trees, and always stopped for one last look at the rest of the street and its uniform bric-a-brac. Whether she could see them or not, a few hand-laced curtains fluttered as God-fearing eyes marked her passage, and church folks chalked up another sin against Maude's house. Violet's bare brown legs, the light glinting off large hoop earrings, her head shaved past a boyish cut so that her short kinky hair covered the roundness of her scalp like velvet and invited a hand to stroke its downy curve. Her already full figure pushed against whatever cheap blouse and skirt she'd hastily thrown on, the closure of her blouse more than likely pinned where she'd popped a button or snapped a stitch. And more than one teeth-sucking *uh-uh-uh* passed judgment on her slovenly ways. At that point, Violet looked tired and fed up with the world. Then she'd lunge toward the house and as the tree-lined shadows dappled her back with speckles of light that danced like butterflies or silvery fish, she seemed to toss the world's damnation into the debris gathered with the leaves at the base of the trees. I always felt torn between commenting on Violet's daily stand against her neighbors' gossip and the mingled smell of dime-cheap toilet water and mold that swept through the door with us. For it was Violet who offered me entrance to Maude's house.

I was eighteen looking twelve, the age I'd been when the house had first reached for me. In part or entirety, the house had begun to dominate my life. I knew what I feared and wanted most rested in that house, seeped into my dreams until I wasn't sure what I had imagined and what I had actually seen—a high ceiling room, an arched threshold, gargoyle downspouts, a yard path slit between overhanging trees, windows slick with moisture and winking in the dim light. At twelve, I had inspected those windows from the safe distance of the playground in the adjacent park, swinging so high, I easily cleared the wall and placed myself in direct view of the upstairs hallway. Sometimes, with luck, I caught a glimpse of Maude's naked back entering the bathroom, or a hand caressing her bare shoulder. My dreams filled in the rest. Those fleeting images kept me pumping that swing to dangerous heights, knees bent until I flew to the very edge of the trees and then pushed down, blood rushing to my head, grunting until my weight forced the swing back instead of flipping me over the rail. At eighteen and out of the playground stage, I grew bolder. I discovered a wrought iron bench half-buried in the sod beneath one of the willow trees where, if I sat very still while the willow branches brushed my face like fingers or the hair of some lover, I could watch Maude's kitchen at the far side of the house. Everyone eventually gathered in the kitchen and for most of the years of my watching, three brothers dominated the house until one by one they left—the younger first, then the others in reverse order until the oldest was gone. Violet lived in the room the oldest had occupied. I dreamed her in his bed, her figure filling the mirror he'd spent so much time staring into.

And it was Violet who caught me staring at her one afternoon as she leaned from the bay window, teasing the liquor store delivery boy, my next door neighbor's cousin who had spent his first summer after high school running his hands up the dress of any girl careless enough to get close to him. My mama said Peck's head was big because he was the first boy on the block to graduate from the desegregated high school, but Peck had always been a nuisance. At school, he'd had as much trouble fitting in as I'd had, law or no law. But on the block, he didn't have to worry about white folks and teachers. He pestered everybody. I watched Violet giggle and lean farther over the window sill. Peck's eyes followed the swell of her breasts inside her half-closed robe. A movement startled me. The willow trees bending, swirling near the edge of the sidewalk. A bird or a squirrel scratching a tree trunk or someone tossing water from one of the back windows. I moved. Violet turned, laughed and called to me in a voice that said she'd known I'd been there all along. "Hey girl."

III

The downstairs hallway was a singular path. Curved inward from both ends of the house, it converged on a stairwell, a shaft that plunged light into the entryway like a commanding finger. From this central shaft, the hallway spread toward both ends of the house like two arms, or if you looked down, two legs straddling the center entryway and softened by oak panelling buffed smooth as skin. At the top of the stairs and on either side of the entryway, the light, dimmed by turn-of-the-century glass, grew dull and furry, but the steps led to one great window—a mosaic of bevelled glass changing light into a carnival of shapes. And the corridor itself was wide enough for ball gowns to pass and only brush each other in the journey. On one side of the hallway there were windows and green shadows whispering against the panes. On the other side, voices were audible behind heavy doors to rooms that faced the back of the house. But neither the doors nor the oblique path of the hall kept out the smells. Thin sad smells and smells that knifed the air. Smells that clashed with those tight family smells I'd brought from my mother's house. The odors in Maude's house left me open to scenes I could barely imagine. The house was ripe with its age. Every corner invaded by one or another of its tenants, and its own decay. It seemed to try on and discard smells as easily as a woman passing rows of perfume bottles on a department store counter. The faint smell of plaster drifted from rips in the wallpaper, one layer stripped to expose another which, in turn, had cracked and peeled to the next layer and below that, still another. The jimson smell of old rugs and overstuffed furniture floated at floor level but remained undisturbed unless someone scraped a chair across the carpet or decided to clean a room. Each room had its own smell. Bedroom smells that, at home, were covered by my pious mother with cologne and ammonia. In the house, I found bathrooms of dusting powder, douche and vinegar, their sources under the sink, hidden by curtains covering the shelves. A kitchen where bacon was fried, even at night, its smokehouse odors barely masking cigarettes and whiskey, chitterlings and jars of pickling. And none of it as pungent as the pomade on the back burner where Maude hot-cooked her hair before choir practice. The flickering light, the smells and noises. The house moving on its foundation, groaning with the life that passed beneath its roof. Wet branches skittering across window glass. Doors that no longer hung level on their frames. The sound of someone coughing or cursing over a game of cards, a moan that could have been male or female, a recording of gospel music—the record stuck in one groove. And no one to tell me I couldn't or I shouldn't.

IV

Every Wednesday and Sunday night, Maude left the house. On those nights, the Temple Tabernacle God in Christ Church rocked. Maude Morgan led the choir. Everyone sang exactly the way Sister Morgan told them to sing. She bullied them with her hands, bruised them with her voice, drove them from one chorus to another with fierce looks that offered them no salvation until Sister Morgan wore herself out on repetitions of a song. Sister Morgan loved her songs. She believed every song held endless rounds of a soul stomping chorus and wasn't about to fall quiet until she sang every one of them. She was as faithful to the choir as she was to food. When she really had them pitched to her frenzy, when everyone clapped and popped their fingers, shouting, "Yes Jesus. Amen," Sister Morgan would gather her two hundred-fifty pounds and jump straight up and down like a Zulu during fertility rites. The heft of her weight added timbre to the congregation's joy as she thumped them from one "Amen" to the next. Folks on the street feared the whole storefront would collapse when Maude Morgan started prancing. The rather straight-laced Methodists shook their heads at her jungle antics, and the organized Baptists prayed to Jesus to guide her to a quieter worship. After all, the ghosts of those images lived in their houses and they worked hard to put those ghosts to rest. But just as they mistook her weight for a deterrent to the physical joys of life, they mistook her enthusiasm for singing as pure faith in the ways of religion. "Don't matter what words you say long as you give your spirit to the music," Maude would tell anyone who warned her about over-exertion. And she never wiped the sweat from her face. And she never cared whether her hair went bad at the nape of her neck. "That's where it ought to look rough. That's the kitchen and the kitchen is where I do my business," she'd say. And I surely didn't need to find the oldest of those three brothers to help me testify to that.

V

Maude Morgan was the kind of woman who could be nosey without ever paying attention to what was going on. She always seemed to know what everyone was doing without really being there. A plum-colored woman smelling of spice and talc that seemed to cling to the folds of her dress, the back of her neck and elbows. Her skin was burnished to a high gloss as if someone had worked down the sides and hollows of her flesh in long strokes, ending each stroke in tight circles to add a sheen to her already smooth skin. And Maude loved to touch and be touched, so it was easy to notice when she wasn't around. Before Maude entered, any room seemed like a space just inviting to be filled. "Com'on in," she'd say once she arrived. "Com'on in over here and give me some of your time," she'd laugh, as if you had just been waiting in that lonely room for Maude Morgan to open her arms to your company. Some folks, especially some of the hinkty, upright church women, resented the way Maude could make a stranger snuggle up to her and feel at home, but other folks felt the Lord had blessed them by putting such a loving woman on earth to give them comfort. True enough, it was puzzling to see Maude make a young man turn away from some young woman with aching eyes just because Maude had brushed up against him, but Maude soon sent him back to the source of his admiration. "Some folks can't tell the difference between needing and having," Maude would laugh. "Ain't no reason to be the same fool in 1954 that I been in 1953. Too much in this world for me to be wanting what I need." Then she'd smooth her dress over her hips, wiping the wrinkles out of the material until you could see the flesh push against her hands. And the palms of her hands, plump and pungent, leaving a dewy streak that, invariably, shimmered just enough to force your eyes to follow its trail along her thighs. That movement always made you aware, once again, of Maude's girth, and how much of her was encased in dress, petticoat and underpants. For no matter how raucous her laughter became, or how many "sweet-loving men folks" she boasted about knowing, Sister Morgan seemed to be full of prissy secrets. She thrived on secrets. When the choir began its chorus of "My Soul is a Witness for My Lord," or "Didn't My Lord Tell Daniel," her breasts quivered with the excitement of what was not said, what was kept unconfessed, hidden, and in the dark. And when Violet and I sat around the kitchen watching her add a little bite of pepper to a pot of stew, or a little sugar to a deep-dish pie, she'd let us in on a bevy of secrets. "Men is funny," she'd say. "nothing makes them come to you quicker than to think you're

happy. Then they get all into your business trying to find out just
what makes you so happy. And you just remember, you don't have
to tell them nothing." Then she'd give us a pinch of something to
lip-test and Violet would nod her head just like she understood everything Maude had said. Whenever she told us a story about a
bad time she'd had with a man, she'd stop cooking. She never
turned the story around to make the man seem worse—not the way
my mother and her friends did—she told it straight, her voice low
and the words humming in her throat like a gospel. And while she
was telling, she'd massage Violet's head, slow and careful, until
Violet looked like she was asleep. The first time she rubbed my
head that way, it felt so good, I almost cried, but I just closed my
eyes and let Maude's fingers pull me against the rise of her belly.

VI

Violet said, "Girl, this job is driving me crazy." The iron sizzled
against the apron of her uniform.

"You only been working there three weeks, I told her."

She burned a brown smear across the waistband. "Don't matter.
Them folks is crazy. Wanting me to work in some greasy spoon for
nickels and dimes."

"Better than what I got." I said.

"Who you?" Violet asked.

I watched her burn the cap. "Maybe you ought to go back to
school."

"I don't need no school for what I do," she laughed.

"You got to be eighteen, Vi. How you gonna strip tease and you
can't even get a drink in a bar?"

"Peck says I look . . ."

"Peck!"

"Yeah. Peck." The iron slammed against the Shepherd's Burger
emblem. "And Peck ain't the only one."

"If your mama finds out, she's gonna be on you like white on rice."

"Damn her!" Violet shouted, then threw the uniform on the bed
and yanked the ironing cord out of the socket. I mouthed a Dance
Fever tune playing on the radio. Violet and I were heads and tails
of a coin. I was an only child and she the middle one in a nest of
brothers and sisters. I spent too much time hiding behind my

glasses and Violet cared less about who saw her do what. But we both agreed on the aggravation of mothers. "Let me show you what I did last night," Vi said. "Bought me some green feathers yesterday, and girl. . . . I'm gonna be the best thing this town has ever seen." She began to undress.

I tried not to watch her—not that it made any difference. Everyone else in the neighborhood could see her through the open windows. Besides, this wasn't the first time I'd seen her undress. Our summer work schedule made it easy for me to visit Violet. My job with the Recreation Department ended at noon. I came directly to the house after I left the park. Vi's job at Shepherd's didn't begin until six, so I had plenty of time to visit before dinner. She was always asleep when I arrived and sometime during my visit, she'd get ready for work, never bothering to turn her back or dress in the bathroom. When she practiced stripping, she took her time, almost unconsciously falling into her routine. "Come on, Thin. Give me some rhythm," she said. As if on cue, the radio switched to a Little Richard heavy-on-the-drums cut. "And now, Miss Vi Berry," she announced as I turned up the radio and began clapping. She pulled her wig off the lamp shade and plunked it on her head. She'd bought it with her first paycheck. A gross brown thing full of oily curls that almost matched the beige tones of her skin. The hair transformed her, hardened her features, made her body seem more suited to the squinty-eyed look she affected. Even the room was right for what she did. The half oval of bay windows a common stage—window panes of old glass, drawn to an uneven thickness, made light turn syrupy and cast rainbows on her skin. Willow limbs cut the light like beacons while Violet's hand snaked out, dropping a garment here, caressing skin there. A caramel doll. A painted trick of eye and imagination. A dream of what I thought I could never become. Even with practice and without the hard thin warnings of my mother echoing in my ears. What kind of a world could grant misery to an eighteen-year-old when it had allowed so many gifts to Violet at fourteen?

VII

Violet and Maude spent far too much time together. I was the outsider. I was in the house but not of the house. Maude spoke in riddles and Violet answered. My tongue was stuck in my mouth. Roles were reversed. I was the one who should know more, who should have the right answers. But there we were—a girl who wanted to be a woman and an almost woman who had never been a girl. Each day I felt more incomplete. At six o'clock, I entered my mother's house and turned to stone. She wanted to know if I would ever speak again. I waited for morning, for the dreariness of entertaining irresponsible children. They played the same games I'd played—Blind Man's Bluff, Little Sally Walker, 24 Robbers. What would it teach them? What had it taught me? I began to live once I entered the house. No matter that the air was stale, or that I would be trapped for twenty minutes by Mrs. Cole, caught as I walked through the door and made to lead her down the stairs and to the kitchen, one arthritic step at a time. If I was lucky, Violet would be awake when I reached her room. If I was lucky I would help with her bath, pour in generous amounts of Maude's bath salts and fill the tub with sudsy water. If I was lucky, she wouldn't mind me sitting beside her, waiting to wash her back. If I was lucky. Or I'd run into Beulah who had a room near the kitchen and belonged to the Ladies Auxiliary. She knew my mother but didn't like her, so she sent me to the store and gave me beer for running her errands. Her husband pinched my arms whenever she wasn't looking. If I couldn't shake Violet awake, I'd drop in on Maude who was always in the kitchen fixing her next meal while she finished her last one.

One day, mid-summer, I opened the door and found the oldest brother sitting at a table. A face from a distance suddenly close up. I felt chilled as if a breeze had blown through the kitchen, but the air was swamped in smoke and heat. He'd taken off his shirt and Maude caressed his shoulders. "Ain't the size of the ship that makes the sailor seasick," Maude said. "It's the motion of the ocean." Then she saw me standing in the doorway. "Come in," she beckoned. "Look who's back." "Back in the women's quarters. Ain't nothing like it," he laughed and pressed his head against the soft mound of her belly, his voice so deep his words seemed to rumble into the roar of water Maude had going full blast in the sink. Maude called him Bud and while she told me where he had been and why he'd come back, he stared at me. Brown eyes ringed in black. A long, square-cut face with a strong jawline and even white teeth. His hair was cut short, almost as short as Violet's, but shaped so it accentuated his strength and neither invited nor discouraged a desire to touch him.

VIII

"I told your mama. I say, Dorothy Nashberry, you had far too many babies to act the way you do about Violet. By the time I was Violet's age, I'd run off from my first husband. Plenty of girls prettier than me still at home working on pin money for the movies. And look at me now, I say. Got me a big house, plenty of friends . . . Ain't that right, Bud? Yeah, and the Lord's good music. But you still worrying about Vi, I told her . . . Now, ya'll wake up. Dealer's choice." We played cards once or twice a week. Bid whist and Violet always bidding as if she could handpick her cards on every deal. Bud watched every move I made, turning now and again to smile at Vi or rub Maude's arm. Violet made far too many mistakes. She barely looked at her cards and each time she needed to make a bid or play a card, she prolonged the game: calling attention to herself, smoking, laughing, brushing her hands across her wig—which she insisted on wearing all the time these days. "Don't you have to get ready for work?" I'd ask. She'd glare at me and ask Bud another question, acting like I hadn't said a word. And Bud would tell us what destroyer he'd been stationed on, about Florida and Mediterranean ports, and how many young sailors would love to be in the room with him playing cards with such lovely ladies, as he called us. "How about some sailors, Thin?" Violet would ask, but when I wouldn't answer, she'd grunt and turn back to Bud. He'd have just enough time to change his expression before she saw him. But Maude would roar, a deep-throated laugh that threatened the already cracked chandelier. "Bud, you ain't changed a bit," she'd say and pour some more sweet wine into the water glasses at our elbows. Bud would say, "Yeah," in a detached way and wink. I'd manage to blurt out my bid without looking directly at him. I'd already memorized his smile, the curve of his neck, the toast brown color of his skin. Most of the time, I knew what he would say and how he would say it, but that didn't seem to matter so much as hearing him speak the words. On other afternoons, we danced. Violet, as usual, starting us with her stripper fantasy and how she'd make everyone remember her when she was a big star. Then Bud would urge me and Maude to get up. Comic relief, I called it. Maude's bulk shifting like oil and water, like a hippo rising from a bath, while I worked to keep my elbows tucked in and my legs from goose-stepping. But Bud always singled me out, always gathered me into his arms. "Just a handful," he'd whisper as he led me through an achingly slow dance. Violet would look sullen, but Maude would laugh and laugh and tell Bud what a stud he was.

Violet missed work more often than not, but one day after I'd persuaded her that she had to go, we tripped down the hall toward her room, both of us more than a little loaded on sweet wine and less than ready for the rest of the bottle Violet had with her. She'd begun to let her hair grow, so after I finally managed to get her wig off, I brushed the soft mass of curls, chiding her about being late for work while I concentrated on aiming the brush for her hair, and not her neck or forehead. We both took swigs from the bottle. She told me Maude wouldn't give Bud a moment of peace. I said yes, and that I'd seen her groping him whenever she had the chance. She told me Bud only stayed because Maude gave him free room and board, and Maude only kept him because it made the other women jealous. I told her she'd better not let Maude catch her leaving Bud's room the way I had the day before.

"Who you telling?" she asked.

"Nobody."

"SO?"

"Nothing."

"You just remember who you came here to see," she said. I was silent. "Hey girl," she said. "That's where it's at, don't you know?" And we rolled on the bed, laughing and drinking wine as if we'd talked about jobs or Peck or Maude's church friends or how many empty rooms there were in the house.

IX

I couldn't go home smelling of wine and Violet was in no shape to dress herself. We didn't just give in—we really did try standing up straight, but no amount of effort could keep our knees from buckling. We thought the August heat had made us silly. Lord knows, we'd been sipping Maude's sweet wine all summer without letting it slow us any. Violet tugged at the window, and with my help, managed to open it a crack. The air was sticky warm, worse than the room had been without it, but we didn't have the energy to shove the window down. Finally, we let the wine take us. As I fell into a soggy dream, one arm flung across Vi who was already asleep, the voices of children drifted from the playground on the other side of Ashland Place. I slept, thinking I was gathering my snaggle-toothed third graders into their favorite ring game, knowing they would collapse in the end, exhausted little rag dolls.

Little Sally Walker, sitting in a saucer.
Rise Sally Rise. Wipe your weeping eyes.
Put your hands on your hips and let your backbone slip—
Oh shake it to the East. Oh shake it to the West.
Oh shake it to the one you love the best.

X

Violet answered the door. She didn't bother to put on a robe and Bud took no surprise in seeing her nakedness. "Maude's gone to choir practice," he said.

"Tell ME," Violet laughed. She watched his hand touch her shoulder, then slide to the curve of her waist.

"Yeah," he said.

I only had managed to open one eye, but I grabbed Violet's robe and sat up. "Vi!" I shouted, or tried to shout. What came out sounded like the moan of a dying frog.

Bud placed his palm against the door as if he expected Violet to close it. "Well, look at this."

"Ain't she cute?"

I was all bones. Knees and elbows. Arms that seemed to extend the length of the bed. I had thrown Violet her robe but left my own body uncovered. Bud smiled. A mister-cool-breeze smile. A piano-player-in-a-blues-club smile. A now-I-see-what-I-want smile. I gulped air. "Oh Jesus," Violet yelled. "She's gonna be sick." I felt her push my head forward. "Com'on, Thin," she said as she rubbed my back. "Don't get sick on me, girl." Bud had conjured up a wet cloth and a waste can at the same time. They sat me on the side of the bed, Violet holding me and Bud wiping my forehead and neck with the cloth. "It's all right," he whispered. "Don't worry." This is jive, I thought. This is not real. I wondered if I should be sick, then let myself go limp as they cooed and cuddled me. Violet let Bud hold me while she lit a cigarette. After a few puffs, she passed the cigarette to him and he passed it to me. Violet held my hand. Without meaning to, I felt the need to cry. We were shipwrecked. We were lost in a haunted house with no way out. A dog barked outside the window, and two kids yelled at it. A woman's voice, shrill, called someone home. Who could know where we were? The house held us inside its circle. Afternoon breezes skirted evening.

XI

Bud leaned forward and kissed Violet. "You ain't right," she told him. Her hand gripped mine tighter, and the world rushed past me all at once. "I have to go," I said and tried pushing my way through the tangle of their arms. Bud pressed his hand against the small of my back and pulled me toward him. Violet giggled and I shut away my mama's face. I could hear Bud talking, murmuring the way he had when we'd danced. I felt the length of his body, muscles too close to the surface and unwilling to fit my palms the way my own body slipped so easily against my hands. I leaned against him and willed myself to fit the curve of his neck, the width of his shoulder. Inhaled the surly sweetness of his skin. The smell of skin in summer has the same tangy odor of warm, yeasty bread, or the smell of a pillow pulling you awake from a dream. Skin can invite you to touch it, dare you. It can pull you in until the only way to stop yourself from aching is to let it take you. Bud's skin was new leather, the way a fine pair of woman's gloves feel when you take them from their tissue wrapping. So sweet and brand new, you almost don't want to wear them. And Violet, Violet was the present I'd been good for all my life, the package wrapped in secret and hidden somewhere in the house. What I'd get on my birthday or some special day when all my chores were finished and I'd said "yes ma'am" in just the right voice. We helped Bud undress, touching each other for every movement he made. And Bud whispered to us both as we slid over and under him. My hand, clutched in Violet's, was a smudge of ink, a tell-tale shape that could have been an elephant holding an umbrella or cannibals over a stew pot. She led my hand across Bud's chest, his waist and below, and she laughed when I wanted to draw back, to curl my fingers into a fist. When I touched Violet and trembled, Bud helped me, and when I turned away, Violet was always there. The three of us knelt together, our bodies like trees twisting toward the sky in a tangle of limbs. One tree splitting into parts or three feeding off each other. The three of us, somehow, balanced on Violet's rickety bed, Bud's clothes falling away like leaves until, in one motion, we began to fall. One body floating against another like clothes falling in a woman's closet. And then, elbows and knees like weapons. Violet yelled, "SHIT!" Blood on her lower lip and my eye already swelling. At first, only the taste of salt—my own tears. Then Bud kissing me and Violet. Then Violet. My hand moving between Violet's legs. I thought of all the words: muff, poodle, beaver. All too ugly to fit the softness I felt. Our mouths turned to sugar. Bud's hand against the cup of my thighs. Violet's nails stroking his back. My tongue tracing the rise of Violet's breast. The sound of the willow tree rustling like silk, leaves swaying like the rocking motion of Bud's embrace. Wherever we were, no one could find us. No children's games, no gossip of movie stars and magazines. Not the watchful eye of fathers watering lawns in the light of the afternoon sun, or mothers preaching about the worst that could happen to us, arguing about whether our retribution would come because of me and Violet or because of the two of us with Bud. No one to find us. Violet whispered, "Hey girl," and Bud laughed his answer. I filled myself with their scents, and laughed at us all while I told myself I wasn't really dreaming. This was really happening. I really could see bright shadows lining the walls, and trees turned rosy, their leaves fuzzy splotches of darkness against the wallpaper's own pattern of fake trees. The house welcomed evening, its timbers popping as it settled in. The smell of murky dampness mingled with body musk, with the jasmine of bath salts and aftershave. The pressure of bodies drew me into muscles that pounded, I thought, mimicking true confession magazines, too much like a heartbeat. "Girl, this is stupid," I said to myself. Then I took a deep breath.

XII

The harsh overhead light sliced shadows without redemption. Maude blustered her way around the kitchen—seasoning a pot of beans, dicing onions, drinking wine. "Lord, it's hotter today than it was yesterday, don't you think?" I agreed, although she didn't wait for my comment. "Isn't Vi going to work today? If she don't, she'll lose that job for certain. I was telling Miz Evans . . . I say, Beulah, young folks don't know what it is to NOT have a job. That's what's wrong with Violet. She ought to learn from you, chile. You keep your head about you, you do." I grunted again and flushed out my solitaire spread by pulling a queen I'd overlooked from the discard pile. "Ain't everything in this world having a good time," Maude continued. "Got to work and got to play." She stopped for a moment to taste the beans, her face, under the cloud of steam from the pot, as dark as the varnished wood in the hall-way. "Precious Lord, take my hand . . ." she half-sang and half-hummed. I reshuffled the cards for another try at solitaire. "You don't seem to be doing so well with them cards today," Maude said. I shook my head. "Mighty quiet too," she added, and peered at me real close. I smiled. She began stripping slices of bacon into a hot skillet. I laid out the cards and wondered vaguely if my mother had started supper. Both Maude and I looked up sharply as three heavy thumps echoed in the hall. "I guess Miz Queen Bee's calling you," Maude laughed. I pushed my chair away from the table. "Spect you be staying for supper too, huh?" I shrugged and gave Maude a kiss on the cheek before I left the room. She was already singing when I reached the door, and into a third chorus of "I Ain't Gonna Study War No More," by the time I reached the end of the hall. Bud was waiting in front of the open bathroom door. "Mercy," he said, as if someone would have mercy on me. As I opened the door, he said, "My love's coming down." Violet threw a clump of bath foam toward us, its bubbles bursting in the steamy hot air almost before they left her hand. "Don't let it get to you," she told him. Then she looked at me and we both laughed. When I closed the door, it thumped along its hinges, sticking for a moment, then slid-ing shut. I sat on the edge of the tub and began to sponge Violet's back. We could hear Maude calling Bud, but no one answered her. Bud leaned against the wall, cleaning his nails, the sound of his nail clippers clicking like a telegraph key. Violet leaned away from me, blowing foam in little puffs of air and cooing in time with the pigeons who pranced in the rain gutters outside the bathroom window. I looked up just as one hopped onto the eave by the window pane. His fat black body almost filled one leaded glass square, and his head was cocked so that one red eye stared into the hot house steam of the bathroom. I cocked my head at the same angle and stared back at that stupid, unblinking eye. After a while, we heard Maude singing again.

Take Mama's Picture out of the Light

THE DEEP CREASES IN THE ROSE PETAL PATTERN of the easy chair seemed to be repeated in the wrinkles of her face. She sat, half slumped in the recesses of the chair, the paper inches from her nose, her glasses dangling on a chain of small brass beads around her neck. The chain itself was almost hidden in the blue-grey shadows of her dark blouse. She tilted her head, squinting words into focus, but no amount of awkwardness and blurred vision ever caused her to push her glasses up so she could see the paper more clearly. Her squinting was almost as automatic and unproductive as the dialogue in the television program droning on the screen in front of her. Occasionally, she lowered the paper and peered at the set, but for the most part, she ignored it.

She had been a fine looking woman once, the perfect image of the sultry female, like those pictures of Billy Holiday and Sarah Vaughan on record jackets in the '50s. And there was that photo of her, taken some twenty years ago and now resting in one of the hidden corners of the house: Rebecca sitting next to a walnut phonograph cabinet, champagne glasses and cigarettes on the table beside her. Rebecca lounging on a plush settee, her black skin softly accented by a white throw covering the chair. Rebecca smiling from the center of a gold-framed photo, her full lips slick with the latest shade of lip rouge, and her hair forced into a crown of croquignole curls that were still shiny with pressing oil. In that picture, her legs were crossed and below the hem of a strapless, chiffon dress, thin dancing slippers seemed to rest casually on her feet. The picture was so perfect, the moan of a jazz trombone could almost be heard above the crooning of the record that rested under the needle of the phonograph: Nellie Lutcher singing "Fine Brown Frame," or Billie Holiday's "Ain't Nobody's Business."

Now it was difficult to imagine how the thin black woman sitting in the dim light of the living room could ever have been that young girl. Now, all anyone could see was the tiredness that showed in her face as she scowled at the blurred newsprint. Her face, when it wasn't pulled into frowns, was still as smooth-skinned as it had been in that old photo, despite the way her mouth turned down at the corners, and the oily curls crowning her head, flat and too hastily combed. Her arms were extended stiffly in front of her, and when she shook her head over the dismal picture the news presented, the fluorescent blue lights of the television bounced against the oily sheen of her hair.

As soon as she finished a news item, Rebecca quickly turned the pages of the paper. For a moment, she glanced at the tv screen. A strident announcer barked out the opening lines for a commercial. She dropped the paper to watch. A plastic dummy exploded onto the screen as the announcer proclaimed the anguish of life filled with pounding headaches. When he'd finished his pitch, Rebecca turned her attention back to the paper, then suddenly raised her head again when she heard a faint creaking sound.

"Who's there?" she called.

No one answered. She removed the glasses from the tip of her nose where they'd gradually settled. Leaves beat the porch window in back of the house, and somewhere a dog, lonely, barked at nothing. The sound was rhythmical and unbroken for three seconds or so, then silence followed by more barking. Rebecca could not determine which neighbor's backyard held the dog. On both sides of the alley, yards blended into each other in one continuous string of debris and broken fences, clapboard back porches and sunrooms that looked so much alike, a wanderer would have trouble finding a specific house. The clock ticked out of synch with the dog's barks. Rebecca could barely see the numbers without her glasses.

"They should have been home," she muttered.

She frowned again, the lines cutting the space between her eyebrows into furrowed rows of black skin. Then she smoothed her hair from her forehead, and immediately had to wipe the oil from her palm.

"Man keeps me up all night," she whispered.

She took off her glasses, lifted the chain over her head and wiped them on her dress. The movement left a smear of oil across one lens and it took on a waxy glow. Rebecca shook her head and replaced the glasses around her neck. Then she stood up and walked into the kitchen.

"Ain't nothing keep a man out this late," she muttered. "Both of them out there. Ain't nothing I'd even pay to see this time of night."

Many people had paid to see Ernestine Cross. She was billed as the "Ebony Queen," and the name fit. She was ebony and the manager of the Club thought "queen" gave him a selling edge— something for the folks to think about while they sipped their watered drinks. Ernestine had just finished a set, her third and final one for the night. She left the stage, her skin flashing oily in the purple light as she entered a small room in back of the bar area.

She was in her late twenties, and although she was hefty in places, her body had that slow cushy sexuality that men liked to imagine themselves sinking into. She was bosomy, with full hips and fleshy thighs that could allow her customers, those who were hung-up on motherhood, to think of her as ripe to have a baby or ready to nurse one. But she was as slick and limber as a snake, too. So the rowdy ones, the men with tattoos and knife scars—or the ones who imagined themselves as tough—dreamed of her introducing them to their fantasies. Ernestine had no intentions of satisfying either of those groups.

In her head, she was as diaphanous as silk, a real performer, and her dancing was just stage work. The costume she'd designed could have put her in an exotic dance revue. It was made out of sleek, wet-looking material that came to life and form once she pulled it on. In her head, Ernestine was an expensive package, ready for Paris, ready for something besides a highway bar. She looked into the cracked dressing room mirror and stuck out her tongue. The chains at her midriff were tangled, but she finally straightened them and shrugged into the cotton stretch tee shirt and jeans she'd worn to the club earlier that evening.

The jeans looked tight, but for Ernestine, they were comfortable, an outfit that allowed her to blend into the crowd, especially when she was entering the club. At that time of afternoon, the Club couldn't hold the roadhouse facade that allowed customers to toss off the knowledge of how little security their flimsy paychecks offered. In broad daylight, it looked as cheap as it was, the outside painted over many times, the last few coats peeking through to the final dingy layer covering siding, boarded-up windows and double-thick doors. Pieces of old posters billing other singers and dancers still clung to rusted nails. But the Club fit the rest of the highway strip: the used car lots, gun and tack shops, massage parlors, hardware stores, liquor stores—the usual fringe trade of any city. Ernestine had worked in at least nine bars like the Club.

She yanked off the platinum wig, heaving it into the box beside the table. The light picked up bits of lint sticking to the short braids of her own hair. In those places where the braids wouldn't hold, her hair had knotted itself into a tight, kinky nap. She avoided glancing at the mirror again until after she'd plunked a dark brown wig onto her head. Then she stared intently at her reflection, wiping moisture from her upper lip with a towel and checking her better-than-real eyelashes. Finally, she slipped her feet into boots, tucked in her pants and laced the boots up to her knees.

When she walked back into the bar, no one paid any attention to her. It was as if they had forgotten how the "Ebony Queen" had disappeared through the same door Ernestine now used. The band was playing off-key, but the musty bodies crowding the dance floor attended to everything except the quality of the music. Red and green lights highlighted sweaty foreheads, exposed contracting bellies, spotlighted male hands on some woman's butt, and added splashes of color to many a slack-jawed female face. The bartender poured drinks and cleaned glasses with the absent-minded look of a man who'd long since given up separating war, sex and booze. Two scars running parallel down the left side of his face announced that he didn't bother to tell the difference between a bar stool and a rifle butt. He had become an observer, and he took refuge in that position.

Ernestine nodded to him and moved down the length of the bar. As she walked past, the bartender remembered an Asian woman near Da Nang whose very body scent could make him forget all caution. Ernestine walked up to a man who was slouched over his drink. She was at his elbow before he noticed her.

"Hi baby," he said. "Sit."

Ernestine shook her head. "Rudy, you look like hell."

"Shit, I'm at my peak. 53 years old and going strong." He picked up his glass and turned away as she signalled the bartender to bring her the usual scotch and water.

"Ernestine, I got to get out of this place," Rudy added without looking at her.

"Ok baby," she smiled. "I'm through for the night. You wanta go home?"

"Naw," he grunted. "I mean out. Out of here. Out of town."

"Like where?"

"Wherever you want to go, baby. Just name it."

"On your paycheck?" she laughed.

Rudy mechanically rubbed his hand across her knee, but Ernestine remembered how he'd snored once she'd finally gotten him to her place the night before. She shook her head. The bartender watched this exchange and turned away, smiling, but behind them, in a booth opposite the bar, a young girl also watched. She wasn't smiling.

Whenever Rudy lifted his glass or rubbed the stripper's jean clad knee more vigorously, the girl in the booth clenched her teeth. She had been in bars like the Club before, but this one was on the highway and off her beaten path. Usually, she was one of the first dancers on the crowded floor. She'd throw herself into the rhythms of the music, her hips rotating in perfect off-time to whatever song the band played. Everyone knew Georgia Rae, and everywhere she went, there was some man anxiously waiting for a chance to talk to her. But tonight, Georgia had insisted on sitting in the booth.

They had entered the Club just as the crowd watching Ernestine's performance had thinned a bit. Georgia was already tired. All night, she'd been hustled by her date, and the chance to sit down allowed her time to avoid his attentions. On the dance floor, the pressure of his body against hers would have controlled her conversation. Sitting, she could watch the crowd and only half-listen to the half-truths he murmured. She'd been content to watch the floor until Ernestine appeared from the back room.

Georgia first noticed the tightness of Ernestine's pants. The jeans seemed to strain in every crease, stretching toward impossible odds against ripping at each step Ernestine took. Even the material was worn in a pattern that had thinned until it was almost white where it was pulled across broad paths of flesh. But somehow, in those lighter areas, deep, almost new shades of blue rested in the creases left by Ernestine's movements. Around the zippered front of the pants, the material was almost zebra striped. Georgia Rae didn't like obvious displays and was about to dismiss the woman as trashy when she noticed the stripper talking to a man who'd been hunched over his drink. After he turned his head to greet the woman, Georgia had been unable to take her eyes off them, and her frowns cut deep trenches into the creamy skin of her forehead.

The guy in the booth beside her became restless. "What's on you mind, sugah?" he asked. "What you looking at?"

"Did you say something to me?"

"Yeah. What's got your eye, Georgia? You haven't said two words to me since we walked in this club."

Georgia turned to him. "Go . . . away," she said slowly. "Two words, right?"

He smiled.

He was so handsome, she almost forgave him for his toothpaste grin. It was his smile that gave her a shock of pleasure when she'd been away from him for a while. She smiled back, pulling her lips slowly across her teeth in what she called her Miss America pose. He arched one eyebrow, and deepened his smile.

"Baby, I could love you forever," he said.

"What about your wife?"

"What about her?" he asked.

"Can't you love her?"

"What's that got to do with it?" His voice was sharp and peevish.

Georgia shook her head and turned back to the bar. In the blue smoke-dulled light of the room, her face was the color of a dark copper penny. When she turned, she seemed to use the light, letting it brush shadows across her face and tilting her chin a bit so that her profile was etched in the glow from the dance floor. She had wanted to be a model, but she thought her wide forehead made her eyes too large and her lips too full. Ashanti features, her father had called them. Now, in the foggy bar light, her face was sharply contrasted by the gold African designed choker circling her throat.

The man next to her leaned forward and kissed her ear. "Baby, you look like one of those Nefertiti heads in the museum, you know that?"

"I know," Georgia answered.

At the bar, the stripper was leaning into her partner's ear. He seemed to be lost in thought, and from time to time, the woman chatted with the bartender while the man on the stool next to hers caressed her leg.

"Humph," Georgia snorted. "Ebony Queen my foot."

"What are you huffing about?" her date asked.

"I said, Ebony Queen! Well, part of it's right. She's pitch black." Georgia lifted the man's hand away from her knee. "Now what do you suppose could be on your little mind?"

"I was just saying how lovely you were, sugah."

"Yeah, take after my mama's profile and my daddy's smooth maneuvering."

"It's a good combination, baby," he said, and leaned over to nibble her ear again.

"Don't," she snapped. "And don't call me Baby. My name is Georgia Rae. I don't want nobody calling me Baby again. You got it?"

He kept nibbling. "Let's leave, baby. It's nearly two and I got to get home. We can run by my brother's for a while. Listen to some records."

"Now that's a lie. We've never heard a record at your brother's yet."

"Yeah," he laughed. "But listening's fun."

Georgia had turned her attention back to the bar almost before he'd finished. The couple were still there, but she wished she could hear what they were saying to each other.

With the next number, the band changed tempo, and even more dancers joined the others on the already crowded floor. Someone sent the stripper a drink and she smiled at the bartender, then turned to the man on the stool next to hers and lifted his hand from her knee. Rudy seemed to shake himself awake when she moved his hand.

He grabbed her arm as she made a move to leave, but never really looked up. Ernestine hesitated for a moment. In that moment, half on and half off the barstool, her jeans were pulled across her thighs until the dark wrinkles blended into the lighter shade.

One seam threatened to give way from the pressure of being stretched to its limits. Ernestine eased completely off the stool, gave Rudy a quick kiss on the cheek and left.

Fifteen minutes later, Georgia also said goodnight, and left before her date could protest.

When she reached her house, her mouth was still in a tight, straight line.

Rebecca had just finished collecting the litter in the living room when the front door opened. "Who's there?"

"It's me, Mama," Georgia said. "You shouldn't be up. It's well past your bedtime."

"I got to wait up for your daddy," Rebecca told her. "He likes hot soup when he gets in late. When he works late, I wait up."

"Daddy working late, huh?" Georgia asked. She took off her hat and pushed her hair into place, then moved across the room and flopped onto the sofa. "Working must be tiring. I know I'm bushed."

"Your daddy has to work late sometimes."

Georgia smiled at her fingernails and ignored her mother's frowns.

"You go out with that Harris boy?" Rebecca asked. "I heard he was back home from the service. Miz Harris told me that at church last Sunday. I wish you'd go to church more often. I don't know who you seeing anymore. You so quiet about it. Miz Harris said her boy asked about you."

Georgia grunted. "I'll bet he did. When he stopped running, I'll bet he asked."

"He's a nice boy," her mother continued. "Thought that might be him on the phone today. That was him, wasn't it? Not that Billy Wallach. I told you to stay away from him. That wife of his got more than her share of troubles."

"Yeah, Mama. I know. See the Harris boy. I know."

Her mother moved into the kitchen. Georgia could hear her heating the soup when the door opened and her father entered.

"Hey Georgia Rae. You still up, baby?"

"Yeah. I just got in."

"You out awful late, princess," he said. He leaned over and kissed her. Georgia turned away from the smell of scotch.

"Yeah, it's late," she said, reaching for the shoes she'd kicked off. When she straightened up, she sniffed the air loudly, her mouth pulled down at the corners. "Guess I'm just a rover like you, Daddy."

"Where'd you go?" he asked as she turned away.

She answered him over her shoulder. "I was with the Harris boy," she said, walked toward the stairs. "Just ask mama."

"Rudy?" Rebecca called from the kitchen. "I'm getting your soup ready now."

"Hot soup every time you work late, hun, Daddy?" Georgia laughed. Then she slowly climbed up the stairs to her room.

Rudy could hear his wife in the kitchen and the noise of the dishes didn't quite drown out her voice as she fixed his late supper. She was singing, and as Rudy settled into the chair his wife had abandoned, he heard Georgia join her mother's chorus as she came downstairs again. His daughter popped her fingers to the rhythm of the tune.

I want to scream cause I never have seen such a fin-ine brown frame . . .

Rudy closed his eyes. He tried to remember the singer he'd first heard sing that song. Heard it in a bar somewhere, he thought. There had been so many bars and so many singers. Too many places, he thought. Too many places and too many women.

When he looked up, Georgia was bringing in his soup. He leaned away from the rose leaf pattern of the easy chair. His wife's voice sounded slightly off-key, but Georgia rounded out the melody, pulling at each word as if the song, written years before she was born, could belong only to her.

Imogene

S HE WAS OUT OF CIGARETTES AND SOMEONE WAS
making love down the hall. Low moans, abrupt intakes of
breath, then fading sounds. She slammed her feet into her worn
sandals, leaning against the dresser for balance.

She had scrambled around the room, turning things over, searching nervously for a cigarette or part of one to calm her. It was happening all over again. Feeling on top of it one minute, and doom the
next. She had been anxious about him last night, unsure of him. So
tonight, she'd waited, waited until she had to go out, until the noise
and her dry throat forced her to the door.

When she looked up from the dresser, the image in the mirror
refused to be familiar at first, then was all too familiar—her face
bloated, her skin faded under lemony shadows.

Jesus, I've gained weight, she thought.

The moaning erupted again and she clutched her stomach, but
by the time she'd reached the stairs, she could hear the couple
grinding into each other once more. The audible breathing, the in-
evitable currents, lowing and building.

It was cool on the street. The night air brushed against her face,
rolled over her and she fell into the comfort of darkness. Despite its
grittiness, it was a California summer's night. The few palm trees
dotting this side of Oakland looked as out of place as she felt, something left over from some other town and dragged to this place to
be ignored by everything but dirt. Her forehead was damp with
sweat and old makeup. She hadn't felt the wetness back in her
room, but now it was heavy, pulling at her, adding extra weight.
She wiped her face with the sleeve of her sweater.

Shouldn't let him see me sweating. Won't!

173

But she couldn't just shake off knowing he hadn't come looking for her. It was late and he hadn't come up to the room to find her.

She glanced back at the triplex. A wooden box. Someone had painted each section in different pastel colors, once upon a time. Now, like all the other houses on the block, it was faded, the paint chipped and windows missing. How many houses like this had she seen? How many one room traps of many rooms? She decided she must be as tired as the building looked. Even the uneven tiles in the doorway reminded her of the rumpled bed she was deserting.

She walked quickly, ducking her head at the slightest movement: a floating scrap of paper, shadows of trees, a flash of light reflected off long, low, chrome-plated cars. She thought she heard someone call her name from the doorway of an all-night convenience store, but she didn't look up. She hurried past it all, toeing in, her body curved, no hips, no bust, not seeing anyone but knowing someone recognized her. They would talk. Say how she'd cut them cold. She'd make it up though. Tomorrow, she'd ask questions, smile. Ask about brothers or cousins. Ask about cars. Questions with answers she'd learned to ignore.

Learn. Humph! What do I learn? All these years and no reason for me to believe he's different.

He wasn't the most handsome man she'd known and it wasn't that she couldn't look for someone else. No, not the most handsome, but style! *I can still pick them. Six feet tall and light on his feet. Moves like a hunter. Like one of those mountain cats. Knows every hidden place. Some college too. And a good dresser. Ohh-hh, he can look good. Fine suits and clean fingernails.*

But it wasn't the way he looked. She could see that in the movies any day. It was the touching, the reaching out and finding him there when she needed him. How many others had she felt, but never touched? He was her man, the one she could love and feel. That sweet-awful feeling of knowing how someone else felt. Not guessing. Not faking. So little to ask.

She walked faster, shuffling a little to keep her sandals on her feet as the uneven cracks of the sidewalk jutted out in front of her. She pulled her elbows into her sides, cutting off the breeze and closing in the dampness.

It was the way he tilted his head. *Yes, that must be it,* she thought suddenly. A kind of unconscious lift just before he smiled. And his hands. *Yeah, his hands. Not the way he held his head. That was it.* Those broad fingers and their sure, swift movements.

Two dogs raced each other across the street. The little one skitterish, running first in front, then behind the bigger one. The big one striding, breaking his stride once to turn and half-heartedly growl at her. She hesitated, narrowed her eyes to a squint and eased out her breath. They moved into the bushes and she stumbled to the next corner. The shadows elongated her legs across the half arc of light from the street lamp. She was pleased to think this added a few extra inches to her short figure.

She wished she'd stayed in her room. She should try to forget him. Not make any excuses to go out, despite the welcome relief of the night air. She should forget all about him, his hands and thighs.

Thighs, that was it. I've always been a fool for thighs.

Her mind clicked on the image of smoothness under pants that gripped muscles. She imagined him under her, over her. Her hands on the long inclines of his thighs, pulling them against her, almost into her. She wrapped her arms tightly around her waist.

Suddenly, the sharp blast of a car horn shattered the rhythms of the street: 5 rapid stabs and 2 steady beats. Shave-and-a-haircut. Always insulting, no matter how many times she heard it. She lowered her head as the driver's wide-brimmed hat turned in her direction.

No need to wave. No reason to speak. Just cruising. A good night for cruising. A clear sky. Maybe he's out here somewhere. Maybe he's gone across the Bay, into the city. Maybe he's looking for someone else.

A man passed her just as she stepped off the curb. *Too easy. A dead mark,* she thought. She could hear him pause, but she didn't turn when he said hello.

By the time she reached the BART bridge, she'd talked herself in and out of seeing him again at least half-a-dozen times. A train whizzed by overhead. The lighted cars let her see the heads of people. *I'll bet he's across the Bay,* she thought. *Gone over before dark cause he knows I won't follow him there.*

She stopped for a second and watched the train disappear around the curve. She thought vaguely about the city, but as usual, she couldn't connect herself to anything she knew, to what she imagined might happen on the other side of the Bay. Even on those nights when someone had taken her for a drive close enough to the water so she could see the city lights and skyline, none of that world connected for her. Oakland. That was enough.

The intersection on the other side of the BART overpass was free of cars. She was the only figure visible in the streetlight. Her skirt tightened as she stepped back onto the sidewalk. The material clutched her hips and the waistband bit her flesh. She pulled at her sweater.

Got to lose weight. Damn skirt's too old. Old skirt. Old me.

She dismissed the thought and pulled her sweater tighter against the swirling wind and its debris. She could sense the man she'd passed still standing on the corner at the other side of the BART bridge. He was watching her walk out of his line of vision.

Goddamn men. Where was he? Dumb. I'm dumb. Why worry? He'll wait. Why shouldn't he? Shit! She knew he could find someone else, particularly if she kept him waiting too long.

She had believed in him, had told him so. She'd believed in all of them, even the one she'd married. *God, he was good. Almost for a month.* That had been a good sign. But he'd left, like all the others. *The good looking ones run faster,* she thought.

And she had known they would, but she'd wanted to hang on, feel secure with them. She had searched their faces each time, hoping for the right one, looking for the final, the honest, one. *Every time.*

She groped in her pocket for a cigarette and then remembered why she'd left her room. Then she remembered her purse, left on the bed. Or under it. She rarely forgot it, but all that moaning down the hall and the dry feeling without cigarettes in that funky little room.

Damn! Need a drink. Get a drink somewhere. If I could just get him to care. We could move. Try another city.

She'd told him that once. She'd told him she was willing to move, to find a good job and work with the sun up, to make friends. And then she'd have the nights with only his lips flush against hers, his shoulders pushing as he turned her over and over.

God, he's good, she thought again. And she thought about how easily he made the whole world turn smooth and silky. How he made her body feel innocent.

The Tambourine was near by, its pulsing neon sign already in sight. She had credit there. He liked the place. He'd be there.

Plots, tricks, plans. She really needed that drink. Across the street from the Tambourine, she stopped and watched the door of the bar for a second. If he was not there, then one drink. Fifteen minutes at most.

The heavy odor of liquor billowed against her as she opened the door. The stale beer and smoke reminded her of armpits and she closed her elbows in and headed blindly for a barstool. Her legs brushed the polished wood as she swung herself onto the seat. She'd seen him immediately and felt the rush of blood behind her eyelids. She forced herself to turn towards the bottles lining the back of the bar. *Double bourbon. Yeah, that's it.* She nodded and ordered.

He was alone, not looking her way, but he'd seen her. When she walked in, she saw him check his watch, then reach for a cigarette. She licked her lips, immediately wiped them dry again with the bar napkin, her fingers brushing the slight mustache covering her upper lip, and in the reflection in the mirror back of the bar, her eyes checked the oily space across the broad plane of her nose.

Bastard! Once, if I could wait for him to come to me just once!

She signaled the bartender and walked to the table, drinking as she crossed the room. Someone reached out, touching her thigh. She caught only the coarse color of denim as the hand withdrew. The bourbon was good and the glass cold. She held the icy surface against her forehead. The glass was half empty by the time she'd crossed the floor.

He had a fresh cigarette already in his hand when he turned to face her. When she'd lowered herself into the chair, he placed the cigarette between her lips and lit a match with one stroke of his thumbnail. She inhaled, trying not to look directly at him, then chased the smoke with a sip of bourbon. His hand brushed her cheek and he pouted a fake kiss at her. She looked down at her drink, trying to wish away the hot feeling left by his hand.

He turned to speak, his voice bone-deep and caressing her weakness like a suede glove.

"Let's take a walk, baby."

She didn't move. He began a smile, then pulled at his shirt cuffs and shifted his body towards her. He took her hand, rubbing her fingers, stroking her palm. Then he pulled her fingers to his lips, kissed the tips, then her palms. She forced herself to smile.

"You're a good woman," he cooed, his voice lower this time, almost a murmur, a whisper heavy with the secret they shared.

Despite herself, she looked up, searching for his eyes but he'd turned to pick up his cigarettes. She dropped her eyes again, the pain of wanting him ballooning like hot steam in her chest, just below her collarbone. She removed her hand from his. Then he got up, taking her hand again and leaning over to kiss her lightly on the cheek.

"Com'on," he said. "Let's go."

She rose halfway out of the chair, finished her drink in one swallow, then let him lead her from the table. He held her hand clear to the doorway. A few people looked at them and she felt protected. When he felt her hesitate, he turned and winked at her. She let herself relax. *He waited,* she thought. *He was here, waiting, all the time.*

He took long steps, his short city boots hitting the floor in a cowboy's cadence. He stopped to maneuver her around a table, his shoulders blocking the glare of the neon sign above the bar. Everything about him suggested even lines: his legs, his arms, the angle of his jaw, his shoulders, even the razor-edge crease of his trousers cupping the bulge that sweetly curved into the nest of his crotch. His body was a little too thin, but he was wearing blue, the outfit she'd bought last week. A powdery blue jacket, the material soft, full of shadows and clouds of color, the nap rippling with each movement of his body. A diagonally cut zipper was partly opened, and his dark silk shirt contrasted with the softness of the jacket. Above the silk collar, his skin was velvety black.

Even in the doorway of the dimly lit bar, the sight of his smooth skin made her feel flushed. He led her to the sidewalk and as the door to the bar swung shut, he turned and waved to the bartender, and she noticed how the faint creases around his eyes and razor stubble on his chin added handsomeness to his face the way a pipe did for some men.

"The car," he gestured, "over there."

Quick. Too quick, she thought. He saw her frown.

"It's cool. Don't sweat it. I'm here, right? Can't stay in that room all night. Easy, baby, easy."

He lead her across the street. She lowered her shoulders from their tensed hunch, trying to walk in long strides, trying to look as if she were about to enjoy the evening. Anyone could see she was

with him. She was his. That was all. Nothing else. He walked close
to her side, and she tried matching his pace, her hips swaying gently under the tightness of her skirt, her sandals flopping rhythmically, breaking the other noises of the street. When she looked down
the length of the block, another BART train whipped past on its
way to the city.

They reached the car. He put his hand on the handle, the gun
metal grey of the door glinting slickly against the knobby weave of
his jacket.

"You ok?" he asked.

She nodded. He gave her arm a reassuring squeeze and opened
the car door. It opened soundlessly, the black leather seats sleek and
smooth, almost breathing into the light that fell upon them. He
blocked her view, the back of his neck catching the light as he
leaned forward, leaned over the front seat toward the rear of
the car.

"Mr. Preston? It's ok. She's here. You been real patient."

He stepped back, standing between her and the open car. His
smile was smooth now, and he patted her cheek again before pushing a stray hair into place, and pulling her sweater squarely onto
her shoulders.

"Fifty bucks, baby," he said. "I'll be in the Tambourine."

Then he kissed her forehead and moved aside, helping her into
the back seat. She didn't turn to look at him as the door shut. She
closed her eyes and pushed her body across the seat. The slickness
of the leather licked her skirt, gripping and holding it above her
knees. As she squirmed over the seat, she wet her lips again,
smoothing the dryness out of the flesh.

She kept her eyes closed, holding onto his image, holding her
squint and letting her face relax so that her lashes touched her
cheeks. The man in the back seat breathed with a sharp intake. *A
scotch drinker,* she thought. The man's rough hands moved swiftly
past her knees to her wet crotch and she shuddered. But her
thoughts were clear: she remembered her man, how he had smiled
and the warm feeling when his hands brushed her face just before
she'd slid into the car and the door had closed. She hoped he would
be in a good mood when she got back to the Tambourine. Her
sweater fell open and she let her body go soft, leaning into the seat,
stroking the smooth leather with her free hand.

Under the Equinox

I HAVEN'T BEEN ABLE TO SLEEP. NO REASON FOR IT except the ache in my bones, the echo in my brain. My brain burns with the desire to do something. I answer the most complex questions with brevity, and reluctantly perform the duties asked of me. "Turn this way, Nicky. Raise your arms, Nicky. Flex your buttocks. Move Nicky, we can't see in this light."

I smile at pink tongues flashing across thin lips. I watch as weak brush strokes are smudged across canvas after canvas. I am satisfied finally when the first tremor of excitement spills a paint pot or splatters a black blot of India ink onto a near perfect canvas.

I watch the north light dim above my head— "pale winter light, the best," they have said in chorus. I watch the magic of it dance in shadows along my elbow if I turn this way, or my knee if I turn that way. I see it dance and I amuse myself with a beam of light here, a beam of light there. I clock the tedium of my four long hours in the center of the studio by the changes in light. I am the eunuch guarding the sultan's treasures; his treasures lick with bright pink tongues and paint grotesque images of me while their minds grow naked on their faces, their eyes ringed in fear, the fear of knowing what it is they want.

I stopped by Bella's place. Boldly announced myself, pushed my lips right into the grillwork of the intercom. "I am here," I boomed. Then I breathed into the speaker, inhaled deeply and exhaled for a full minute, I believe. I am still weak from my last bout with flu. "A new strain of germs," the doctor said to me. "Strong active germs." My gift to Bella and all her pretty friends. I went up the stairs, lightheaded and happy for having left a gift in the grillwork.

Bella was waiting for me on the landing at the top of the stairs, her silhouette looking like a bright smile in the center of her open arms. Her little pointy ears fairly twitching. Oh Lupus, oh Bella my pretty wolf, your teeth should drip red, drip blood. How many victims have you caught today, pretty pigeon?

I let her rub me with olive oil until I could almost see my reflection on my back in the mirrors. My face reflected on my back like a visual black echo. My face in the glass—black; my back—black and gleaming with the reflection of my face—black; the reflection bent and distorted when I flex my shoulder muscles. And Bella behind me, caressing my thigh, my shoulder. She has developed a dozen new flowery phrases. Her eyes still slant and narrow when she fantasizes what we are about to do. The pupils become as green as a cat's, positively electric, day-glo green, glimmering inside deep sockets set into that pallid white face.

When I left her, she was still spread-eagle and wet. Her face cold, and beads of sweat caught in the hairs of her uppper lip. I watched her for a moment before I closed the door. She seemed almost dead. Then I could see she was breathing, but her breath was as shallow as an old dog's.

Feb 15

I went to the cathedral today. Gregory saw me before I could leave. I hadn't seen him since the last time we were arrested in Washington Square for protesting the war. I could hear the tremor in his voice as he called to me: "Nicholas—Nicholas—Nicholas— Nicholas." The echo bounced from the altar to the pews, to the statue of Our Lady, to the door, until it weakened and died against the stained glass window above the vesper candles. Gregory rushed from the chancel and clutched my body, asking if I had forgotten to bring him a copy of the cantos. Yes, it has been a long time, I thought to myself as I shook my head, but I couldn't admit having deliberately ignored him. I joined him for a few minutes to ease his obvious pain over my answer. His eyes still come alive and lose their innocence when I stroke his cheek.

I asked him to show me his newest translations, the tedious Old World poems he so delights in, the same poems that bored me when we met as novices in the Order eight years ago. He works so hard and needs the praise. I was mildly surprised when he declined; yet I stayed to hear him play, letting the notes shuffle past my ears, more engrossed in the slow motion speed of his fingers on the keyboard, and the afternoon light dancing in and out of the long golden pipes above his head than in his somber melodies. Gregory could lull a forest with his melodies. I left without saying goodbye.

Mar 7

Bella has called.

Mar 8

My mind is as grey as the rain. I must do something soon.

Mar 12

I wonder if Canada misses me? I saw a wine bottle in the gutter today—his label alright. I will look for him one day soon. He is as easy to find here as in any other city. I will help him chase away the rats, and let him tell me once again how the world began. I will hold him to me and sing as I rock him past his sweating bouts of chills and fever. And we will laugh again. I am trapped; Canada is free, free in his baggy clothes, free from the handcuffs of schedules and coffee breaks.

He can not remember owning a watch or lying with a woman. He watches the pigeons and shares their secrets. How Hillary hated him, despised his freedom. Hillary is such a utilitarian. She hoards her passions like her father hoards great sums of money in his five banks. Hillary wanted me to break the evil spirit of the dragon, wanted me as the Black Knight who would crack the spell of the sorcerer, but I was not the proper catalyst. I would not take the banner into battle against her father's five banks, and his eighteen cashmere suits, and his white shirts and spit polish shoes. I could only share Canada, his philosophy and his freedom. She only smelled his stale sweat, saw his shoes stuffed with newspapers, and his scalp full of sores and lice. All I could really give her was my name, and she still has it. Has to use it to introduce herself, or sign checks or charge books on her library card. I am still with her until I decide to take back my name. Ah, for an honest woman. My kingdom for an honest woman! One without a seraphic smile and the smell of a sarcophagus. Canada, you opened the door to all my troubles. You with your grizzled chin and yellow broken teeth, and I did not have the strength to step across the threshold and fall safely into your arms.

Mar 15

Bella has been in my room. She scribbled my name eight times across the scratch pad by the bed. Nicholas—Nicholas—Nicholas, on and on in her thin even letters. Then she scratched them from the page with thick strokes of a felt-tipped pen I left beside the pad. "Nicholas," executed eight times with the blunt stab of a blind pen. Oh Bella, soon . . . soon . . .

Today, I shaved my head.

Mar 17

The weather is cloud burst warm and the ground is turning sweet with the promise of flower buds and new grass. I saw Gregory standing at an intersection. He looked so forlorn and hopeless. I watched him for a full minute before I joined him. We crossed together on the green light.

When he saw my head, he thought I had become penitent and was delighted, rubbing my bald scalp again and again as he sang praises to its shape and blackness. I hated to disillusion him, but finally suggested we share a bottle of wine. His breath already smelled faintly of wine, and Gregory was easily swayed, as usual.

We found Bella's list of scribbled "Nicholas'" with their felt pen death strokes. I told him what and who, when he asked me. He sat there, half nude, the top sheet pulled up under his chin with one hand. "How can you do that with her heart?" he asked. "With the same ease I used to rent this cheap room for us, and with your money, my Jesuit friend," I told him. "I have never presumed to be your casuist, Nicholas. We are too close for that," he snuffled. Gregory becomes so androgynous when he is angry. His eyes, female and full of tears, their long lashes wet and stuck together, his chin raised, square-jawed into sharp right angles with his thick neck. I snatched the sheet from under his chin, tore the cheap material in half, and fashioned myself a loin cloth from it.

Mar 22

I have been translating Rene Depestre. It has not brought me closer to what I need, but I love the feel of French sliding off my tongue. I read aloud on the second floor balcony for effect, lifting my voice skyward to drown out the incessant clanging of cable cars at the bottom of the hill. I disturb the pigeons, and fewer people walk on our side of the street, but I address the crowds anyway. Yesterday, I stayed on the balcony for three hours relishing the rhythms of Senghor and Dumas. English is so blunt, a hangman's noose, a useful tool if you're in the mood for Baraka or Lee. French is a rapier, a fine poignard.

Mar 26

I enjoyed the last three hours of work today, actually smiled. I bathed in the light as I never had before, my limbs supple and my skin as smooth as an obsidian against the white backdrop curtain. I posed as if Tweedledum and Tweedledee were Michelangelo and van Gogh, rather than pasty little wife-dumplings from the suburbs. My scalp was on fire, but I did not raise my hand to it once. I know it will be scarred tomorrow, but the scars are gifts from the sun. Before facing the cold light of the studio and the anxious twitchings of would-be artists, I meditated in the park at North Beach. The meditation eased my soul, the full sun was deliciously warm, but my scalp withered and burned. I have been a Western man too long; my scalp demands a shield of hair.

Mar 27

I fled to Bella's again. She bathed my tender head and gave me the warrior's name, "Shujaa," as she rubbed my scalp with a baking soda solution. I let her cradle my head between her breasts, licking her nipples from time to time, but I wouldn't answer to her cooings of "Shujaa." I have been one woman's warrior and failed;

I have tried the monastic ranks and failed in a war in the name of
the Trinity. It is foolish to try again.

Mar 29

There has to be more to life than a strong North light. I left after
forty minutes in the studio. I was told I could be replaced. Crowell
lifted his nose and sniffed, "I can find someone else, you know."
That insouciant shit thinks I'm dense. He stays to watch me twist
this way and that under the skylight, but he never lifts a pen or
brush. I see the dreamy looks when I flex my ass to make the
shadows dance. I know I can go back next week and he'll never
blink an eye, just pull my time card and check off four hours like
always.

Tweedledum and Tweedledee fluttered about while I dressed,
bubbling and gesturing, "What did we say? Oh my, did we do
something? Oh dear, did someone say something nasty? Call you
names? Oh me! Oh my!" Their pudgy wrists floated out of their
blue smocks like bread dough from a baker's tube. "You will come
back, you will, you will," said Tweedledee. "We must catch you in
the last of the North light before spring," said Tweedledum. "Fuck
the North light," I said.

April 12

Gregory came to see me today, excited over an old article about
some African who received accolades from the Order years ago. He
had translated it from a moth-eaten copy of *Stimmen der Zeit.* Sometimes he is so serious, he believes himself. Oh Gregory, one day
they will find you out; catch you when you have some young choir
boy spread over the credence table.

April 23

Bella had a party, Bella and her pretty little friends. Invitations
were sent: *A Saturnalia in Celebration of Spring/8:00 P.M. MY PLACE!*
The floors were waxed, the thirty mirrors cleaned, and new candles
discretely placed in niches along the shelves. The place was filled
with smoke when I arrived. I pulled a joint and made a quick trip
to dreamland before joining the others. We fingerpainted Dulcine's

wide ass and flabby back for two hours. Juicy Ducey! She looks better in oil base than acrylics. I got first draw on her and she squealed with pleasure, telling me as we wobbled toward the bedroom: "Oh, I can get fucked and blessed at the same time!" I wouldn't wear the cross to bed, and although she was fat and happy when I finished, I admit—my heart wasn't in it.

April 23

Dulcine, Stanley, and I stayed at Bella's after the others left. Dulcine and I slept in. When we woke up, she found a half empty lid and some eskatrols. We tripped out, and I decided to give her the full compliment of my style. She's better for fingerpainting after all.

I tried convincing Bella of that when she broke in after pounding on the door. Bella was none too pleased that Dulcine had locked the door. Her nails left tracks across my back after I pulled her off poor, fat Dulcine. I got a toke from Stanley and fled to the loft. I could hear Bella's voice bouncing against the locked trapdoor as she screamed insults. The loft was deliciously cold and bare, the last cold night of the season, according to a weather report I heard later. I let Bella scream herself silly, and lying spread-eagle above the trapdoor, enjoyed Stanley's toke.

I must have been there for some time when I heard my mother's voice. It came to me through the supporting beams and the skylight, shrill and harsh as ever. I knew the old man would be close by, so I looked for him. He was hiding behind a trunk in the corner, holding the loose end of a length of rope in his fist, the other end of the rope secured to an overhead beam.

Bella said it took them nearly an hour to cut me down, get me back to the bedroom, and slap me alive again. She licked the rope burns on my neck, her salty saliva cutting the pain deeper into my skin. She told me not to listen to my old man's voice anymore, murmured how she would never leave me. I don't know how I can stop listening to him. Whenever I find his voice, I know I will soon feel the weight of his hands, the blows bouncing off my head and back punctuated with curses. "Stay home, nigger—slap. Be good, nigger—slap, smack. I'll beat some sense into you yet—smack. You'll do as I say or else—hit, slap." That was what he told me in the loft. "Do as I say, nigger." That was what I'd heard before I put the rope over my head, pulled it through my tears, past my mouth and around my neck, then stepped off the dusty trunk into a blinding sea of red.

"Yes Papa. Yes, I'll do it."

May 2

I left while Bella was shopping. At last I have heard Him! Yahweh spoke to me last night, His voice coming through the bones of my head. I answered so loudly, Bella woke up and hugged me to her, keening in her foggy half-sleep. I tried telling her it wasn't a nightmare, but Bella has a small mind. So I waited until I could leave without her endless questions trailing me.

I walked down to North Beach, just as He had told me to do. He said I would know when I'd found His messenger. I wandered around for a while, held the hand of an old wino as he slipped into his self-made coma. He had nothing to tell me; he was not Canada. When I found myself in front of the art gallery, I knew I had to go in.

She was standing in the center of the gallery, standing in light that was egg-white pale, her shadow bending across the floor and against the far wall, giving substance to that pastel blue wall. She was standing in front of Dulac's *Arabian Night* series. I walked up to her and turned to the canvas, reading the inscription below it aloud, my voice resonant and strange even to my ears.

"As he descended the daylight faded from view." "Lovely, isn't it?" she said. I let her watch me for a few minutes. Her belly was beautifully round, pushing against her green smock and obviously blossoming with the child she carried—my child, the messiah. She flushed when she realized I was staring at her, when she saw how I was smiling widely with the delight of finding her. I saw her eyes go to my head, watched as she tilted her head a bit to the left as if she were seeing a bare scalp for the first time.

"You're not wearing a ring," I said. She began to walk away. "No, wait," I said. "What is your name?" "Leslie," she said. I let it roll from my tongue: "Leslie—Leslie." I asked her to have coffee with me. She said she had to leave. "To meet your husband?" I asked. "Well, I'm not wearing a ring—so . . . what husband?" Her voice was husky and throaty as she laughed at her own answer. Then she turned and walked to the door. I let her go. I knew I

could find her. I knew I would know where she was. He has told me
I would know. Yahweh has told me what to do. I will talk to her
again tomorrow. And she will answer, because she is carrying my
son; my son who will chase away my father's voice, who will quiet
the pleas of Gregory and silence the echoes of Hillary, who will help
me as Canada was unable to do, and rid me finally of Bella. My
son! I shall drink of his blood and he will free me. I will eat of his
flesh and be free.

I will laugh when I cry, cry when I laugh and walk close to the
edge of the world. There is no sky. Colors are all one and I am one
with colors. Time is only the distance between me and destiny, and
Leslie—Leslie, you have my destiny. When the sun bakes the
earth, we will stand above its filth and my son will lead the way.

I fell to the floor and wept, Dulac's Aladdin riding his white stal-
lion across the skies of the canvas above me. I left when the gallery
director broke the spell, calling me a "damn hippie" and shrilly de-
manding an explanation for my tears. How could I tell that hard
face I had found life!

A Dance With a Dolly
With a Hole in Her Stocking

THE GATES ARE LOCKED, MECHANICALLY SEALED
so that when the catch is released, the latches whir, unlacing
and wheezing like the breath of an asthmatic old man. But that
sound, so final and scientific, is wasted since once the clicking
stops, the guard has to swing the wrought iron gate to the edge of
the driveway and chain it to a half-crescent spike sticking up from
the curb. I listened as the bus driver and gatekeeper exchanged
words, hoping that somehow they'd find a reason to deny our entrance, but a few seconds later, the locks began to slide and twist,
the long metal posts rubbing against the sockets in a rapid succession of firecracker explosions: WHACK WHACK-WHACK
WHACK!

I sat in a busload of students whose faces I knew well enough to
never forget. My neck ached but I didn't want to move. This
morning's sudden chill had forced me to wear a jacket, and after
the loose fit of thin, summer dresses, I couldn't seem to get my
body to accept itchy winter wool. And now, this place with its
wrought iron gates of twisted, double filigree grillwork, like the
fences at Ash Hill Cemetery or the front entrance to Anheuser
Brewery where Papa had worked. And on each side of the gate,
concrete posts holding brass plates inscribed, *STATE HOSPITAL,*
the words centered in the metal rectangles like invitations to a wedding. Or warnings.

As soon as he had the movement underway, the gatekeeper
grabbed a section of chain swinging at the end of the crossbar and
turned his back on us, dragging the gate behind him like a farmer
snatching a dumb ox down the trough of an already plowed field.
But over his shoulder, he watched us, his face wall-eyed and heavy

with suspicion—one eye turned outward toward the gate and the road back to the city, the other turned towards the hospital grounds.

Oh, he was pleased to see us, his smile said, but his eyes held the flat dull light of a winter sky. Once he'd secured the gate, he motioned us past. I watched him as the bus pulled away. He was still smiling, but one eye stared at a spot somewhere near the rear hubcaps while the other had already dismissed us and was aimed at the gatehouse. I tried to relax, tried to catch some of the excitement the others showed. I'd finally made it, made something of my life, as my mother would say. With a little healthy prodding, I was here. But I felt paper-maché, flat and as lacking in detail as a pen-and-ink outline. "Will the real Josephine Ethel Barron please stand up?"

Who was I fooling? This is where I'd been heading most of my life. This is where I'd been heading ever since the fifth grade when all the kids on the block had heard about circus fire-eaters and decided to run away and join a side show. I'd been bound for this place ever since McKinnely Turner put a snake down Rochelle Watkins' senior prom dress.

Rochelle had been stand-offish and hinkty. Not as snooty as the Dunlap girls or Monica Frasier, but Rochelle still had been hinkty. That took some doing in a school where the most cliquish girls were near-white. Rochelle was almost blue-black and pretty as a preacher's hand during baptism, but country and tight-lipped. Full of nasty-nice words and soft eyes that made the boys come running. But she was a good Baptist and kept her legs crossed as tightly as her mama had kept that rope-thick hair of hers Dixie Peach straight. McKinnely Turner's snake put an end to Rochelle's prissness.

Rochelle had screamed so long, her voice broke and vanished in her throat like water sucked into a downspout. Even after the sound ended, her mouth stayed open, screaming although she was the only one who could hear the noise. Her eyes had rolled back to white, but she hadn't fallen to the ground the way Miz Lucy Bates' brother did when he had fits. Miz Lucy's brother had died having one of those fits, squirming away his life on the ground right in front of their house, but Rochelle had gone through her seizure standing up, her body rigid and her head thrown back as if she were calling to something up in the clouds.

"Say she ain't nothing but nerves," the old women had whispered that summer. "Jumpy as a cat."

And that fall, I heard Rochelle was going to be sent South. "Where some of her kin can look after her," some said. But my mama said, "They found one of those homes for crazy folks to put her in. One that accepts black folks. It's a sin and a shame to be black and crazy in this world, God knows. Then you ain't got no mercy from what the white folks can do to you."

After that, I started visiting Rochelle every week. Sometimes Monica Frasier went with me and sometimes I went alone, but the visits were always the same. I'd read and Rochelle would stare at the window. Or the wall or whatever her chair happened to face.

"They blaming it on that boy," Mama had humphed, "but that child was always kind of sickly. No good for anything now."

When it was time for Rochelle to leave, when they'd loaded all of her belongings in the car and tied them up so they wouldn't come loose during the long ride, I was sorry to see her go. When the car pulled away, I'd waved. Rochelle had raised her hand. She hadn't actually waved, but she'd looked directly at me.

"Lord have mercy," Miz Lucy had said and the rest of the women stared as if I'd done something special.

Now I was here, trying to look as calm about the whole process as the other students. Acre after acre of close-cropped lawn, unrolled with landscaped precision, like those incredible mazes in the gardens at Versailles. When the bus stopped at the staff entrance to the main building, I followed the others to the doorway, then turned back for one last look at the front gate. The lawns were pablum smooth, unfolding toward the horizon as if they stretched the length of Crévecoeur County and beyond. When the door closed behind me, that world disappeared.

Inside, I found Bill Madero talking to a short plump woman in her mid-forties. *Miss Thayer,* the name tag announced. The woman eyed us suspiciously, her glance picking up every flaw, every rumpled sleeve or frayed hem or missing button. She ushered us into a corridor, a long tunnel of shiny, unmarked aluminum with several dim recess areas feeding away from the main stem. We passed a door leading to an office complex, then moved into an adjacent corridor that led to a patient wing of the main building. The hallway deflected light so that its entire length seemed unbroken and smooth. Then I realized only the lower half of the wall was metal. The floor was grey linoleum tiles shined to a buff that reflected the aluminum as brittle light. The floor itself seemed metal, and in that stark light, the entire hallway was bathed in aluminum—clean and unyielding.

As we clumped along behind the doughy Miss Thayer, Terri Morton, who always signed "Terri" with a heart over the "i" instead of a dot, skipped to catch up with me. Her dimpled blondeness bobbed at my shoulder and I made myself remember that we'd lived through many a night of study sessions. My close-mouthed acceptance of her giggly eagerness somehow reached a balance, a fulcrum we'd used to speed up the tedious hours of memorizing and researching. Blonde or no, she'd been there when I needed her. Not just for sneaking movies, or sharing a steak dinner, but helping each other sound more professional. "Getting rid of the corn," as Terri put it. She'd spent hours coaching me to say *length* so that it didn't sound like *lint*. I'd spent just as much time pulling her Kentucky accent out of words like *celery* and *salary* so they didn't sound like *sale-ry*. But both of us still said, "Little *awf'un* Annie *awf'un* goes to the store." And here, in my starched uniform and well-oiled elbows—("You'll scare somebody to death with those ashy arms and knees, child. You spozed to be helping folks," Mama had chuckled.)—here, my black skin, pimples and all, would be under the same scrutiny as Terri's sugar-coated paleness.

"Well Josey, this is the tombs. Spooky, eh?" Terri wrinkled her nose.

"Folks in my neighborhood don't use the word *spooky,* Terr. You cutting close to home, girl." Terri quickly blushed. "But it's scary as hell," I added.

She laughed then, keeping pace as we passed a ward. The upper half of the door to the ward room was reinforced with hexagonal links of wire. It was a locked ward, and there was a calculated atmosphere of cleanliness for people whose minds were cluttered with the debris of a lifetime. I could see clusters of ghostly figures shuffling across the room. They all had the appearance of clouds on a day pregnant with rain—grey and barely moving. And there seemed to be no real differences between males and females. They were all mottled with grey tinges. Even their washed-out blue housecoats seemed to have a grey overcast. And everyone was white.

I moved deeper into the group, trying to hide my blackness in their whiteness but all the while, recognizing my skin color more acutely than ever. Terri halted my flight, almost deliberately blocking my maneuver. "They're all so pale," she whispered. "Like they're dead. White and dead."

I couldn't resist. "Spooky, eh?" I mumbled. Terri may have answered, but I heard my mother's voice telling me, "Take the good with the bad, chile."

I shook myself free of the memory and tried to pay attention. Miss Thayer was rushing us into an alcove, telling us as we filed past that for the convenience of the orientation, we were to be divided into two smaller groups, one led by her and the other by her assistant, a large boned, horsy woman who'd followed us down the hall. The assistant motioned several members of our class to follow her back to the entrance. "Witness another lesson in bureaucracy," I whispered to Terri. "In order to go back to the beginning, you must start in the middle."

"Whatever it takes to let us know who's in charge," she muttered. "Hup two, three.."

After the others had filed out of the alcove, eight of us were left to face the crisp directions of Miss Thayer. She was the most symmetrically round woman I had ever seen. Her surgically manicured hands and landscaped hair made her figure look more like a solid uncooked dumpling. Only her mouth seemed alive and was, to me, a Clara Bow kiss done to perfection. There were no smile lines, but the lips seemed always about to smile. Or pout. Her little piped-in speech to welcome us aboard was so smooth, I expected her to start quoting Civil Rights legislation, but she only pursed her lips and said, "Good Luck."

We followed her to the end of the corridor and suddenly, we were confronted with an elaborate set of double doors, impressively large and ominous. "White folks build doors to keep people in, not out," my mother had muttered.

Terri inhaled and said, "Christ, look at those padlocks!"

The double locks linked an interlocking section of the inlaid design. I tried to imagine how many sets of doors we would pass before the day was over. Mentally, I rushed Thayer's speech to its end, craving the smell of grass and trees visible through the windows on the other side of the door.

"Most of you will be stationed in the intensive ward," the director said brightly.

She sang it, her voice rising to a lilt at the end of the statement, and the way she said it, intensive ward sounded more like solitary confinement. Immediately, I thought of incarceration and a host of fears. Back in my neighborhood, the loss of freedom was always imminent—ghetto mentality, the experts called it, as if it were a product of the imagination. But the ghetto was real. Weren't we here to prove it? Terri, Bill Madero, Thelma Johnson—all of us shoved into a slew of special courses and squeezed out of the other end to become statistical evidence of equal opportunity. And everyone of us had broken down doors to get here.

So what was I doing here where walls and doors were all that mattered? Healing the body heals the mind, professors told us. *You must remember: a hospital is not a dumping ground for errant souls; you will not be a giver of mercy, but a giver of life.* "And some of us are complete fools," my mother's voice echoed without prompting.

When we entered the courtyard that connected the main wing to the adjacent one, we gulped air, trying desperately to do it silently. We sucked it in, gently but definitely, then stalled. A few patients crossed the courtyard, blending into the shadows of plants and wooden benches the same way they blended into hallways and waiting rooms. They moved without any apparent effort, gliding ghostlike but shifting the pattern of light and shadows while keeping the basic design intact. Bill Madero pulled his shoulders down and jammed his hands into his pockets. Terri started to comment, then changed her mind.

"Let's move on, Miss Lady," I told her in my mother's voice.

Terri motioned me to follow Thayer. In the entryway to the next ward, Thayer waited for us, her tight little enchanted forest smile somehow appropriate for the sharp acrid smells of medicine and disinfectant. After the fresh air of the courtyard, the odors seemed to hang in the air like fine powder. Bill Madero was the first one to step into the ward. An old man approached him. Bill made a halfstep backward, then stood his ground. The books never covered this, his eyes said. He looked at the patient, then the director. She offered no help. The man drew nearer. He drooled slightly but made no move to wipe his mouth. His eyes flashed blank, then recognition, then blank again. His cloth houseslippers were silent and his hands were folded into the sleeves of his robe. Bill nodded, then said in a clear voice, "Hello."

The man stopped, his legs moving slightly although his feet were still. Then he turned and walked away. He moved as if his body had no volume, no mass. As if his arms and legs were controlled by wires. I remembered the lessons on tranquilizers and their effects on the postures of heavily sedated patients. They all just seemed to be nice words to remember, nothing more. Terri touched Bill's arm and he jumped in startled reflex, then quickly recovered, nodded, and pulled back his shoulders to acknowledge passing the first test of proper ward behavior.

The director sighed. "Well, this is the intensive wing," she said. "Well, poop-dee-doo," Terri whispered. I nodded.

Thayer explained how we would need to sign in and out each time we left the ward for anything, no matter how small. She emphasized "small," as if she could not foresee any reason for us to leave the ward for anything at all. A nurse, sitting behind the glassed-in desk, arched one eybrow, then dropped her head back to her charts. We watched her scribble little notes on the daily log sheets. Her hand moved rapidly and the lines on the sheets increased at an amazing speed in the magical language of pills and patients written for doctors only. We moved past the desk. The nurse did not look up again as we left. In the far corner of the room, a television was encased in a wooden cabinet hinged to a board against the wall. The cabinet was painted the putrid color of dull Georgia clay. The director explained that only the nurses were authorized to change stations. "Not even doctors," she laughed.

I rolled my eyes toward heaven and gave Terri a vaudevillian grin. As the director detailed the rules for watching television, we studied the patients. A few sat in chairs facing the set. They seemed to be barely breathing. One was at the writing table in the corner, his head buried in his arms. The inkwell was dry. Nothing else was visible on the table. There were patients perched in window seats facing the wall or on radiator panels facing nothing. Suddenly, in the corridor adjoining the othe side of the sitting room, a half nude figure paused in flight, glared at us and rushed by. Seconds later, three other figures followed him: a ward nurse with a robe held open in poised pursuit of its fleeing owner, and two orderlies whipping the air with frantic gestures from a Marx Brothers movie, blue and white hospital towels trailing from their hands like flags. They did not pause.

Thayer interrupted her talk on the importance of television privileges. "Oh, that's Jeremiah. He was trapped in a mine cave-in. Cerebral damage to the right hemisphere. He's a post-traumatic schizoid. Primary insult to the occipital lobe. Subject to respiratory arrest when excited." She rapidly clicked off symptoms that were the sum total of Jeremiah. "He absolutely hates a closed-in space and it's bath time," she added, twittering slightly at the end. "Come along then."

We fell in step behind her, imitating her crisp efficient pace like ducklings—another medical services team, eager and trained to give precise meaningless answers. Only a few patients seemed to even notice our presence. One was an old woman sitting in a chair by the door facing the hallway. She was hunched into an almost "U" shaped position. I smiled. She tried returning the smile, but somehow never made it before her head tilted forward and her eyes closed. In one move, she seemed to disappear, blending into the tattered creases of the naugahyde chair. By the windows, an old man tortured the ends of his hair with mindless combing motions. I nodded. He returned the gesture, then beckoned as if asking me to join him. I saw myself in his eyes, the nurse's eyes. Even Thayer's eyes. So far, I could not recognize what I saw.

I could feel myself withdrawing into that easy stance where the world was divided into "them" and "us," and on the ward, there were a lot of "them" and a bare minimum of "us." Everyone I saw seemed old, old and not worth the effort.

"Even *you* can live long enough to be old or dead, sister woman," my mother had told me. And whenever we had to visit Miss Owida Granberry, my mother's old Sunday school teacher who was even older than Claudia Lumpford, who was the oldest woman at church and claimed she'd seen Marcus Garvey in the flesh, I knew what folks meant when they said "older than dirt." But old or not, both Owida and Claudia were still as sassy and meantempered as ever, not like these patients, who looked old and transparent, almost without color. I don't mean white—Thayer was white—the patients were like fossils, preserved remnants of some life that no longer existed. Too old to be contrary; too old for spit and vinegar; just plain too old.

I must have said that out loud, because suddenly, I heard Thayer snap. "Miss Barron! I was addressing you. Old? Define old?"

"Josey . . . I mean, Miss Barron," Terri offered. "She just feels she should know the patients, Miss Thayer."

Thayer smiled her flapper girl smile. "I hardly think you need to *know* these patients, Miss Morton. Whatever you need to *know*, you should have learned before you arrived here. Or at least, I sincerely hope so. But," she smiled, "that remains to be seen, doesn't it?"

Terri cleared her throat. "Coxitic scoliosis. The woman in the chair, that is. Symptoms of advanced senility too. Dysphasia perhaps. And that one . . . the one by the window . . ." She paused, running out of textbook words.

"That will do for now," Thayer concluded. "We have the rest of the wing yet to view."

Terri slowly exhaled and smiled at me. I felt as if I'd just flunked a Stanford-Binet. Terri pulled me in step with the rest of the group.

By contrast, the next ward we visited seemed to contain patients who were of no particular age. And we had been there for only a few minutes when I realized we had become as much of a curiosity to the patients as they were to us. Then I noticed two of them walking directly toward us: a gaunt, almost skeletal man, and beside him, a woman. Not really a woman but a girl, and girl or woman, her skin was raisin brown, despite the greyish tint from the harsh light. It wasn't that I hadn't expected to see black patients here, but she seemed to have materialized out of the grey pallor that pervaded the ward.

She nudged the man with her elbow, poking him sideways as if to keep him moving in the same direction. My first impulse was to say she didn't look crazy. "Hard to tell when black folks got an attitude or when they just gone out of their heads," my mama had said. But I couldn't deny Rochelle and her nightmares of snakes. And there was Thelma Wooten's Uncle Raymond, shut up in his room for days, and the Greens, who carried their oldest girl as a child on the welfare records for nearly thirty years. But all of them were at home and didn't we take care of our own, as Mama would say?

As the two moved closer, I could see the girl looked no more than sixteen or seventeen. They stopped in front of me. At least the man's feet stopped, but his scissoring legs threatened to pull him past us into the hallway. And the girl pumped her arms up and down like a passenger on a bus signalling for a stop. Below her hairline, there was a jagged scar, raised and shiny. Keloid, I thought. The mark of my people.

I whispered, "Lord Jesus, we might have been in the same demonstration." Civil disobedience, they called it. Is this the punishment?, I thought. Hers to be patient, and mine to be keeper? I threw a brick in the air and if it landed . . .

"Be careful," Terri warned. "Thayer's watching."

The girl began to make noises, poking her tongue in and out although her lips barely moved. Thayer chuckled. "That's Agnes. She likes people. They brought her in here after the riots in St. Charles. Sometimes she has convulsions, but usually she's friendly. Aren't you, Agnes?"

"How stable is she?" I asked.

For a moment, Thayer's smile faded but her bright, "Beg your pardon?" was pitched to a musical lilt.

"Has she shown radical change in symptoms?" I asked again. I heard Bill Madero clear his throat. Everyone was quiet, so I shifted my position until I stood somewhat apart from the group, centered between Thayer and the patients.

"If the initial insult was sustained during the riot," I continued, "With a subdural hematoma, we might see some changes in her behavior. If the doctor can predict some specific symptoms . . ." I shrugged.

Terri moved beside me and whispered my name, but made no other move to interfere. It was comforting to know she was there. Then Agnes moved closer. She raised her hands to my hair, and began to smooth loose hair into place as if she needed to make each kinky hair fit perfectly. Then she put her hands to her own hair. I smiled at Agnes.

"Comb your hair!" my mama had yelled. "Looks like a rat's nest," she'd said. But Uncle Roman had laughed and said my afro reminded him of the baby feathers on a buffle-head duck, and Miz Claudia Lumpford had said my hair looked like the ruff of kinky fur around a buffalo's neck. Acoording to Miz Claudia Lumpford, I wore my hair the way colored women had when the slaves were heading West on the wagon trains, after they'd been freed by the Emancipation Proclamation. "Miz Lumpford's surely right," my grandmother had said. "I 'member my mother telling me bout it.

They was starting out from Kansas back then, close to the Missouri border, and Mama used to go down to the wagon trains with her pappy to give them folks victuals for the long road ahead. There was black cowboys in them days and they called them women Buffalo Gals, on account of their nappy hair."

I smiled as Agnes patted down the thick mass of her hair.

"She still has seizures," Thayer said in a flat voice.

Agnes smiled back at me, her eyes bright with medication.

"We've been trying to get Agnes to cut that mop of hers for months now," Thayer continued. "Maybe you can help there, Barron."

"Who will do my hair?" my grandmother had asked each Friday in the memory of all my years, and too tired to tolerate the cold, she had sat by the stove as Mama tugged and braided her thick grey hair into exacting sections. I remembered something I'd heard women reciting to make themselves brave during a sit-in.

Mother to child, sister to daughter
And I lay my hands upon her hair, combing,
And think how women do this each for the other.

"What?" Terri asked. "What did you say, Josey?"

I started to answer, but Thayer's glance silenced me. Instead I recited the symptoms so obviously attached to the gaunt man who accompanied Agnes. "Somnambulist is the old term," I intoned as I mentally checked disorders and symptoms. "Dyskinesia algera is a more commonly used diagnosis." I tried the words on, rolling the sterile sounds across my tongue the way some professors mouthed words like *insidious* or *supercilious* or *environmentally deprived*. Syllable by syllable, I pulled at the catalog of symptoms as if the gaunt man would deny the connection between the words and his sleep-struck stare. As if the words would deflect everyone's attention from Agnes.

"You might enjoy working with Agnes," Thayer said. "She was our test case for a long time. I suspect she is ready to make the shift to the rehabilitation unit. This hospital now covers four counties instead of three and we need the space. It's not often we get someone a patient like Agnes can immediately trust." She paused as I listened to what she had not said.

"Don't worry," Thayer continued. "You'll be seeing quite a bit of Agnes. But now, it's on to the food center."

I saw Agnes with her hair combed. Smiling again.

"Let's hear it for progress," Terri muttered at Thayer's retreating figure. "Just what *did* you say to Agnes, Josey?" I shrugged.

"A poem. Something I remembered, that's all." I looked for Agnes, but she had vanished into the knot of patients at the other side of the room. I saw the gaunt man. He was seated in the middle of the sofa under a poster of a sea gull which carried the message: "Come rest on the shore."

"It was just a poem," I repeated. "Nothing else."

"You can tell me about it later," Terri whispered. Then added in a louder voice, "Step lively, Miss Barron."

A blue line painted on the floor of the hall intersected a red line that led to the courtyard behind us. The blue line indicated the direction of the dining area. Terri danced in the narrow space between the two lines. "Only one tv program each evening," she chanted. "Clean linen on Tuesdays, Thursdays, and Saturdays; movies on Mondays, Wednesdays, and Fridays. No magazines in the North wing; no coffee in the Chapel." Her voice assumed the same unnerving gaiety Thayer used. "Come along, Miss Barron. It's off to the dining hall with you," she giggled.

I watched the manicured lawn slide past the diamond-shaped pattern of wire mesh embedded in the windows. We were near the last set of windows when suddenly, automatic sprinklers clicked into motion and my final glimpse of the rolling lawn was clouded by twirling umbrellas of water spouts. As we entered the double doors of the main dining hall, streams of water slapped against the windows, the sound picking up its own music: *Miss La-dee, Miss La-dee.* My mother rapidly clicked her tongue against the roof of her mouth as if to hurry me along.